PRAISE FOR KID STERLING

"The author's thoughtful rendering of dialect accurately captures the vernacular of the era, lending an authenticity that draws the reader in."

—Andrea Kortenhoven, PhD Linguistics, Alumna, Stanford University

"A well-paced and gripping narrative that excels not only at capturing the young protagonist's deep love of, and commitment to, jazz pioneer Buddy Bolden's music, but also at offering us a powerful, and often very moving, account of some of the kinds of struggles, particularly around issues of race and class, that would have been part of the context of the day for a young boy, like Sterling, growing up in New Orleans."

—Professor Ajay Heble, School of English and Theatre Studies, University of Guelph; Director, International Institute for Critical Studies in Improvisation; Artistic Director Emeritus and Founding Artistic Director (1994-2016), The Guelph Jazz Festival

"Of a time and place, not only of a culture... the story is convincing and respectful of the characters and their humanity."

—Chris Benjamin, Managing Editor, *Atlantic Books Today*; Canada Reads Top Essential Books list, *Author of Drive By Saviours*, winner of the H.R. Percy Prize

KID STERLING

CHRISTINE WELLDON

Red Deer Press

Published in Canada by Red Deer Press,
195 Allstate Parkway, Markham, ON L3R 4T8

Published in the United States by Red Deer Press,
311 Washington Street, Brighton, MA 02135

Library and Archives Canada Cataloguing in Publication
Title: Kid Sterling / Christine Welldon.
Names: Welldon, Christine, author.
Identifiers: Canadiana 20200181785 | ISBN 9780889956162 (softcover)
Classification: LCC PS8645.E447 K53 2020 | DDC jC813/.6—dc23

Publisher Cataloging-in-Publication Data (U.S.)
Names: Welldon, Christine, author.
Title: Kid Sterling / Christine Welldon.
Description: Markham, Ontario : Red Deer Press, 2020. | Summary: "In this poignant coming of
age young adult novel, Sterling Crawford is a young African American kid living in New Orleans in
1906 learning about jazz, the legendary Buddy Bolden and forced to face racism, a loaded justice
system and racial barriers that divided a nation" -- Provided by publisher.
Identifiers: ISBN 978-0-88995-616-2 (paperback)
Subjects: LCSH: Race relations – United States-- Juvenile fiction. | African American jazz musicians
– United States -- Juvenile fiction. | Bolden, Buddy, 1877-1931 -- Juvenile fiction. | BISAC: YOUNG
ADULT FICTION / Historical / United States / 20th Century. | YOUNG ADULT FICTION / Social
Themes / Prejudice & Racism.
Classification: LCC PZ7.W455Ki |DDC [F] – dc23

Red Deer Press acknowledges with thanks the Canada Council for the
Arts and the Ontario Arts Council for their support of our publishing program.
We acknowledge the financial support of the Government of Canada through
the Canada Book Fund (CBF) for our publishing activities.

ONTARIO ARTS COUNCIL
CONSEIL DES ARTS DE L'ONTARIO
an Ontario government agency
un organisme du gouvernement de l'Ontario

Canada Council   Conseil des arts
for the Arts   du Canada

2 4 6 8 10 9 7 5 3 1

Edited for the Press by Peter Carver
Text and cover design by Tanya Montini
Printed in Canada by Houghton Boston

www.reddeerpress.com

To young musicianers everywhere

King Bolden, now,
there was a man could play.

—Robert Sargent, *Touching the Past*

Part 1

KICK IT OFF

ONE

"Need a shine, Mister? Get a mirror shine right here! Mirror Shine!" sang Sterling Crawford to the high-top boots, the brogues, and the army boots of men who hurried or sauntered by. They were headed to the gambling joints and pleasure palaces of the city, but Sterling managed to grab someone's attention now and again.

"Thanks, Mister," said Sterling to a customer who stopped to rest a foot on his stand. Sterling bent to deliver the polish he promised, paying half his attention to the job, and half to gazing out at more boots and shoes coming his way.

His eyes searched for a certain pair of low-top leather shoes with a fine pedigree, and he listened for the gentle voice of a special musicianer—King Buddy Bolden. Every afternoon, Buddy walked along

Basin Street toward one of the saloons in the District, and Sterling set up his shoeshine stool, the horsehair brush, the boot black, and the grease, right in his path.

Sterling owned this sweet spot on Basin Street near the train station. His brother Syl had used his fists and feet to win it fair and square from a boy twice his size. It was only a few feet of ground, but its location was prime.

From the river close by, the City of New Orleans spread outward, its beat pulsing with colors and sounds that blended with the aromas of frying fish, sweet beignets, rotting fruit, and a hint of salt from the marshes beyond. And around him, the melodies of street vendors swung crazily into a ragged harmony that set up catchy tunes inside Sterling's head.

"Ap-PULS, le-MONS, fine le-MONS, madamma, straw-BERR-ies," warbled the lady fruit sellers.

"I got O-kra, got CELery, got TURnip greens picked o'ny YESSerday," the vegetable man rasped. "Got CREole tomatoes, get it all HYEAH!"

"Best shine in town!" Sterling would sing against the backup rhythms of freighter blasts, streetcars, and rattling coal wagons, the tin horns of rag men, and the bellowing paddlewheelers that crossed the great Mississippi River.

Sterling finished his shine and reached out a hand for his nickel, scarcely paying attention to what coin his customer placed there, because, at that moment, he saw Buddy Bolden walking with his long, easy stride along the street toward him. Tall and slim, good-looking too, Buddy was dressed like a rich man. His tailored suit was pressed to perfection, his shirt starched to crisp whiteness. He placed importance on getting a high shine to his shoe leather, and Sterling felt proud to supply the finishing touch.

"Hey, Mirror Shine!" Buddy said, stopping to rest his foot on the wooden stand.

"Hey, Buddy. Teach me some licks sometime?"

But Buddy's answer to Sterling never seemed to change. "Kinda busy now. Just got time for a little shine. Keep on practicin'."

Sterling swallowed his disappointment, spread the boot black with extra care, and got to work with his brush. Buddy's silver cornet was tucked under his arm, flashing in the sunlight. He never went anywhere without it, wouldn't allow anyone to hold it, not even the pretty girls who often ran after him. "Play me a tune, Buddy!" they called, and offered to hold his beer while he played them a special love song on his horn.

"Where ya playin' tonight?" asked Sterling.

"The Globe. You gonna come listen?"

"Nah. I'm gonna get in trouble if'n I stay out late."

After some spit and polish, Sterling stretched out his hand for payment. If he polished Buddy's shoes before a performance, he'd be lucky to get a nickel tip, but sometimes, when he caught him on his way back, that was another story. One time, Buddy tipped him twenty cents, and Sterling hid it away with money he had put aside to buy a new trumpet. He had eight dollars saved and needed only a few dollars more.

Two coins dropped into his palm. "You still savin' for that new horn?" asked Buddy. He didn't wait for an answer, his polished low-tops already moving along.

Sterling looked down at the coins. Fifty cents! "Thanks, Buddy!" he called. "You the King!" Buddy gave a backward wave as he turned the corner.

It was true. Bolden was King! Everybody knew it. That man could blow horn like no one else in New Orleans, but Sterling Crawford hoped that one day, it would be him up there on that bandstand, playing his own horn as good as Buddy.

Or maybe better. Because when Buddy played horn, the girls came running.

And the King played loud! Sterling imagined those clear notes of his wending their way over the muddy Mississippi, past the barges and ferries, curling around the fancy boaters on Lake Pontchartrain, mystifying the dicty white passengers on their way across the lake to Algiers, laughing at them.

You think you the boss? Well, think again. No way you ever gonna play music like me!

At sundown, Sterling carried his tools to Paulo's fruit and vegetable shop, where he stored them every evening. Strains of brass band music filtered in from the street to tempt him. He forgot his promise to his mother to come straight home, and not to stroll along the streets near Congo Square.

He lingered outside tonks and clubs, listening to music that blared through open windows, then walked with purposeful step toward the Globe Ballroom. He was already late home, but his feet took him on to an alley behind the building.

It was raining—a lush, warm spring rain that did not discourage him. He leaned close to an open window to catch the liquid tones of Buddy's horn, rising up into the moist, velvet darkness. The piece ended, lingering on a plaintive note no keyboard could match. Sterling tasted the applause, the yells and whistles for more, and waited for the next tune.

"Boy! What you doin' there?"

Sterling looked up. The dark form of a man filled the back entrance, his cigarette describing a glowing arc, highlighting the fine profile. Buddy Bolden himself!

"Jus' listenin'."

"You like my music? How old is you, ten?"

"Goin' on eleven." He stood and moved closer to stare up at Buddy. He could just make out the cornet tucked under his arm.

"I know you, don't I? Mirror Shine! So, you come after all."

"Name's Sterling." *About time the man know my name.*

"Well, Sterling. This your lucky night!" The King swung the door wide open and waited for him to pass through.

Sterling stood still, scarcely breathing, mouth half-open, feet stuck in place.

"You scared a-come inside?"

Scared? His nerve endings jangled for a grab at this chance!

His brain sent a message to his feet and he bounded over the step. At the threshold, he hesitated. *He funnin' me?*

In answer, Buddy's hand guided him in. Sterling followed him up some steps toward golden light and brassy music that spilled out through an open door. Buddy ducked through with Sterling close on his heels. He was in!

TWO

An explosion of cheers and whistles pounded in Sterling's ears. Hands pushed him gently forward into the saloon, patted his head, touched his cheek. A woman in a sparkling green dress reached out and hugged Sterling to her. "Ain't you just the sweetest thing!"

Sterling, dizzy from the noise and lights, felt he could drown in her warmth and perfume, but Buddy's hands lifted him out of her arms and up onto the bandstand. He led Sterling back behind the drummer for a view of the band and the crowded dance floor beyond, then took his place up front.

King Bolden put the cornet to his lips, stomped three times, and his band came in on the fourth beat and took it away. The dancers grabbed their partners and Sterling swayed to the beat. He could feel the crackling energy of the man and sensed the strength that he channeled through his horn, like kindling to the flame.

Up this close, the notes from Buddy's cornet were cannonballs that shook Sterling's bones, the tone clean and pure, teasing and lusty, till he felt himself lifted up and away, a catfish on a hook.

Buddy finished the tune and paused a moment, head lowered. The women screamed for him. "Play it for us, Buddy! Play it!"

He lifted the horn again to play a melody that was pure sweet and low down—the beginning notes of a church hymn. Sterling recognized it from sitting on hard benches at the Sunday Baptist service. But Buddy suddenly ragged the beat and morphed that tune into the blues. His horn gently persuaded the churchy music toward seduction and devilry, as if Satan was stealing that hymn to suit his own self.

The King swayed in a trance, looking as if he was right inside the music and the music inside him. He played the bluesy tune and then he played notes that were frills; playful licks that danced around, under and over the tune, but in Sterling's head, he could still find the threads of it.

Willie Cornish answered on trombone, and Jimmy Johnson's bass embraced them like the throb of a heartbeat. The dancers clung to their partners, slowly swaying till Buddy's playing hit a peak and ended on a note that confused the crowd. They stopped dancing and listened. The low fading moan of the cornet seemed to gather in all the people, understand their losses and defeats, all the bitterness and hurts, and, yes, their triumphs, too.

The note touched something deep inside Sterling. It answered the secret parts of him that were confused, even angry, and it held a faint promise. In the hush that followed, Buddy lowered his horn, but the crowd would not let him stop.

"Buddy! Buddy! Play it, Buddy!"

Sterling felt someone's eyes staring at the back of his head and glanced into the shadows behind. Someone stood there, watching. From the looks of him, Sterling figured he must be the boss. The man jerked his thumb, meaning, *"Get off the stage and outta here."*

Willie Cornish noticed and winked at Sterling, then put down his trombone.

"Boss wants you out. It's kinda late. You got a momma

waitin' for you at home, I guess?" He took Sterling's hand in his own and led him off the stage. Cornish was a big man, and Sterling's hand disappeared inside Cornish's fist.

Outside, the rain had stopped, and the night air was heavy with the fragrance of jasmine.

"You a musicianer?" asked Cornish as he leaned against the doorway and lit a cigarette.

"I got a spasm band," answered Sterling. "I play horn."

"That right? Maybe I come hear you play sometime. What's your name?"

"Sterling. You think King Bolden got time a-teach me?"

"Happen he could. I teach music if you want a lesson. You run on home now, Kid Sterling, fast as you can."

Sterling turned to do as Willie said, but someone brushed by him and paused a moment at the doorway.

"Who you, boy?"

The young man looking down at him had a neck as thick as an ox and the shoulders and arms of a fighter. Next to him, tall Willie looked small. His name was Black Benny, and Sterling knew his reputation. The police always kept clear of him unless there were four of them to take him down.

Sterling once saw him aim a rock and knock over a man standing a block away. A known jailbird and thief, Benny was a prizefighter, too. And he was one of the best bass drummers anyone ever heard in Congo Square. When he played, people felt the beat right down to their feet, and they remembered *Africa!*

"C'mon, boy. You can talk, can't ya?"

This close, Sterling stood at eye level with Benny's knuckles, swollen and scarred from the fights he won on the battlegrounds of the Ward. Benny bent down to look closely at him.

"What your *name*, boy? You look like my nephew Tony, same build, same face even. You related, maybe?"

Benny's large face filled every corner of Sterling's vision. He tried to speak but his tongue was stuck in his mouth. He shook his head, no.

"Tell him your name, kid. Don't worry. He ain't gonna eat you," laughed Willie.

"Sterling Crawford," he blurted.

"Good kid. He play horn," obliged Willie.

Benny held out his hand and Sterling took it, prepared for a grip that could crush, but no—the handshake came firm and gentle.

"No relative of mine, but you the *spittin'* image of my Tony! He sick with the fever and my sister don't hold much hope, 'cause the doc say he ain't gonna beat it. She already plannin' the funeral. They let me out o'jail today so I can say goodbye."

"My cousin die that way," said Sterling, finding his tongue at last in a rush of words. "Only five year old. My momma say she jus' too little and weak to fight."

"It a awful sickness." Benny agreed. "The only Crawford I know is Syl. Tall, light-skin. You can't be no relative of his'n?"

Sterling was about to say *Yes*, but he stopped himself in time and shook his head.

"Well, I might need your help. I let you know."

"What kinda help?"

"Funeral work," said Benny. "You interested?"

Was he! Too thrilled to speak, Sterling managed a nod.

"How do I find you again?"

"Got a shoeshine stand at the station, Basin Street," said Sterling. "An' I play at the park after school."

"I'm gonna look out for you," said Benny as he turned to go inside.

"Run along," said Willie. "Watch out for the police. Don't stop for nothin'. I see you aroun'."

Sterling took off through the lighted streets, his chest close to bursting with excitement. He couldn't wait to tell his brother about this night's events—King Bolden! And now Black Benny, too!

He remembered the time his brother took him to see Black Benny fight in a "battle royal." The ring was set up near a clearing in some trees, away from the eyes of the law; just some wooden stakes in the ground and a rough rope. The rules were simple. Put on a blindfold and start punching.

Not many had the courage to get in the ring with Benny Williams. His bare-knuckle fists could knock out a man's brains. Sterling had watched the meanest, dirtiest fighters of New Orleans climb into that ring, and they all sneaked a peek under their blindfolds to see where Benny was standing. And Benny just stood there, cool as you please behind his blindfold.

The bell clanged and the men went in fighting. When they met up with Benny's thick paws, one-by-one they folded like tarpaper shacks in a New Orleans hurricane. The crowd was eager for blood that day, and for Black Benny's most of all. Sterling found his voice shouting with the rest, "Kill 'em. Knock 'em dead!"

A few foolhardy souls who went down, staggered back to their feet—what did scars or broken noses matter when the purse was a big one? With luck, their flailing fists might connect where it counted. But there was blood and vomit in the dirt that day, and none of it was Benny's.

As Sterling ran now through the streets, a refrain in his head beat time with the hollow thud of his feet on the boards:

Syl Crawford! He my brother!

Syl Crawford! He my brother!

It would make him proud to say it out loud to Black Benny, but Syl had warned him: *Don't tell nobody that we brothers.* The only people who knew were his friends at school. No one else would ever believe it.

"How come you so short and he so tall?" his friend Clancy would tease. "You the runt?"

Sterling guessed his brother was passing for white. Syl's light skin and wavy hair gave him entry into places that coloreds could never go in New Orleans; a key that unlocked any door. And if whites knew he and Syl were brothers, that key would no longer work.

Along the street, music poured through every door and window. Sterling ran by stoops where men sat and shared buckets of beer; past a boy perched on an empty whisky barrel, playing a sad tune on his harmonica; on by the stink of unsold bananas left brown and rotting in the gutters; and past the cribs where sporting girls stood at open doorways, their flimsy wraps open to show naked breasts.

"Boy, go fetch me a half a can?" called one from her door, closing her wrap with sudden modesty.

Sterling figured he could get a good tip for bringing her some beer, but the police were out with their nightsticks. They watched for boys in short pants past curfew. He'd be risking a blow to the head or, worse, a night in jail.

And anyway, he had no time. He could hardly wait to get home and tell Syl about Bolden, and he'd never believe that Black Benny wanted *him*, Sterling Crawford, to play along with him. Better watch out, get ready to step aside, King Bolden!

The future lay just out of sight around that next corner. Sterling imagined he could reach out his hands and touch it if he ran hard enough. A burst of speed and he could almost glimpse the glow of it, waiting up ahead. He left the gleaming lights of Rampart Street and plunged into the darkened streets beyond. The night engulfed him and, for a moment, the old uncertainty came back. *Bolden don't care none. Black Benny, I bet he already forget.*

He ran on down Marais Street toward his own front door. His mother might scold, but she'd have his hot supper waiting. And in the warm glow from the front window, he sensed it again—the future—so close that it shimmered and beckoned like the snaking river they lived on, full of temptations and secrets and dangers.

If only time would flow faster, *faster!*

THREE

Sterling heard his mother's rich low voice as he walked into the kitchen.

I wring my hands and walk the floor,
Till I see you come through that front door.

The blues came on whenever something worried her, and she had to sing them out. She sat at the table, her troubled look fading at sight of him. He noticed how young she seemed, even with the lines in her forehead and the skin of her hands dry and cracked. She worked for well-to-do Creoles in Frenchtown, washing and ironing their fine linens. Sterling often stared at the crisp white shirts and delicate lace tablecloths that his mother laundered and hung on the line. He wondered how it would be to live easy and spend money on quality things.

"Sterling, where you at, all this time? School tomorrow! Syl jus' out lookin' for you."

Sterling sat down with her. He daren't tell her he was inside a tonk tonight.

"Out listenin' to some music."

"Don't do like your brother, always into this thing an' that, all hour o' the day and night."

Syl was seventeen, much older than Sterling, and he sometimes took work as a stand-in drummer for the bands around town. Bandleaders liked him because of his good looks that drew the girls. It was easy work, and fill-in drummers did not need a drum of their own. But Syl had another, secret, life that Sterling knew about. Syl never talked to his mother about his night-time jobs working for Paulo di Christiano, and she never asked.

Sterling always stored his shoeshine stand in Paulo's grocery store, and knew first-hand that Paulo and his gang of thugs took protection money from grocers around the city. Sterling's Uncle Ned had to pay a pizzo every month to run his grocery, to prevent hassles from di Christiano's men. It was a part of doing business in the city. No one could escape it.

"Never tell Paulo we brothers," Syl would warn,

laying a finger against his lips. "I'm your boss. That's all Paulo need a-know. Our secret."

When the freight boats came into port, Syl worked through the night to supervise the unloading of Paulo's fruit and vegetable shipments. At sunrise, he would slink home from the shadows of gutters and alleyways, the sour odor of river mud and sweat and dirt rising from his pores, like an alley cat come home to lay quiet till its next hunt.

Sterling's thoughts came back to the present as his mother put a plate of rice and beans on the table. "You eat that up, then go on to bed. I'm so tired I gotta go lay down." She went to her bed, still humming her sad song.

But Sterling had no appetite. His head was full of other things. He went to the room he shared with Syl and picked up the battered trumpet he kept in a drawer. He imagined this time the crowd was screaming for him. He stomped on the floor three times to set the beat, just like the King, and pretended to blow his horn as he strutted around the room. Buddy always wore tight pants to please the girls, and Sterling remembered how, tonight, one of his britches was hanging down so casual, and his pressed white shirt half open to show a red undershirt, the sweat gleaming on his face and neck. In his head, Sterling could hear the music that Buddy had played to drive the crowd wild, and that last bewildering note that caused such a hush. He wished he could play like Buddy! Wished he could lose his own self to create a golden note that lingered in the room, even after he'd lowered the horn from his lips.

The back door slammed shut and Syl strolled into the bedroom, flushed with excitement from whatever he had been up to that night. He wore a fine linen suit that hung well on his tall, slim figure. Sterling figured he'd been playing Kotch at the Twenty-Five joint. The brothers kept his gambling a secret from their mother. She would march Syl straight to the church pastor to get a sermon about fire and brimstone.

"Hey, where you at tonight?" Syl asked. "I done look all over. Even the river."

For once, Sterling had something to share.

"I got news! Buddy Bolden brung me inside a tonk, right up on stage with 'im! An' Willie Cornish say he gonna teach me on horn! An' that ain't all ..." Sterling paused to deliver the best part yet, but Syl did not seem to be listening. He had turned away to open a drawer, drop a package inside, and close it tight. His mind was somewhere else, figuring out some deal, trying to beat the system one way or another.

"I gotta eat," he said. "Come in here, tell me 'bout it."

Sterling followed him into the kitchen and sat, as his brother dished up his meal from the pot.

"So, King Bolden?" He settled at the table and began spooning food into his mouth. "You can make a ton of money with the Bolden band. He ask you to sit in?"

Sterling looked at his brother's face to see if he was making fun, but saw only a lively interest there. "No, but some day ..." He got up from the table, grabbed his horn, then strutted around the room and blew a blast, trying for a sound like Buddy's.

"Hush, you gonna wake Momma!"

"An' Willie Cornish gonna give me lessons!" Sterling repeated, leading up to the big news. "An' ... an' Black Benny want me a-play for a funeral!"

His brother's eyes grew big and he stopped in mid-chew.

"You playin' with Black Benny? Ain't he in jail? Well, you gettin' famous, for sure! Where'd ya meet him? Don't tell Momma. She ain't gonna like it." Syl put down his spoon and held out his hand. "Say, le' me see what you got today."

Sterling reached into his left pants pocket and took out the coins to hand over. He kept his tips in his right pocket to add to the savings in his drawer. His earnings went mostly toward rent, but Syl always took a cut because it was his stand and the location was prime.

"Benny, he talkin' to me about his nephew. He dyin' with fever. I maybe gonna play at the funeral! That money ... it gonna buy me a new horn, for sure! I got eight dollar saved," Sterling said. "I only need two dollar more for that horn sittin' up in Jake window."

"Whyn't ya just put the money down and take the horn?" asked Syl.

"Momma say I gotta pay in full."

"Nothin' wrong with the horn you got." Syl got up to take down the tin box from the kitchen cupboard.

"It sound fine, but it all dent, an' the finger keys make a noise. I'ma be a musicianer, I gotta have better." He sat down to watch Syl add up the coins.

A smile crossed Syl's face as he counted them out. "Benny tell ya 'bout the time we all in the tonk, stuck in there 'cause a gang waitin' for us outside to beat on us? He went out an' fix 'em good, an' by the time we got outside, that street all clear and Benny, he set down on the curb, jus' a-restin' an' a-hummin' a tune."

"No. He never tole me," said Sterling, beginning to prickle inside.

"One time, he took his good suit out o' hock an' put it on all proud, high-steppin', a-primin' an' a-preenin' like some kinda cockatoo, but the police come an' git him. 'I ain't goin' a-jail today,' he says to 'em. 'I ain't even wore this suit a whole year, and I sho' ain't gonna wear it a-jail.'" Syl bent over laughing. "He drug them police down the street like he some kinda bull, till they just fall over like skittles and give up."

"He never tole me 'cause he don't know I'm your brother," answered Sterling with a leap of anger. The memory still rankled—that moment of denial to Benny.

Sterling remembered he had a message to deliver. That afternoon when he had gone to collect his shoeshine stand from Paulo's grocery, the man had called out to him, "You see your boss, tell him I got a job for him. Tonight."

"Okay," he had answered, glancing back as he left the store. The man's unblinking eyes had made him think of an alligator waiting in the dark.

"That fat old man Paulo want you for a job tonight," he told his brother. "Tole me be sure an' tell ya. Why ya workin' for them gangster? They jus' bad."

"'Cause, donkey, I have to get us out o' this dump." Syl put the box away. "I gotta take what I can. Ain't nobody gonna give us nothin'." His mouth tightened, a scowl darkening his features.

"You passin' for white all the time now, I bet," persisted Sterling, seeing the danger signs on Syl's face, but charging ahead, anyway. "You gonna be like Daddy some day and jus' walk out on us?"

There! He had said it. That worry always nibbling away at him. He hardly remembered his dad, but what if Syl might one day step out the door and never come back?

"Stop, now." Their mother appeared at the doorway, wiping the sleep from her eyes. Sterling figured she knew a storm was about to break; she had maybe sensed a change in the air while she was sleeping. Syl's moods could charge the atmosphere in a second, like one of those thundershowers that soaks New Orleans with rain and noise, then leaves in a hurry.

But it was too late.

Syl went for Sterling and, in a flash, Sterling found himself tipped over, chair and all, his head ringing, and Syl's angry face over him.

"Whatever I do is for us! For us, dummy! If you don' like it, don' take my money. Starve!" he snarled. "You so high and mighty. What you ever done? Blow a tin horn for pennies? Shine shoes? That all you can do?"

"Syl, leave him be!" His mother yanked on Syl's arm. "He jus' scared for you is all."

"Okay, okay!" Syl pulled Sterling to his feet and righted the chair. "I gotta go out."

"This late? What time you comin' home?" called his mother, but like a quick slice of bad weather, Syl was out the door and gone.

Sterling sat down and rubbed his head where a bump was starting. But Syl's words hurt even more.

"Tell me what you been up to," said his mother. "I know somethin' goin' on."

She sat down at the table with him and waited. She could read him too well and he could not lie. He told her about being onstage with the King, about Willie Cornish, and Black Benny. When she had heard everything, she slowly nodded.

"Seem like music the only way for us folk to get ahead in this city," she sighed. "But that Bolden, he a drunk and a crazy man. I think he gonna blow his brains out some day, he blow that horn so hard. You got no father to guide you, boy—sorry for that—but don't be puttin' Bolden and Black Benny in the place where a father oughta be."

Sterling stared down into his bowl of food. "You think he gonna come back, ever?"

She shook her head. "Done grab his chance. Up north somewhere. I ain't hope a-see him no more." She nudged Sterling's plate toward him. "We all doin' fine without 'im. Eat up, now."

"Ain't hungry."

She got up from the table and tipped his meal back into the pot. "Then go to bed now. And go get a lesson with Willie Cornish some time. I'ma find some dimes to pay him and send your aunt Ruthie along, too. But you ain't missin' school for no funeral, and you won't never be mixin' with Black Benny Williams."

"But I tole Black Benny!"

"Then you go tell the man I say no!"

Sterling said goodnight and slunk away to bed to wait

for sleep. Outside the bedroom window, a man walked by, whistling a jaunty tune to the beat of his footsteps on the boardwalk. Sterling listened for a moment, grabbed onto the tune, humming it to make it better, added frills, changed the melody a little, slowed the beat. Sometimes, the music inside his head wouldn't let him be, especially those strong, clear notes of the King's cornet.

"She can't stop me," he muttered. "I'ma take that job, no matter what."

Then one day, he vowed, it would be him up there on stage and the crowds shouting his name. "Kid Sterling! Play it!"

FOUR

"Time will pass, Sterling. Will you?"

Mr. Trask had caught Sterling gazing out the narrow classroom window. No breeze stirred the shades. It was that time of day in New Orleans when the clock always beat slow, so slow. Sterling willed it to tick away the few seconds left till noon.

A brass band marched along the street, its sound growing stronger, till it blared into the classroom and cut through the stale air. The students whispered and fidgeted. Lips mouthed the lyrics to "Get Out of Here and Go Home." *I used to be a dreamer* ... Forty-two pairs of feet softly tapped or jiggled in four-beat time.

He could hear the power of Buddy Bolden's horn among the brass, as the band moved on past their window. His sound just could not hide.

Sterling caught his cousin Barrel's eye, then glanced over at Sydney and Clancy. Their bodies were hunched forward, ready to spring out of their seats at dismissal time. The marching band passed on down the street, and the steady rolling *OOMP OOMP* of the bass drum grew fainter and faded away. Mr. Trask lifted his pocket watch and waited for the minute hand to tock into place. He snapped his book closed and put down his chalk. In the waiting hush, it rolled loudly from desk to floor. One of the juniors made to go and fetch it, teacher's pet, but his teacher stopped him cold with a look as good as words: *I dare any one of you to lift your butt from that chair till I give the signal.*

Every eye fixed on him, every pair of feet tensed for motion.

"Class dis ... missed!" he pronounced in three hisses.

Freed, Sterling scraped back his chair, raced across the room and out the door, Clancy, Sydney, and Barrel at his heels. Pounding down the stairs, they shoved the juniors aside, reached the street, and turned this way and that, ears straining to hear, bodies poised to run.

"Where they at? Which way?"

The marching music echoed somewhere in the

District, maybe toward Basin Street. Waves of sound teased their ears as the boys navigated in their wake, like tugboats bobbing after a ship.

"That way!" shouted Barrel, but he was a beat too late. The others were already racing past him.

"Over there!"

The tail end of the second liners rounded a corner, those dancing folk who would follow behind a parade. With a holler, the boys rushed along to dance and strut and get closer to the heart and joy of it. Sydney and Barrel stayed at the back, but Clancy and Sterling pressed forward. Sterling dodged around second liners who clapped and danced and beat on tambourines, till he was right up tight with the band.

King Bolden led the horns, and tall Willie Cornish blew his slide trombone at the rear. Sterling slipped in behind Willie, then stepped to the beat while the music swept him along.

The marchers turned corners to chase the Grand Marshall. His long sash flashed scarlet, as he strutted and turned and twirled his baton. Faking left but pivoting right, he led the band on and on through the streets, the second liners marching and dancing along behind, till the band stopped outside a saloon. There, stepping in place, they blew out their last tune.

"We gotta get back, Sterl," puffed Barrel. "We ain't got no dinner, and now we gon' be late for singin' class."

Barrel was always hungry. His father, Sterling's Uncle Ned, owned a grocery store on Rampart Street. They all called him Barrel because he loved to eat, especially pickles. Whenever the wagon delivered barrels of them, his cousin was right there to dig in.

"Jus' wait awhile," said Sterling, edging toward the King as the band finished their last song.

"Hey, kid," said Buddy. He stood wiping the sweat from his brow. "Got a special job for ya. Keep this for me while I go for some refreshment." He held out his cornet. "Won't be but a few minutes."

"Sure, Mr. Bolden. I'ma take good care of it!" said Sterling, feeling a leap of excitement to be given this important job. "When ya' gonna teach me some licks?"

Buddy took off his cap and wiped the sweat from his brow. "Might I could, but things real busy now. We see about it later." He placed his cap on Sterling's head. "Keep this for me, too."

He walked into the bar with Willie. Sterling cradled

the shining instrument, and polished some fingerprints off the metal surface with the tail of his shirt. He would ask the King again when he came out. He would not give up.

Barrel called to him. "Sterl, me and Sydney leavin'. You bes' c'mon along!"

Sterling could see Sydney's skinny form running barefoot down the street. Clancy was long gone.

"You all get along," he said, proudly adjusting Buddy's cap over his forehead. "I gotta keep this safe for the King."

"You gonna get in trouble," Barrel warned.

"If'n I ain't come back, meet in the park after school."

Buddy stayed in the bar for more than a few minutes. Through the open door, Sterling watched him drinking beer, shoulder to shoulder with the rest. The sound of his voice rose above the rumble of talk as he told a lively tale. Sterling glanced about him, then he dared lift the cornet to his lips and blow a faint sound. Willie wandered out of the bar, cup of beer in hand. He reached for the instrument and cap.

"Thanks, kid. You run along. I'll keep these for Buddy. He gon' a-stay a while. How long you been playin' horn?"

"Goin' on three year, but I need a-keep learnin'. Ya think Buddy can teach me?"

Willie turned to look toward the saloon. "He mighty busy these days, son," he said with a faint grimace. "He gettin' some bad headaches. But like I tole you, I give lessons. Got some time free a week Monday. Come after school. Your ma know you want lessons?"

Sterling shrugged and dodged the question. "I got some money save to pay ya."

"No need to pay me, Sterling, 'cept maybe some tobacco now and then. We can work that out later, when you famous. You know where I live?"

"Sure—on Perdido."

"White house on the corner. I'ma give you a little tip right now. Start spittin' beans or rice, get your muscles in good shape."

"I spit beans every day." Sterling always grabbed a handful of dried red beans on his way out the door each morning.

"You better hurry on back to school," said Willie. "See you next week. We gonna make a ace trumpeter out o' you."

Sterling ran along the streets and slipped inside his school by the side door. A chorus of voices, some flat, some on key, echoed from the meeting hall, and he peeked in to look.

"A rollicking band of pirates, we ..." The students belted out the verse and swayed to the rhythm. Lucky for him, everyone was rehearsing *The Pirates of Penzance* for an end of term concert.

And even luckier, Rose was at the piano.

Sterling slipped in and squeezed through to stand beside Sydney. Love had struck Sterling the minute he first saw Rose Piron, a gentle-natured, slender Creole girl. She was training to be a nurse at Flint Medical College. Playing piano and teaching helped to pay her fees. She lived downriver near Frenchtown—a better part of New Orleans. He was just a kid in short pants, but that didn't stop him from dreaming.

"Who, tired of tossing on the sea, are trying their hand at burglaree," sang the boys. *"With weapons grim and gory ..."* Sydney brandished an imaginary cutlass.

"We gonna practice after school?" Sterling asked him softly as he joined in with the boys.

Sydney nodded. "I got some time before work."

Sydney worked on a coal wagon with his dad, his skinny arms straining with the effort as he delivered his wheelbarrow of dusty black rocks.

Mr. Trask tapped on his stand for attention. "Look

fierce, now," he called. With a pirate's prance, their teacher bent his bony knees, swung his fists, and aimed a kick at a sailor thug. The boys snickered. Sterling glanced at Rose to see if she was laughing, but her expression was serene as ever.

When school was done, Sterling lingered for a moment after dismissal, to watch Rose put her music away.

"Go on. Talk to her! I dare ya!" said Clancy, giving him a shove. "You such a yella belly."

He plucked up his courage and walked over, while the boys nudged each other and giggled. "You need help packin' up, Miss Rose?" he asked.

"Thank you, Sterling. You are a gentleman," she said sweetly.

He began folding her music, looking at the lines and dots on the pages.

"Do you read music?" she asked.

"I sure do wan' a-learn, but I only read words. I like makin' up tunes but don't know how to write 'em."

"My brother Armand composes and writes," she said, her soft brown eyes looking into his. "It is a gift to make up your own tunes."

Sterling looked down at his feet. He had no more

words, only a lump in his throat as big as a calabash. With a muttered goodbye, he slipped away out the door. Clancy and the others waited for him outside.

"What all she say? She gonna meet ya later?" laughed Clancy.

"Shut it," said Sterling. "I got some news!"

He told the boys about his talk last night with Black Benny. "He maybe gonna ask for my help, 'cause I look jus' like his nephew that died."

"You lyin'! What kinda help?" asked Barrel.

"Blowin' horn. I'ma be a musicianer, for sure!"

"King Sterling!" said Clancy, bowing. "You gonna have your own band mighty quick, I know it."

The boys ran home to fetch their instruments and snacks. Back when they first began playing for pennies, some three years ago, they used a kazoo, a cigar box banjo, and a drum made out of a chair seat. A chair leg worked as a drumstick. But now they had real instruments—a hand drum stood in for the chair seat; a bent clarinet for the makeshift banjo, a battered trumpet for Sterling's comb and paper. Sydney was clever on the mouth organ, too poor to buy anything better. He had joined their band only last year, when his mother had been taken by yellow fever. Syd and his father had moved into a neighborhood down a back alley in the poor side of town.

The park was full of people idly sitting or strolling, finding coolness in the late afternoon sun. An organ grinder played some cheerful hurly-burly nearby. Syd unwrapped a sandwich filled with banana. No money for meat in Syd's house that day. When they finished eating, they heard a vendor's cry: *"Achetez les plaisirs."* The aroma of her crisp pastry cones tempted them. Still hungry, they jangled the change in their pockets.

"Hey, let's get one," suggested Clancy. Barrel nudged him, his eyes glancing at Sydney. Syd was too proud to let them pay for him. They turned away from the wagon to save his feelings. A kind lady who sat resting in the sunshine offered them some ginger cakes from her picnic basket, and they washed it down with water from the fountain. At the bridge, they peered down into the creek for minnows, before beginning "Maple Leaf Rag." Sterling played his trumpet loud, the way King Bolden played.

"Hey, you playin' real loud," said Barrel. "Keep it light."

"That boy, he in love. He playin' so Rose gonna hear him 'cross town." Clancy doubled over laughing.

"Stop that. I got a new tune for us," said Sterling. "I call it 'Bouncy Feet.'"

He hummed the lively tune he had put together from watching Clancy's feet in class—never still, always jiggling. Sydney came in with some soft and perfect harmony on his mouth organ. He understood it and knew what it needed. Sterling believed that if he tried, Sydney could play just about any instrument, and be better at it than any of them, he was that good. No one who looked at his puny body would believe he could blow out such sweetness. He secretly guessed why Syd's ears stuck out— they kept growing bigger to suck in all the tunes he could.

The clink of a large coin hit the pennies in the hat. As one, the boys looked down at the quarter, then up to see who had tossed it.

"Good playin', boys," said Black Benny. He jammed his fists in his pockets, his brows drawn together in a fixed frown. The boys gaped up at him, eyes round. He jerked his chin at Sterling.

"Kid, I got some business with you. My nephew jus' pass an' I'ma talk with the preacher. I want you in the funeral parade tomorrow mornin', like I said. Give you fifty cents."

"Okay, Benny!" Sterling felt a thrill of excitement. But he remembered a little boy had died. "Sorry 'bout your nephew. Where I gotta come?"

"Over at Union Sons Hall, nine o'clock. You good for that?"

"Yes! Sure thing!"

"You so lucky," said Clancy after Benny had walked on. "Playin' with a real band. I'ma take off from school and be a second liner. You comin', too?" he asked Barrel and Sydney.

Sterling felt too excited to play anymore today. "I gotta go an' work now. And don't tell my aunt nothin'," he warned Barrel. His aunt would tell his mother, and his mother would tell him no.

On his way, he stopped at Jake's Pawn and Loan to take another look at the horn he wanted. When musicians spent their money on too much liquor and women, they took their instruments to Jake, but on Fridays, they lined up outside Jake's shop at opening time, ready to get their trumpets and trombones out of hock for weekend dances. No one had ever come for the horn Sterling wanted. It looked like its owner wasn't coming back for it.

Uncle Jake's was just up Rampart Street. All kinds of instruments sat in the front window—trombones, trumpets, clarinets, and some strings, too: a violin and a big double bass. Jake never took on instruments that were too big. Someone tried to hock a piano once, but Jake wouldn't take it. Sterling peered in the dusty display window. There were a couple of trombones and a drum or two, but the spot where his trumpet had lain was empty. He pushed open the door and went inside. Maybe Jake had put the horn on one of the shelves. Jake was bent over his counter, writing in his account book. As the bell over the door tinkled, he thrust something that sparkled into a drawer.

"Ah, it's you," he said, squinting at Sterling. "You got the money for the trumpet? You're too late. Someone bought it just an hour ago."

"But you done tole me you keepin' it for me!" said Sterling. "I about got all the money save."

"I can't live on 'about got,'" said Jake. "But I have another beauty here. I'll show it to you. The ticket expired last week."

He lifted his stepladder and climbed up to reach the top shelf. Sterling caught the flash of gold as he brought an instrument down. "Have a look at this."

Sterling drew in his breath when he saw the trumpet in Jake's hands. Polished brass, no dents, and the finger buttons were inlaid with a silvery white sheen.

"Here you have gold brass, with mother of pearl inlay on the finger buttons, from the shell of a pearl oyster," said Jake. "For this, you must grease the slides every week and put mineral oil on the keys. I can let you have the case for a special price."

Sterling took the instrument in his hands, admiring its curves and shine. The finger buttons moved easily up and down. He daren't ask how much.

"The price is twenty dollars, but for you, fifteen dollars and another two for the case. Why don't you try the instrument for sound?"

Jake nodded in encouragement, and Sterling raised the trumpet and played a few notes of "Bouncy Feet." The tone sang out, warm and mellow, and the finger keys slid easily up and down. Sterling knew he had to have it.

"I got jus' eight dollar," he said.

"That is not a problem," said Jake. "I run a loan shop. You give me the eight dollars, then pay me weekly till the loan is paid off."

"So, how much I gotta pay every week?" asked Sterling.

"That depends on you, but I charge interest for the loan."

Sterling shook his head, not understanding.

"Interest is like paying rent for the loan. So, every week you pay me extra to cover the interest charge. For you, a special offer. If you pay two dollars every week, you add just ten cents interest till the loan is paid."

Sterling did some calculations in his head. His shoeshine tips brought him about a dollar every week. He must get a second job to cover the dollar and ten cents more to pay each week for the horn. Maybe he could deliver newspapers like some of the other boys he knew. He had missed out on the first horn by waiting too long. He couldn't let this one go.

"Okay," he said, gulping back his doubts. He must do it somehow. He just must. "I'ma get my eight dollar, if'n you keep the horn and the case right here."

"It'll be here," said Jake. He polished the instrument with a square of cloth, and Sterling looked hungrily at it.

"I'ma come right back," he said, then hurried out the door. He imagined playing it in King Bolden's band.

With that horn, no one could say he wasn't a serious musicianer.

He ran past his school and glanced down the street as he hurried by. He stopped and stared at a couple walking slowly along at the end of the block. Was that his brother Syl walking next to Rose? Sterling felt his heart thumping. He stared and stared, not wanting to believe it was true. They had their heads together, laughing, and Syl's arm was around her waist. They turned the corner, out of sight.

His steps now slow and dragging, Sterling went on home. No one was about, and Sterling went straight to the drawer where he kept his savings. He felt for the familiar lump of coins among his things and did not find it. He pulled the drawer out and dumped its contents onto the floor. Nothing! The money was gone! He searched in Syl's drawer. There was a small sack lying under some clothing. He picked it up and shook it. Nothing jingled but, curious, he untied the string around it and looked inside. White powder. Cocaine. Was his brother using? He retied it and put it back, then continued his frantic search under the chair, in the cupboard, even peering into the cistern of rainwater in the back yard, till things were upside down and scattered every which way. Someone must have walked in and stolen it. He sat on the floor, his head in his hands, then got up and started searching all over again.

"What's all this?" Syl came in and stared at the mess.

"My money got stole!" Sterling said. "It ain't in my drawer."

"Stop worryin'. I done borrow it. I'm gonna pay ya' back next week." Syl strolled into the parlor. "You bes' clean this up 'fore Momma get home."

Sterling blocked him and jabbed his finger at his brother's chest. Syl took a step back. "You done stole it? Give it back or I'ma kill ya!"

"Hey ... hey ... wait now. I jus' borrow it a couple days. You gonna get it all back. Promise."

"You ain't never ask. You jus' stole it and I want it now."

Syl opened his mouth to protest, but Sterling had no use for words. First, Syl took Rose, and now he'd taken his money. With a growl, he put his head down and charged at Syl, butted him right in the belly. Syl lost his balance and fell backward onto the floor.

"Oomph," breathed Syl. He sat there, his eyes wide with surprise. Sterling pressed his advantage and pounded on his head with closed fists, getting in some good punches before Syl shoved Sterling off him, flipped him over like a crawfish, and pinned him to the floor with his body.

"Stop it or I'm gonna knock you cold," he snarled. Sterling struggled to get him off but Syl was too strong. He felt the tears come and hated himself.

"Jus' give it back," he sobbed. "That's my money. I work for it a long time."

"I promise a-give it back."

"Le' me up!" ordered Sterling, panting, trying to get out from under his brother.

"If'n you stop beatin' on me."

"Okay, okay, jus' le' me UP!"

Syl let go of his arms. Sterling stood, then took a sudden swipe at his brother's face. "I hate you, you bastard. When you gonna pay me back?"

Syl blocked the punch. "In a week. Jus' a week, Sterl. I owe some money. I'm sorry, sorry—okay?"

"Then you pay me back the interest," said Sterling, remembering the rent he had to pay to loan the money from Jake.

"Hell, what? You want interest?"

"Yeah, the rent you owe me for usin' my money. I want one dollar interest." Sterling wiped his sweaty palms on his pants and stuck out his chin.

"Okay. You gonna get your dollar interest. Now clean up this mess so Momma don't see it. And you keep it to yourself. Don't rat on me, y'hear?"

"I'ma rat on you if'n you don't pay me next week. And you clean this up. I gotta go an' work."

Sterling stomped out the front door. For the first time in his life, he had told the brother he loved and looked up to that he hated him. It felt like his whole world had turned upside down.

FIVE

Finding Black Benny in a crowd was easy as finding an oak tree among saplings. Sterling had pretended to go to school that morning, but instead had hurried toward Union Sons Hall on Perdido Street. Benny stood at the back of the large room, while musicians dressed in black milled around him, waiting to be called to order. As Sterling came up, the man was talking to a musician, and jabbing a thick finger at his chest to make a point. The musician nodded in nervous agreement and scurried away.

"Hey, Benny. I'm here to play."

Benny stared at Sterling's trumpet. "You ain't gonna play, you the lead marcher."

"But I brung my horn," said Sterling, disappointment rising.

"Someone gonna look after that horn, maybe later you play, but first, you leadin' the band, right out in front, an' keep your step in time with my drum, y'hear?"

Benny noticed Sterling's disappointment. "That's jus' the right face for marchin'. Real sad like that. You maybe never knowed my little nephew, but he look like you, same size an' all. C'mon over here; we got a special mournin' suit for ya."

Benny took him over to a rack of clothes and picked out Sterling's costume. There was a black jacket, a starched white collar to fix to his shirt, a child's black knicker-bockers, and a black straw hat with a long black ribbon.

"Put 'em on, then come outside an' find Joe Never Smile. You gonna march in front, but not too fast. Like this." Benny took some slow steps to demonstrate; his thick legs and large feet tamed into a mincing walk.

Sterling was not happy about the knickerbockers, and hoped his friends would not skip school to follow the funeral march after all.

"Here," Benny took the trumpet from him. "I'm gonna keep it safe."

Sterling put on the clothes. The jacket fit fine, but the knickerbockers did not cover his knees. Was nothing going right today? He went outside to find Joe Never Smile. Two black horses had drawn up to the front entrance, hitched to the funeral wagon. A fine white lace covered each horse's back, to show this funeral was for a young child. Joe was wiping around the horses' eyes with a rag that he was dipping into a bottle of liquid.

"Hey, Joe. Benny say I'ma walk out in front."

"That's good. We about ready," said Joe. His eyes stared blankly at Sterling.

A trumpet sounded three double notes: ta *ta,* ta *ta,* ta *ta.* At the signal, the musicians, looking smart in marching-band uniforms, filed outside and formed rows behind Black Benny.

"We all gonna pick up the coffin first, so get ready," Joe said.

Sterling petted one of the horses, stroking its nose. "Hey, this horse cryin'!" There were tears trickling down the horse's nose, and the animal whinnied faintly and shook its head.

"That's 'cause he at a funeral," replied Joe, and gestured that Sterling move out front.

Sterling could smell something pungent. Onions. He looked for the bottle Joe had been holding, but it was tucked out of sight somewhere. Black Benny began to beat his drum with a slow marching step, and Joe pushed Sterling firmly out in front of the horses, then climbed up on the wagon.

"Where we goin'?" asked Sterling. "I gotta know, if I'm leadin' the band."

"Two blocks straight, then turn right, Baptist Church. Get along now; we all waitin'."

Sterling stepped in time with Black Benny's steady rolling drumbeat. He thought it would be a good thing to cry like the horses, but he couldn't force any tears to trickle down his cheeks. Next time, he would have an onion ready in his pocket. As he marched, he kept his eyes lowered and his head bent. The family was waiting outside the church, along with some dozen men, women, and children. They wept as Benny's drum sounded and the funeral parade marched toward them.

A little girl with a black kerchief hid behind her mother's skirts, and peeked out at him as they stopped in front. Three band members went inside with Black Benny, and came out bearing the little wooden coffin to place inside the wagon. Sterling felt some sadness at sight of the coffin. Benny started the drum beat and a trumpet began to play "Nearer My God to Thee." The family stepped in behind the band as the wagon slowly moved onward. Sterling led with slow steps. He heard the women and men behind him weep and wail. Where was his trumpet? He turned his head to look back at the second liners.

"Eyes front," hissed Joe, but Sterling glimpsed his horn tucked into Black Benny's waistband. How he wanted to play!

The band stopped at the cemetery gates, as the family and preacher went on inside. The sun blazed overhead and sweat trickled down his face. Sterling worried his mother might find out he had skipped school. She had gone to work early, before school time, but she might be home by now, waiting to give him his dinner. An hour passed. At last, the mourners walked back through the gates. Maybe the band would play "Didn't He Ramble." Sterling liked to play the tune and swing it just like the King. It was about a bull that rambled around town to visit different places, but at the end, got struck down by lightning and killed. The music always started nice and slow but ended up louder and faster. They would blow out the Ramble tune till it was the happiest music anyone could hope to hear.

The preacher always had a kind word, no matter who was in the coffin. Even if a man had lived a life of crime, shot up a bank till he got shot and killed by the police, the preacher might say. "Didn't he ramble? Didn't he shine till he was unjustly shot down on Rampart Street?"

Benny came up to Sterling. "C'mon up and march back with me. You done a good job, today."

"Didn't he ramble?" called the preacher on cue. "Didn't little Tony skip and dance like a little lamb? Didn't he laugh and spread happiness till the fever got 'im?"

"Can I play along?" asked Sterling, his shining eyes on the trumpet still tucked into Black Benny's waistband.

"You know it?" asked Benny.

"Sure does!"

"Here, then. Take it." He handed over the trumpet

Benny's drum sounded and the band began to kick it up to Benny's beat, stepping lively as they strutted along. The mourners danced behind them, through the park and down by the creek. Sterling imagined Tony playing tag with his friends and crawfishing after school. The music was speaking for little Tony, viewing the places he loved, rambling for him one last time. Sterling lifted his trumpet and played right along, swaying to the beat and letting his music out. He knew he sounded good, that his notes were strong. All that bean and rice spitting had paid off!

People lining the street jumped into the parade, high stepping or dancing the buck jump, banging on tambourines, shaking cow bells, and tapping on beer bottles. And Black Benny's drum, swinging and joyful, made Sterling's spirits soar. He felt sad for the little boy who had died but, right now, he was still living and glad for it. Death hadn't caught *him* yet, and he felt good to be alive and able to do the thing he loved most—play his horn.

Back at the family's home, the mourners prayed in the parlor. Sterling slipped into the kitchen, and his mouth watered to see the sandwiches and cakes. He grabbed some meat sandwiches and gobbled them down.

"You hungry?" Black Benny walked in. "You done good on that horn. Guess I'ma give you a dime extra for the fine playin'. Folk really enjoy that." He reached into his pocket and gave Sterling some coins.

"You got more work for me, Benny?"

"Gotta git back in jail in two minutes. You look me up soon as I'm out. See what I can do. Eat up, now, 'fore everyone finish prayin'. Go see Joe Never Smile. He got more jobs for you if'n you don't mind funeral work."

"Thanks, Benny. I don't mind, long as I can play my horn."

Sterling grabbed a piece of cake and left, the money jingling in his pocket. It was almost dinner time. He could just make it home in time if he hurried. He ran to the hall to change out of his clothes, then on to Joe's stable. He found him talking to the horses, brushing them, and making them comfortable.

"You got more work for me, Joe?"

"Yep. You marched real good. Looked good. Kep' good time," Joe said with his blank stare. "This fever is goin' around again from them skeeters. Tell me where you live and I'ma tell you soon as another child gon' be ready to meet its maker."

"Well, I'm sure gonna feel bad if'n a child die," said Sterling. "But I'ma come an' ask from time to time. My momma sick and don't want no visitors," he quickly invented.

"Stop in here now and then," Joe said. "Always somebody dyin'."

SIX

"Auntie Ruthie, hurry up!" Sterling muttered. She was late and today was Monday, time for his first lesson with Willie Cornish.

He felt lucky his mother hadn't found out he had disobeyed her and marched in that funeral band. This morning she told him to wait for his aunt, or there could be no lesson without her company. He paced the sidewalk, feet stamping the boards with impatience, and walked up to the corner to catch sight of her. Still no Aunt Ruth. His feet turned of their own accord in the direction of Willie's street across town, and he began to run. This lesson was too important to miss. Perdido Street was some distance away, but Sterling did not stop for a rest till he reached Willie's neighborhood. He slowed down to step over the sewage lying in the gutter, dodged around a horseshoer at work, walked past honkytonks toward a cluster of two-room cottages. Strains of horn music drifted up toward him. Those notes could only belong to one man!

The King perched on Willie's stoop, wearing his signature derby hat and blowing his cornet, his eyes closed. Two pretty young women stood beside him, swaying to the beat. He played a hymn, but so slow and loose and bluesy that Sterling stood listening to every note in wonder. Just plain church music, but the King could change it up to something so new. The playing faded into silence, and Buddy looked up and noticed him.

"Hey, Mirror Shine!" called the King.

Sterling wished the King would remember his name. He didn't aim to be a shoeshine boy for the rest of his life. But when King Bolden called him "Mirror Shine," he couldn't help thinking that shoeshine boy was all he would ever be. The King took a swig from his cup. A woman picked up Buddy's horn and held it for him while he drank, adoring him with her large brown eyes.

"I come over for a shine yesterday but you ain't there."

"No, I come late 'cause I got chores," said Sterling. "I got a lesson with Willie today." He hoped Buddy would take an interest, but Buddy massaged his forehead as if in pain.

"Suzie, go to the druggist, get me a pick-me-up for this headache. Be quick, darlin'," said Buddy, handing her some coins.

Down the street, Sterling saw a barefoot boy running toward them, his thin reedy body hurtling forward. Sydney. What was he doing here?

"Hey, Sydney? You comin' for a lesson?"

"No, I jus' come a-see you play," he panted.

Sterling frowned. "Why ever? You never play horn."

"I jus' wanna learn about it." Sydney wiped his runny nose on his hand and brushed away the dirt from his scratched knees. Some blood trickled down his leg. He must have taken a tumble in his hurry and opened up a scab.

"We all gonna ask Willie. But don't git in the way. Come on." He led Sydney up the steps and tapped on the open front door.

"Afternoon, Kid Sterling!" Willie stooped beneath the door frame, as he stepped out to greet him with a kind smile. "Hey, Sydney. Your dad doin' okay? Come on in."

Sterling guessed Sydney and his dad delivered coal on this street. As the boys followed him inside, Sterling glanced back at Buddy and hoped he might come in to listen, but he was laughing and talking to the girls. He sure knew how to attract women. They were landing like flies on a Mardi Gras King cake.

Willie's house was comfortable, with a saggy old couch and a few chairs. The front room served as both kitchen and parlor. Calendars decorated the walls, some with scribbled pencil notes. There were some feminine touches, too—white lace covers on the armrests of the chairs, a vase of magnolia blooms on the kitchen table. Sterling guessed that Willie lived with a woman.

Willie pulled out two straight-backed chairs from around the kitchen table.

"Syd jus' gonna watch," said Sterling.

"Well, you take a seat there, Sydney, and let's hear you, kid. What ya got?" Willie sat down with Sydney and turned his chair to face Sterling.

"Play any tune you like."

Sterling planned to play solemn and steady for the first few bars of "Didn't He Ramble." Then he would make the beat raggedy, sliding the notes, the way Buddy played it. He felt his body suddenly tremble with nervousness at the King, sitting right outside the door. He raised his horn. His lips stuttered out the first few notes. He had the music in him, but it was not singing the way he wanted.

Why I ain't playin' good for King Bolden? he wondered. *This dumb old trumpet!*

Willie stopped him in the middle. "I'm gonna give you a tip right here, kid." He took the horn and raised it to his lips, then played one note—long, unwavering, clear. "What I'ma do, just this one note, I'ma give it respect, see? Make it the best one note I ever play. I'm gonna finesse it, reverence it. When I got that down— maybe it take a few tries, maybe it take a day, a week, however long—then I'ma play one half-note above and keep playin' that note till it sound good like the first."

Willie played a half-note higher to demonstrate. "Then I'ma play that first note again an' compare, make sure they both good. Keep doin' that till you got the whole scale, every note perfection."

"That horn ain't too good," muttered Sterling.

Willie examined the horn, his long fingers pushing the finger keys. "This a rackety old horn, but that ain't no problem. The tone jus' fine. You ain't gotta feel nervous. You got a fine beat. I know you got the music in your head." He took his slide trombone down from the counter. "Play that tune again, now. Stand straight. Get your mouth ready."

As Sterling began again, Willie added some notes that helped his own sound begin to stand up and show its importance. Sterling glanced out the front window and wished Buddy might come inside, give him some tips, but through the lace curtains, he saw the musician giving all his attention to the group of young ladies.

"Better," Willie said to Sterling. "You got a good rhythm. I can tell you feel it."

"That boy, he make up his own music, too," said Sydney. "Play 'Bouncy Feet,' Sterl. Go on, play it for Willie."

Sterling tooted out the cheerful solo he had made up about Clancy's jiggling feet. Willie seemed pleased. "That's some catchy tune! Let's hear it one more time."

As Sterling began again, Willie played along with him, balancing the horn's high notes with his trombone's low mellow sounds. Sterling felt thrilled to be playing his own tune along with Willie, and that it sounded so good. *Hope you listenin', King Bolden!*

They finished their duet and Willie smiled his approval. "Fine tune, Sterling! You sound real confident that time."

He turned to Sydney. "Now, young fellah, how 'bout you?"

"He play real good on mouth organ," Sterling quickly answered for him.

"D'ya ever play horn?" asked Willie.

"No, but I think I know how."

"That right?" Willie turned to Sterling. "Give him your horn, kid. Just while I hear him play."

If Sydney knew how to play horn, it was surprising news to Sterling. He handed over the horn and Sydney lifted it to his lips. He blew a note so strong, clear, and true that Sterling's mouth fell open. Who would have thought that scrawny kid could finesse a note like that, first time!

Willie grinned. "Hey, now, this kid got real chops! I think he a natural like the King!"

Can't be! This lesson ain't goin' so good, thought Sterling.

Willie taught them some nonsense words to help strengthen their playing muscles, and he showed Sydney some fingering, then told both boys to listen, as he played a lick of notes in a pattern. Some were slow, some quick. He asked Sterling, then Sydney, to play that same melody back at him. Sterling had no trouble at all.

Syd leaned in to watch Sterling's fingering closely and, when it was his turn, his sound sang clear, the notes round and full.

"Sock it out!" said a voice from the front doorway. The King had quietly entered. His eyes were bright, and it seemed his pain was gone.

"You got chops, boy," he said to Sydney. "When you older, I'ma come lookin' for you when I need a good second horn in my band."

What about me? Listen a-me!

The King turned to Sterling. "You soundin' good, kid. You in good hands with Willie."

"Now, when you back home," said Willie to Sterling, "practice on that one note like I tole you, till it perfect, an' it stay in your head forever. An' practice the lick. Make the notes thick, just like the King here. Quality counts."

He turned to Sydney, "You ever git your hands on a horn, Sydney, King Bolden better watch out, 'cause you gonna take his crown."

Sterling's heart felt heavy enough to fall down into his shoes. Buddy stood writing with his pencil on a wall calendar, and Willie looked over at him.

"Now, I gotta work. Fix our calendar for this weekend.

See you later ... An' Sydney," Willie nodded to him. "You come along next week, too."

"Thanks, Willie," said Sterling. He wanted to get out of there fast, and hurried past Buddy Bolden. "See ya, Buddy."

Buddy gave a casual wave, scarcely glancing his way. Sterling ran by the ladies still waiting outside and hurried on down the street, taking all the shortcuts to put distance between himself and his friend. His feet hit the sidewalk with a hollow sound that kept pace with his pounding heart.

"Sterl, wait for me!" Sydney called.

He pretended not to hear and kept going. He just could not speak to Sydney right now. Maybe not even for a long time. Syd called again. His voice grew fainter as Sterling ran faster, till it was just the sound of his feet thumping the boards.

SEVEN

"GA da da GA da da GA," Sterling muttered the nonsense words the way Willie had taught him, fast as he could to get his tongue in shape. Each morning on the way to school, he spit beans or rice to make his lip muscles stronger.

Every evening after his shoeshine work was finished, he sat on the front stoop and practiced just one note, trying to reach perfection but never being satisfied. He measured himself against Sydney and felt himself failing. Syd had known how to play on the very first try.

Two weeks had passed since his lesson with Willie Cornish. His mother found out from his aunt that Sterling had gone without her. She had given him extra chores and chided him long and hard. He hadn't seen Sydney at school since that day. His friend often missed so he could help out his father, but never for this long. He soon learned why Sydney hadn't come for so many days.

"Syd got hurt," said Clancy, running up to him on the street. "They done took him to hospital 'cause he fell under the coal wagon. It like to take his head right off!"

Sterling noticed that he was looking up at Clancy. He used to be at his eye level not long ago, but then, over time, Clancy's body gradually seemed to push and strain at the seams of his clothing in its need to grow. His body was taking a while to get used to all the growing. He moved like a puppet with its strings always tangled, making him lopsided. All his clothes were hand-me-downs, and he was waiting for the next shirt and pants from his older brother. Sterling wondered when his own growing was going to start.

"Aw, come on. That ain't true."

"No, but he almost. The wheel run over his foot. Stuck all over with shells."

Syd didn't own shoes. The roads in town were made of broken oyster shells, ground down underneath the traffic of mule carts, streetcars, wagons, and people.

"That must a-hurt bad," said Sterling.

"Let's we go see him after school," said Clancy. "I bet his foot swole up like a balloon!"

"Yeah, let's go. He in hospital now?"

"No, they ain't got money. He at home, I guess."

When school was done, Sterling ran home to get his trumpet. He thought Sydney might like to practice the lick Willie had taught them, and he felt sorry for running away after the lesson. The two boys met at the corner, Sterling with his trumpet and Clancy holding a beignet.

"I got chores," said Clancy. "But Pa said go visit Syd awhile."

They walked on toward Sydney's street. After Sydney's mother died of the fever, he and his dad moved into a one-room courtyard cottage to save on rent. It bordered on the District where prostitutes kept their cribs. Like the ingredients in a jambalaya, Syd's neighborhood was a place of bold flavors that simmered with life. Honky tonk piano jangled out of open saloon doors; men shouted harshly inside gambling joints; and young girls beckoned and called to customers. Tonks nestled comfortably beside hock shops, and old wooden stables leaned crookedly over cheap eateries, their odors and aromas blending in grudging agreement with one another.

Sterling and Clancy stopped awhile to look down an alleyway, where a bandleader held an audition.

Musicians lined up along the wall, taking their turn to play. They had only a few seconds each to make an impression, before the leader either accepted or dismissed this trumpeter or that trombonist with a curt motion of the head. The boys listened for a while, placing bets on which luckless fellow would receive a nod or a shake, then walked on toward the narrow alley where Syd lived. They hurried by a group of ragged boys loitering on the corner, who turned to stare at them with mean-spirited looks. Sterling held his trumpet close to his body to keep it out of sight. On their way down the alley, they heard sweet horn music drifting toward them.

Is King Bolden visiting Sydney?

Sterling hurried ahead of Clancy and turned the corner. Sydney sat alone on his stoop, a trumpet held to his lips, his injured foot a fiery red from toes to ankle. He was playing a slow church hymn and his horn told a story, lingering on some parts, building layers of meaning.

This ain't just anyone's story, said the horn. *It is special—it will change you, so listen good.*

Sterling walked up to him, but Sydney did not notice. With eyes closed, he looked all lit up from inside out.

All the rags, scabs, and grime of him faded away as the horn took center stage, its notes crystal clear. Sterling sat down on the stoop to listen. He gestured for Clancy to be quiet and stared at his friend, noticing the way his fingers moved so confidently on the finger keys. Each note he created was flawless. How was he doing this without any teaching? And that horn, so polished and sleek! It looked just like the one ...

Sydney reached the end of the piece and looked up. "Sterl! Hey, Clancy! I been practicin' on this horn my father done buy me."

Sterling noticed the creamy white covering on the finger keys. "Mother of pearl," Jake had called it. "Nice! Where ya got it?"

"Some hock shop."

"Jake?"

"Yeah, think so."

Sterling felt a dull ache in his gut, the kind that meant he was wishing for something he now knew was impossible. His brother still owed him that money. They were speaking again, and Syl had promised he would pay it any day now. But what was the use? The horn was no longer his to own.

Sydney waited for his approval. Sterling bit back the words he wanted to say. That horn was meant to be his.

"I like your playin'," he said, swallowing his bitterness. "Willie Cornish right. You a natural!" He looked down at Sydney's red and swollen foot. It was covered with a greasy poultice.

"That foot look real bad," said Clancy. "What's all that grease?"

"Hog lard and turpentine."

"Bet you scream real loud," said Clancy. "What they done a-you?"

"Got a real bobo. About a thousand shells stuck in it," said Sydney. "They got them tweezers and pull out every one, an' it hurt bad, but I ain't holler, not a once."

"It look swole," said Clancy. "Bet I can make it go down—jus' stick a pin in. Got a beignet for ya, here." Clancy held out the pastry. "I jus' took the one bite."

"I brung you my horn, but now you got your own," said Sterling. He felt impatient to know more about Sydney's horn. "How your dad come by that one?"

Syd chewed the pastry. "My dad save up a few dollar. He know how I always want to play horn. He put some money down an' paid a little every week. Said it gonna help make my pain better. You like it?" He turned shining eyes to Sterling.

Sterling took a breath. "I like it fine."

"Can you walk?" asked Clancy.

"I gotta lean on the stick and hop a while. What y'all doin'?" asked Sydney.

"Practicin' for Willie. You remember the lick he teached us?"

"Yeah, I remember it," said Sydney. He wiped his sticky fingers on his shirt, then tooted out the tune. Sterling found the same notes on his trumpet and played along with him, while Clancy pounded on the wooden steps with the walking stick, to beat the time.

"Ya gonna come for another lesson with Willie?"

"Can't. I gotta stay around home maybe a couple week." Sydney gestured to his cane.

Clancy leaned on the stick and hobbled around like an old man. "Lucky! You gonna miss school for two week!" he said. "Hey, I'ma go home." Clancy's long body was poised to leave, now that there was not much to see. "Gotta do chores."

"An' I got my stand," said Sterling. "We all be back, maybe tomorrow."

Sydney looked sad they were leaving so soon.

"I maybe show you some more fingerin' tomorrow," said Sterling, "but you so good, maybe you don't need no help."

"Sure. Come on back, then. I sure do need some help."

As the boys turned to go, Syd's crystal notes followed them down the alleyway. "He playin' real good," noted Clancy. "Maybe he gonna be second horn in our band."

"First horn, more like," agreed Sterling, the knowledge heavy on his heart. "I think he gonna be a real musicianer, jus' like the King say."

Outside on the street, the gang of three boys waited. With their dirty ragged clothes and snaggly evil smiles, they looked ready to fight, and Sterling felt the hairs prickling along his arms.

"Hey, Shrimp, you gotta pay for usin' this street," the tallest boy called. He walked toward them, a scowl on his face, and the others followed. "Le' me see that horn."

"Run!" hissed Sterling. The two turned and ran for it. Pounding footsteps followed them. Sterling felt a sting as a rock hit his back. Up ahead, a streetcar clanged to a stop at the corner, and the two boys leaped on, just as the car was gathering speed. They ran past the driver to the coloreds' seats, and sneered and waved through the back window at the boys left behind. The gang shook their fists and made cutting gestures across their throats. Clancy gave them the finger.

"Hah! We jus' too fast for 'em," said Sterling. "Man, we sure lucky."

"Yeah. Lucky we still alive. You see that boy got a scar down his neck? And that other one, look like he got a empty space where his eye missin'.."

"Naw, I never seen that. You funnin' me, right?"

"You never seen 'im? He real scary lookin'. No way we ever gonna beat them boys in a fight. Good thing we run."

"Yeah, good thing," agreed Sterling. The streetcar came to a stop, and the driver turned an angry face toward them.

"Get out! No money. No ride!"

He put them off, spitting curses because they could not pay. Sterling said goodbye to Clancy and ran toward Paulo's shop to collect his shoeshine stand. But, as always when he felt troubled, he found his feet turning toward the river. At the dockyards, he dodged around loaded wagons of fruit and vegetables, then ambled toward a sternwheeler, smoke belching from its funnels as it took on a cargo of crates and barrels. Neat rows of cotton bales lay piled along the wharf, and small drifts of raw cotton spilled out of torn sacking, light and white as goose down. Workers sat or lay, resting on bales, talking idly, and smoking pipes.

Sterling, unnoticed amongst the hustle and bustle, perched on a sugar barrel to watch the barges and oyster luggers along the shore. The moan of the ferry horn, the chants and calls of the stevedores offered a cradle of music that helped take his mind off his troubles, and the river sang to him its special song. Even so, he could scarcely enjoy the scene that usually brought him contentment.

The river's music played sweetly enough, but another sound played even sweeter, as it lingered in Sterling's memory—the blissful notes that Syd had created on his horn. As if in answer, King Bolden's mellow sound drifted over the city, like a gull wheeling and diving on the breeze.

His worries about his brother and the stolen money peppered his thoughts. For the second time, he had lost the chance at a good horn. Sydney owned a fine trumpet that was meant to be his, and he felt a stab of jealousy.

It ought to be him holding that very same horn now, pushing those fancy finger keys, enjoying that mellow tone. It was all his brother's fault. Syl had promised to make good on his debt, but he still had not paid one cent toward that eight dollars.

EIGHT

"You two fightin'?" asked his mother, as he ate his bread and molasses at breakfast the next day.

"He just got out o' bed the wrong side," answered Syl with a warning look at Sterling. The two brothers had not spoken much since the fight. Losing the horn made the old anger come back to Sterling. He could scarcely look at Syl, thinking about the pawn shop trumpet he wanted so badly and now he couldn't have. He was still carrying his shoeshine earnings from yesterday. Syl never asked for them, so he figured his brother meant for him to keep the coins.

Today was Saturday. Before he began work outside the train station, he planned to take his horn and meet Clancy to play together in the park. But Clancy was late, so he found his feet heading to the river to sit and watch the loaded freighters come steaming into port.

"Hey, Sterl, ain't we goin' to the park?" Clancy called. He always knew where to find his friend if he wasn't at home. "Got my drum. Let's go!"

"Hey, you wanna go crawfishin' first, or maybe go out to Johnson Park, play some music there?" he asked. He fingered the coins in his pocket.

"Hell, yeah, let's go to Johnson! You got any money?" Clancy asked.

"I got a little, but I got plenty enough for a wiener bun, an' we can take the streetcar, easy. You got money?" he asked Clancy.

"Some."

"I bet the King playin' at Johnson today!"

The two took off at a run to the streetcar stop and boarded a car. They found seats at the back. Clancy glanced at Sterling before turning his head to gaze out the window. "Bet you mad at your brother," he muttered.

"Huh?"

"I seen your brother with that Rose Piron. They all walkin' in the street together. If'n he my brother, I sure do some damage to his head."

Sterling did not want to be reminded. "Hey, mind

your business. Shut up now, if you comin' with me today."

"D'ya hear about Buddy Bolden?" asked Clancy, quickly changing the subject. "He hit his ma with a pitcher couple days ago. I bet he in jail. Hey, you think that balloon man Bob Bartley gonna be there today?"

"Can't be. Bolden hit his own mother? Where ya hear that?"

"My dad read it in the paper. I hear he maybe gone crazy. Hey, maybe we ask that balloon man for a ride?"

"Nah. Never happen. The King ain't never gonna hit his mother. I don't believe it. Bob Bartley, he the crazy one."

The streetcar reached Carrollton Street, and the boys leaped off and ran toward Johnson Park.

The sounds of brass instruments drifted toward them on the spring breeze. Picnickers had spread their blankets and baskets of food close to the bandstand, and an ice cream wagon advertised its wares with tinkling music.

"Hey, you want a ice?"

"Yes!"

As they ran toward the wagon, a band on stage played its last notes, and the musicians gathered their instruments.

"I want strawberry!" Clancy said, looking at the

pictures of ice cream scoops in pastry cups painted on the side of the wagon.

"Me, too." Sterling collected his change, his eyes on the bandstand to see who was next up. They licked their ice cream and Clancy tugged on his arm.

"Come on, let's go see the balloon show."

Across the field, the red and white striped hot-air balloon slowly rose above the park. The boys ran closer and gazed up. Bob Bartley leaned over the side, waving at the crowd below, and throwing paper streamers that fluttered down. Higher and higher he went. The boys waited for the exciting part, when an actor with a gun pretended to shoot a hole in the balloon. The crack of a rifle shot sounded, then another, and the balloon began to descend. Had the marksman really shot a hole in the balloon? Sterling hoped it was all pretend, because the balloon was coming down in a controlled way, except ... it came very close to a rooftop and the crowd screamed and pointed as the basket briefly touched the roof, bounced, and wobbled crazily. They could see Bob Bartley hanging on to the ropes for dear life. Then, like magic, it righted itself and floated on down and out of sight.

"Let's go look. Maybe his head split open," urged Clancy.

"He okay," said Sterling. "It jus' pretend. Let's start playin' a rag, get us some more pennies."

They set up under the shade of an oak tree and began a cheerful tune. Sterling played the melody loud like the King, and Clancy gave a good beat on his drum. In the distance, band members walked up onto the stage. They wore the formal boxy blue jackets and striped pants that told everyone they belonged to Bolden's band. Sterling stopped at the end of his tune. "I wanna hear Bolden. Come on."

"King Bolden! Give us the Funky Butt!" shouted the onlookers.

Willie was there with his trombone, and Sterling waved to him, but there were too many in the crowd for Willie to notice.

"How they all get in them skinny pants?" said Clancy.

The King grinned, carrying himself with a sway to his hips that made the girls scream, as he strutted in a circle. He took out a red handkerchief and wiped the sweat off his face, then tossed it toward some women out in front, and they all rushed to make a grab for it. He stomped three times on the floor and took the first song away with a rousing rag.

The King played so loud that the whole city must hear it. Sterling imagined the King's sound reaching the white neighborhoods, all those men and women lifting their heads to gaze up and wonder just where that sound came from—it probably sounded like it was coming down from the sky.

"Hey, you wanna buy us some beer?" Clancy pointed over to a beer wagon.

"Nah, hate the taste."

"Aw, come on. I'ma get us some. You got a dime?" Clancy thrust his palm out and Sterling fished in his pocket. "An' a nickel for cigarettes?"

"Why you want cigarettes an' beer?" asked Sterling, as he swallowed the last of his ice cream.

"You old enough now. Come on."

"Okay. I'ma try it." Sterling gave him the coins, then turned back toward the King.

He could hear strains of music from Lincoln Park a few blocks away, where the uppity Creoles went. John Robichaux had a smart Creole band that played mostly cool waltzes, nothing hot like King Bolden's music. The

King must have heard the music from Lincoln Park drifting toward him, because he got off the stage and walked toward the fence.

"Come on, Willie. Gon' call my chillen home," he called out, and he blew a few bars of a loud hot number through a knothole in the fence, while the crowd followed behind and cheered.

Sterling felt pretty certain that would bring over the crowd from Lincoln Park and, sure enough, after a while, people started drifting toward Johnson Park, enticed by the hot ragged beat.

Clancy held out a lit cigarette to Sterling. "Here, you try it." He waved the cigarette in front of his face to get Sterling's attention, so he took it and inhaled. He felt his throat seize up.

"Wash it down with that." Clancy put a cup of beer in his hand and Sterling gulped it down to soothe the pain in his throat. The beer's bitterness made him twist his face with disgust. "Now take more smoke," advised Clancy. "Go easy, now."

Sterling smoked some more, then gulped some beer. He felt the music pound into his head and he staggered, dizzy and feeling sick, caught in a blue whirlpool of sound. Clancy puffed on the cigarette, holding it between his thumb and finger and blowing smoke in a casual way, while Sterling sat down suddenly on the ground and leaned his back against the trunk of a tree. His stomach began to heave.

Someone was standing over him and he looked up to see his brother. Behind him stood Rose.

For a moment, Sterling had a conversation with his stomach, but his body wasn't listening. "Not now, no, no ..." but his stomach wasn't doing what he asked, and he crawled behind the tree and threw up.

"Clancy, what you doin' a-my brother?" said Syl. "Givin' him booze and smokes." He laid his hand on Sterling's forehead. "Why you ain't doin' the stand? Come on, kid. You all goin' home. You got too much excitement today."

"Aw, he okay," said Clancy. "You okay, ain't you, Sterl?"

Rose took out a handkerchief and bent to gently wipe his face. "Come on over to the fountain. Have a drink of water and wash your face—you'll feel better."

Sterling let her lead him across the park. The uneven ground made him stagger and she put her arm around his waist to hold him steady. It seemed like his dream of having Rose notice him was coming true in the worst way ever, and he groaned out loud.

"Here you are." Rose dipped her hand in the water fountain and wiped his forehead to cool him. "Now take a drink," she urged, filling the metal cup on its chain with cool water.

Sterling bent to the cup and felt his head begin to spin. He gulped some water down. "Thanks. I feel okay now," he lied.

"I'll ask your brother, let you stay with us today. Come on, he won't be angry; you were just trying something new," she whispered, as they came up to Syl and Clancy.

"He's fine," she said to Syl. "Let him stay. He can come around with us. You, too, Clancy."

Syl was laughing now. How easily she had changed his temper. "You sure lucky, Rose feelin' sorry for you," he said. "Now you all gonna get special treatment. Maybe you take care of Rose for me. I'ma stand in for Black Benny, right after King Bolden finish."

"He a scary guy," said Clancy.

"Nah, Benny mostly gentle like a lamb," said Syl. Whenever Benny was in jail, Syl often stepped in to take his place at the drums.

Sterling's head was starting to clear and he felt better. The King's band finished their last number and packed up. He could see Buddy coming down from the bandstand, weaving this way and that, drinking from a cup, the women flocking around him.

"That man always drunk." Syl's eyes followed Bolden's swaying progress through the crowd. "He better watch that stuff or it gonna finish him."

Sterling wanted to ask his brother why he kept cocaine in his drawer, but did not dare. His brother might get mad and punch him.

NINE

"You brought your instruments today," Rose said.

Syl had left them to play drum on the bandstand, and Sterling sat with Rose and Clancy, listening to the music. His head had stopped whirling, and it felt good to be in Rose's company, even though he had behaved like such a fool.

"We playin' for pennies," said Clancy, and beat a rhythm on his drum. "But Sterling easy make up his own music. He so good. You gotta hear his tunes sometime."

"I have to leave and get ready for work. Why don't I take you by to meet Armand? He already knows about you—I told him you are a composer. Would you like that?"

"Yes!" said Sterling. "I got so many tunes in my head. Maybe he gonna teach me a-write 'em on paper?"

"We could ask him," said Rose. "What about you,

Clancy? You want to be a musician just like Sterling?"

"Nah. I'ma marry a rich girl, won't never have to work."

"Clancy, you just talkin' nonsense," laughed Sterling. "No rich girl gonna marry you."

"Just you wait," said Clancy. "I'm so good lookin', I'm gonna get the girls jus' like the King."

Rose waved goodbye to Syl, and he nodded from the bandstand and blew her a kiss.

"You comin' along, Clancy?" asked Sterling.

"Nah. I'm gonna stay awhile." Clancy was eyeing a picnic table full of sweet pastries, laid out near the bandstand.

Sterling followed Rose onto the streetcar and, as they rattled along, she told him about her studies to be a nurse. Sterling soon found himself chatting easily about his own plans, to be a musicianer like the King.

"This is our stop," said Rose and pulled on the bell. They walked into a neighborhood of trim cottages on the better side of town. Sterling believed most Creoles were uppity and proud, because they never mixed with the poor folk uptown. But his friend Sydney was Creole and not uppity. He lived in a neighborhood that was home to all kinds of people—colored, Italian, Irish—and it didn't seem to matter to anyone. He began to feel nervous about meeting Armand. He had lots of tunes in his head, but he could hardly remember any of them for worrying. What if Armand hated all of them, and him, too?

They stopped at the gate of a small white cottage with a red front door. Rose led him inside into the parlor. Sterling looked around the room. Two violins lay on a desk, and an upright piano stood along one wall. Under his feet lay a thick patterned rug. On the other side of the room stood a long velvet-covered couch and plush armchairs. Sterling went over to look at a stuffed bird on the sideboard, with cruel talons and beak, and brilliant green and brown plumage. He was startled to notice an older boy, sitting bent over a desk in the corner, his back to Sterling and Rose. A crutch leaned against the desk.

"Armand, we have company," said Rose.

The young man turned, and a pair of brown eyes stared at Sterling, for a moment unfocused, as though his thoughts were miles away. His forehead was wide and high, the hairline far back at the top of his head, the nose long and finely shaped. His gaze took in Sterling from head to toe, from his worn cotton shirt and knee pants to the scuffed trainers and the trumpet in his hand. After this silent perusal, he nodded to him and raised his eyes to Rose's face with a questioning look.

"This is the boy I was telling you about, Armand. Syl's brother, Sterling. The one who composes. Maybe you can help him?" She smiled at Sterling. "Armand is a good teacher. If he agrees you have promise, he will help you to write your music down in notation form."

"Don't make promises to the boy I may not be able to deliver," said Armand.

"Don't let him frighten you," she whispered to Sterling. "But work hard! I'll go and make some lemonade."

Armand's face showed boredom. "My sister Rose thinks you show promise as a composer. Is that what you want to do with your life?"

The question was an unexpected one, and Sterling needed time to digest it. "I wanna play like Buddy Bolden," he blurted.

Armand grimaced. "While you're in this house, please do not mention Buddy Bolden, or express a wish to play in his atrocious barrel-house style. Do you read music?"

If atrocious meant "bad," Sterling did not think he would like this young man. "I read words on paper. Is readin' music the same?"

Armand got up from his chair, reached for the crutch, and limped across the room to the piano. He sat down on the bench, facing Sterling. "Play one of your tunes for me."

Sterling raised the horn to his lips, and paused for a second to get his mouth ready, the way Willie had taught him. He hit the first notes of his tune about Clancy's bouncing feet with a strong sure touch, proud of the catchy ragtime tune he'd composed, thanks to the boy's fidgeting.

"What do you call that tune?" Armand asked when he finished.

"'Bouncy Feet.'" Sterling tried to read his face. Did he like it? "An' I got more tunes. 'River Rag' 'n lots more."

"That piece is simple, but I like the beginning, middle, and end, just like any good story." Armand turned to face the piano and gestured to Sterling to sit down on the bench with him. He played Sterling's tune on the piano with his right hand, and added notes with his left that made the tune sound even better.

"That's just the way I hear it in my head!" said Sterling. "It sound real good with all them notes together!"

Armand stared at him. "You can hear the entire melody, with the harmony added?"

The word "harmony" was puzzling, but Sterling nodded his head.

"Mozart used to say he wrote music as a sow pisses," mused Armand almost to himself. "Perhaps you have a little of that talent."

"I ain't no sow pissin," Sterling protested.

"I believe he meant the writing of his music was just a mechanical exercise. He could hear the complete composition in his head, then he let it flow outward, to be written down and played. Is that how it works for you?"

Sterling guessed this was so and nodded. The tunes fell into his head from everywhere—the street vendors, the bands, even the rattle of coal carts had a special song. Armand took a sheet of paper from a pile that sat on the piano. With a pencil, he quickly drew some dots on a piece of lined paper beside the keyboard.

"That's how my song look on paper?" asked Sterling.

Armand placed the music on the stand and sat with

fingers poised over the keyboard. "I want you to listen and watch as I play your notes." He gestured to one line of musical notes. "Concentrate, and when I have finished, tell me what you notice about my melody and what is written down."

Armand's long fingers moved up and down the keyboard. Sterling felt anxiety rising in his chest, as he stared at the sheet music and then at Armand's hands. Somehow, he was expected to do something he had never been taught—read those black dots on straight lines and understand what they meant.

Armand came to the end of the short passage and paused, his fingers resting on the keys. "Now, one more time," he said, and began again.

Sterling stopped looking at Armand's hands, but stared only at the music as he listened. "I got it," he shouted before Armand had finished. "If'n you play notes that go high, them dots go up! You play music low, they go down." Sterling stared at the page of music. "Why, I can see my whole song, just lookin' at them dots! My own tune on paper, right from inside my head!"

Armand placed some printed music on the stand and began playing a slow piece. Sterling listened. "That ain't no kind of ragtime I ever heared," said Sterling. "It ain't for dancin'."

"This is a classical piece by Mozart. He was a young boy of five when he composed his first piece, over one hundred years ago. He would turn over in his grave if he heard Buddy Bolden's gutbucket style." Armand closed the folder of music to show Sterling the cover—a drawing of a dicty white musician with curly hair and a high sissy collar.

"Bet he can't play the King special notes," Sterling persisted. He remembered Bolden's musical note that had hushed the crowd, that night he had brought Sterling up on stage.

"Special! Bolden's music has no structure or discipline. His notes would fall into these cracks between the keys, worthless. I doubt anyone will remember Bolden one hundred years from now."

Sterling looked at the narrow spaces between the keys. It seemed to him Bolden already could play amazing and magical notes from those spaces. He bet Mozart never did that.

"So, *you* can't write the King notes neither, with them dots on paper," protested Sterling. "All my music that I hear in my head got them special ones. How can I write *them* notes?"

Armand sighed. "My sister tells me you are gifted, and it is musical theory you lack. I respect her opinion, but my time is precious." He paused for a moment. "You're here because she has some affection for your brother. I don't care for any alliance with someone not of our class."

"I respec' my brother, too," said Sterling. "An' you ain't no better'n us! My momma say we all people, an' we all the same. Just 'cause you Creole don't mean you better."

A slow smile crossed Armand's face. "You have much to learn. We will start with the simple key of C." He struck the key on the piano. "If you are a musician of any worth, and know the sound of middle C in your head, you will soon be able to hear any note and name it from memory, without need of a keyboard."

'Cept them special notes Bolden play that don't have no name, thought Sterling, but he knew not to speak his thoughts out loud.

In the hour that followed, Sterling forgot his shoeshine stand, his missing money, even the time of day. Rose had left for work long ago. Armand finally laid down his pencil and closed the piano lid. He handed the page of music to him. "That is enough for today."

Sterling gazed at the notes he and Armand had placed there.

"Come back next week at this same time. We shall see how you progress."

"You think I got the chops for a musicianer?"

Armand stood and stretched, then picked up his crutch. "You can be a common two-bit musician and play in street bands. To go further, you need to work very hard. You have a long way to go, and not much time to get there. Talent is only a small percentage of what is required."

He walked over to his desk and sat down to bend over his work. "Dedication and passion count for much more," he said as he picked up a pen. "Goodbye for today. You can show yourself out."

Sterling ran home, holding the music carefully in one hand and his trumpet in the other. He burst through the front door of his house, and the aroma of his mother's gumbo filled his nostrils. He could hear voices in the kitchen.

"... too young," his mother said. "I forbid it. There is people out there, cruel folk. It ain't safe, you two alone."

"What you all talkin' about?" asked Sterling.

Syl came over to him. "We havin' a disagreement. What you got there?" he asked, looking at the paper Sterling held.

"My own music! Armand Piron done wrote it out for me. 'Bouncy Feet.'"

Syl took the paper and held it up to show his mother. "You see? This boy gettin' some schoolin' outside school. He learnin' more about the world when he outside school."

Sterling looked from one to the other. Something was up.

Syl waved a letter at him. "Cousin Laura, Plaquemine way, she got a birthday Saturday week, an' she invite us all, but Momma can't go. I got some work that same day, in Plaquemine. You wanna come along? I can take you to Laura before I start."

"Aw, please? Le' me go with Syl?" Sterling begged his mother, his quarrel with his brother forgotten.

"You too young. When you thirteen, then I let you decide. But you not even eleven. I say no."

"But it ain't a school day. Right, Syl?"

"No. Just the Saturday and Sunday." Syl sat down

across from his mother and took her hands in his. "You know I'ma look after him. I'm gonna get a rope and tie him to me, if it make you feel better. An' I'ma write Laura. Make sure she come an' meet the train and take Sterl along."

"Well, if you mean it." His mother began to smile. She could never resist Syl's charm. "You take your necktie and tie it round that boy's wrist. I mean it. You don't let him out o' your sight."

"Bring your horn an' play your song for the birthday party," said Syl. "Now you got a job, too. We gonna make a musicianer out o' you yet, kid. Get you some long pants, for sure."

"An' I gonna bring you back a present, jus' you wait," said Sterling to his mother.

"Jus' bring back your own sweet self," she answered, and seemed to look beyond him to a place he couldn't see. "Listen to your brother and keep close."

Part 2

TRAINWRECK

TEN

"Sterling, git over here." Syl stood with a few passengers at the end of the platform, obeying the signs over the waiting room doors—one read "Coloreds Only" in black letters on white, while another read "Whites Only" in white on black.

The train chugged into the station, belching smoke. Syl stood ready to jump on the Jim Crow car next to the engine. He waved his tie to signal that if Sterling did not stick like glue, he would leash him like a puppy. Through the crowd, Sterling saw Barrel and Clancy, come to see him off.

"Wish I was comin' along," said Barrel. "Here, I brung some fritters from home that mom made, and some pickles."

Sterling took the offering tied in a square of cloth. "I got some food, but this gonna be good for in between times."

"Where ya get them long pants?" said Clancy.

"Syl." Sterling had changed his short pants for a pair of his brother's cast-offs, the bottoms rolled up for size.

"We playin' in the park tomorrow," said Clancy. "Maybe Sydney, too, if he feelin' better."

Sterling hoped Syd's foot was better, but felt a pang of worry that Syd might be taking his place on horn. Syl beckoned to Sterling again, as the train slowed to a halt. The whistle blew two short blasts amid clouds of steam.

"See you Sunday," Sterling called to the boys. He hurried to join Syl and the other passengers: bonneted women with picnic baskets, a tangle of children around their skirts; the men in straw hats, bundles slung over their shoulders.

The boys climbed into the smoking car where the baggage was stored. Inside, a white man spat a wad of tobacco onto the floor, close to Sterling's feet. A chained black prisoner sat hunched near a guard, head lowered, eyes swollen shut, the bruising purple and red. The guard had nodded off to sleep, and his breath came in rumbling gasps, with a few snorts that made his jowls quiver.

Sterling stared at the chained man and wondered why he was being punished. He willed the prisoner to lift his head, so he could smile as he passed, give him some encouragement. His mother always said a smile goes a long way, but the man did not look up. Syl nudged his brother to look away and get to his seat.

He pushed Sterling down into a window seat and sat beside him. The train slowly pulled out of the station, and Sterling leaned out to wave to Barrel and Clancy, as it gathered speed and left them behind.

"Pull your head in, or you gonna lose it," said Syl.

Smells from the toilet fought with acrid smoke flying through the open window. Orange cinders arched into the compartment from the boiler up front. Syl got up and slammed the window closed. He pulled his hat over his eyes to take a nap, lulled by the rocking motion. Suddenly curious to see into the next car, Sterling squeezed past his brother, glancing back to catch the baleful stare of the white man sitting nearby. He peered through the dusty window of the door between the cars, where the white passengers sat in plush chairs on carpeted floors.

"Outta my way, Sam," said the white man, shoving him aside to go back to the Pullman car. Sterling remembered his mother's words of caution that morning. "Never look a white man in the face," she had warned. Sterling kept his eyes lowered.

Their train left the city behind, crossed the river by train ferry, and chugged on up through bayou country. Sharecroppers bent over their work in the hot morning sun. Glimpses of the brown Mississippi caught Sterling's eye, singing to him as it snaked alongside the track, before winding away to hide behind fields of cane.

Sterling had never before seen the river out in the wide world beyond New Orleans. It gave him a feeling of connection to his home. The *chugga chugga, clink clink* of the train danced its melody into his head. He conjured the long, low note of a horn fading in and out as the river came into view, then became lost among the cane, only to offer a glimpse of itself again, slow and sinuous, ever present.

Two hours went by, and the scenery began to change from sweeping cane fields to citrus groves and clusters of cottages.

"Ten minutes to Plaquemine," announced the conductor, as he came through to punch their tickets.

Sterling opened the window and gazed out. The brown Mississippi glinted in the distance; a freighter sailed upstream. At last, the train chugged down the town's wide main street, lined with stores of every kind, and slowed to a grinding stop at the station. This street was not as fancy as Canal Street, but wrought-iron lamp posts and pots of flowers showed a town that took some pride in its appearance.

"Cousin Laura aroun'?" Sterling asked. "You see her?"

"Happen she be there waitin'. I wrote her we gonna be on this train."

The guard yanked his prisoner upright and pushed ahead of them, the shackles on the prisoner's ankles and wrists clinking. Sterling tried to catch the eye of the man as he shuffled toward the door, but he did not look up. It seemed as though the world no longer held any interest for him.

Syl collected his bundle and placed Sterling's horn inside, with the packed lunch and a square of embroidered linen, a birthday present for Cousin Laura. They stepped down onto the platform and looked around for her. On the walls, Sterling saw the same signs that he had seen in the waiting rooms in the New Orleans station. Black passengers exited by their door onto the street. Minutes ticked by, but there was no sign of Laura.

"No loitering." A white station official pointed to the sign on the station wall. "Can't you boys read?"

Syl took his arm and led him toward the exit.

"But Laura s'pose a-meet us right here," said Sterling.

"Happen she jus' late. We bes' go on out to the street, wait there." Syl patted his pocket. "I still got this tie," he warned his brother, "so stay close."

They walked past the porters, and on by the fancy carriages lined up along the street. Behind these stood a Black Maria with barred windows. Maybe the prisoner from the train sat inside.

"Move along!" shouted another official. "No loiterin'!"

"Where she at? She know I gotta leave you with her and play with the band." Syl turned this way and that, searching the street. "We better just walk for now, like we know where we goin'."

Sterling felt a nervous flutter in his chest, but felt eager for a taste of the new world outside the station.

On the street, a horse-drawn billboard wagon trundled past them with a poster pasted to its side.

She Had the Soul of an Angel

the Face of a Saint

and the Heart of the Devil!

Sterling stared at the drawing of a white woman in a flimsy gown. She gazed into the eyes of a man with a neat moustache, dressed in work clothes. As the wagon rumbled on by, he noticed another poster pasted to its back.

The Painter Saw Her Naked Soul!

"Don't stare at nothin'," said Syl. "Just keep walkin'. Laura gotta be here somewhere."

They passed a hardware store and a theater, as their train chugged past them down the main street, on its way out of town.

"I'm so thirsty," said Sterling, his eye caught by a sign in a grocery store window:

Sparkling Lemon Soda 5 cents.

"Let's all get somethin' a-drink?"

"Go on in and get some, then," said Syl and put a coin in Sterling's hand. "Leave your horn with me. I'm gonna wait out here, watch for Laura."

Inside, the soda jerk was busy with a customer and Sterling waited, looking hungrily at the ice cream machine that had two flavors, strawberry and vanilla.

Voices came from the far end of the shop and he glanced that way. Amidst shelves of canned goods, three young white men in shirtsleeves stood around a young colored man. One of the three spoke in a taunting way, while the other two leaned toward the man, who shook his head in denial and mumbled his responses.

Sterling felt scared. *That boy don't have a chance,* he thought. A punishment was coming, no matter what he said. He could see it in the eyes of the men, a look of hatred. And something else as well. The joy of the hunt. The same as when he and his friends hooked that trophy redfish, and it struggled and flashed its silver underbelly, but they knew they had it, no matter how much it jerked and quivered on the hook.

Sterling felt his skin prickle and decided he was not so thirsty, after all. He began to sidle out, pretending he'd had his look around.

"You, boy! Git over here."

He looked back. One of the men was talking to him.

"Yes, you! Over here!"

Sterling looked out the store window for Syl. The man was coming toward him now, and Sterling stood, wanting to run, but his feet just stuck there.

ELEVEN

Up close, the man smelled of sour sweat and whiskey. Lank yellow hair fell over one eye, and there was stubble on his chin. He had a stocky, muscular build, and seemed like someone who enjoyed getting into fights so he could win. He fished in his pocket and pulled out some change.

"I'm gonna give you this money. You run to Neubig's hardware store up the street, get me twenty yard o' strong rope. You come right back—don't make me come lookin' for you."

Sterling took the money. "Yessuh," he said.

"Twenty yard. Fetch it right back here, now."

Sterling hurried out the door.

"Syl! Syl!" he called.

"Here," said Syl, coming out from the shade at the side of the shop.

"White man in there, tole me a-fetch twenty yard o' rope from the hardware store. He done give me some money for it."

"Hell, what he want that for?"

"Some boy in there in trouble."

Syl's face showed his alarm. "Lawd, we gotta get away from this place. This ain't good."

"He say he come after me, if'n I don' fetch it."

"Then let's go fetch it quick. The store is back a way by the picture palace."

The two hurried back the way they had come.

Neubig's was a grand hardware store, with large windows displaying tools and ladders. Syl opened the door.

"Jus' wait here out o' sight while I get the rope," he said, and went inside.

The five minutes that Syl was inside seemed like an age to Sterling. He paced and paced, trying to look like he had somewhere to go, till Syl pushed open the door, the rope in a large coil over his shoulder.

"Why ya took so long!?" asked Sterling.

"Explainin' what I'ma do with all this rope," Syl said. "Tole him it ain't for me but for some white gentleman.

There warn't enough money in the coins he gave you. I done pay out o' my own pocket."

They turned back in the direction of the grocery store. Sterling wished with all his heart he had never asked for a soda.

"Look here," said Syl when they reached the store. 'I'm gonna open the door. You put your head inside, shout, 'Got your rope, Mister,' and I'ma drop it through the door, and we jus' walk away fast, no runnin'. Can you do that?"

"I guess."

"If'n he come after us, we both good runners, but I don't think that gonna happen, 'cause I guess he got other things on his mind."

Sterling did exactly as Syl told him. He opened the shop door, shouted, "Got your rope for ya, Mister!"— too afraid to look toward the men and the poor colored who was in such big trouble. Syl tossed the rope inside without showing his face, and the two turned and walked as fast as they could, away from there. It was all Sterling could do not to run.

On they went, past the hardware store, still searching for their cousin. A theater stood on the corner with a large marquee in front. White people were filing through the glass entrance doors.

"Best coon show on the planet, I hear," Sterling overheard one white man say to his wife as he passed by them. He noticed a crowd of his own people, men and women, lining up to enter a door at the side.

Someone gave a low whistle and he looked around. In the shade of the marquee leaned a slim older boy, dressed in a top hat set at an angle on his head. Striped pants and a black weskit gave him a carefree air.

The boy looked about the same age as Syl. Sterling could see a certain knowledge of the world behind his eyes, a look of wisdom, along with all the good humor, on his large round face. He felt certain this boy did not attend school and had no interest in scholarly matters.

"Don't I know you?" he called to Syl. "Ain't you Syl Crawford?"

Syl stared at the boy. "Clarence? Clarence Williams! Yes, I should say you do know me." Syl bounded forward, shook the young man's hand, and slapped him on the back. "Long time since I seen you! Where you bin all this time?"

"Just around the world and back again. And who is this young fella?"

"Clarence, this my little brother, Sterling."

Sterling felt a leap of joy. At last, he did not need to pretend they were not brothers. Not here in Plaquemine.

"How do," said Clarence. His eyes moved from Syl to Sterling, then rested on Syl. "Where you goin'? Sit down a minute. We got some catchin' up to do!"

"Can't. I'm lookin' a-find my cousin Laura, lives on Barrow Street. I gotta take Sterling over there, then I gotta play drum for a party in town. You know where is Barrow Street?"

"Why, that's a ways from here, down the railroad track, 'bout a mile or two near the edge of town. What time you have to get there?"

"Right about now," said Syl.

"You got no time to get there and back. But whyn't you just hurry along to your appointment. I can take care of your brother while you gone."

He pointed to the marquee. "See there?"

The boys looked up at the sign.

Billy Kersands
Melodies and Dances from the Old Plantation
With Louise Kersands, Clarence Williams

"I happen to be in that show with Billy, just like it says—Master of Ceremonies." Clarence turned to Sterling and snapped his fingers. "Easy to slip you inside! Watch the matinee for free, huh? If anyone can do it, Clarence Williams can." He slipped off his hat with a wide flourish and bowed. "At your service, boys."

He punched his hat down and it folded like an accordion.

"Sterling gotta stay with me," said Syl, catching hold of Sterling's arm.

"Don't you worry. He will be plenty safe with me."

Syl opened his mouth to protest, but Clarence interrupted. "I ain't taking no for an answer, Syl. You done me a few favors back in Nawlins. Here is one for you." He turned to Sterling. "You ever see a minstrel show before? Well, you deserve to see the full show in fine style."

Syl gave up. "I'm gonna be aroun' two hour."

"That's just fine," said Clarence.

"You go on then, Sterl," said Syl. "You can trust him. Do what he say. Stay out of trouble. Wait here after the show."

Syl took his drumsticks out, then left his bundle with Sterling, and hurried back the way they had come. Clarence led him down the alley and through an entrance marked "Stage Door."

"Watch your step," he warned as they walked along a dark passageway. He opened a door at the end, and they heard the sounds of a band tuning up.

Black actors wearing britches and farmers' hats, and in various stages of dress, wandered about, mumbling lines. Their mouths were painted white. Straw stuck out of their pockets and from inside their hat bands. As the boys passed, the men reached out to rub the top of Clarence's head for luck.

"Fall on a pitchfork," said Clarence to one. "Lose your britches," to another.

Clarence led him up some steps and between two plush gray velvet curtains. Dust bit Sterling's nostrils as they edged through the narrow space.

"So, you from Nawlins," he said to Sterling, by way of making conversation.

"That's right. Where you from?" asked Sterling.

"Born here, in Plaquemine," answered Clarence, "but I been tourin' the world with Billy these last five years. Was only twelve when I left my home town," he continued. "Just turned seventeen now and I'm tired. Too much drink. Too many girls. I plan to settle in Nawlins after we're done here in beautiful Plaquemine. Five years on the road is about enough for me."

"How you know my brother?" Sterling asked, curious.

"Run away to New Orleans when I was just a kid, only nine year old. Stole money from my mother's purse." They reached the end of the curtains, and came to a tall wood panel that rose up into the darkness above them. "A gang of kids robbed me, beat on me, and left me for dead. Syl picked me up, took me to the train station, and bought my ticket back to Plaquemine." Clarence picked up an empty crate and placed it on the floor. "Just a year older than me, but even back then, he ain't never short of money," he chuckled. "Never forgot that kindness." He took Sterling's bundle from him and put it down. The trumpet made a metallic sound as it hit the floor.

"What's that you got?" asked Clarence. He didn't wait for an answer but opened the cloth bag. "A trumpet! I mighta known it. All the coloreds in Nawlins are musicians, or wanna be.

"Up you go. Stand on that crate and tell me it ain't a good view."

Sterling stepped up. He was at eye level with a round peephole. He found he was gazing out onto the stage from one side. There were bales of straw with pitchforks, a wagon filled with bundles of hay, and a wheelbarrow loaded with cornhusks.

"Mr. Williams. Where you at? We need you in five minutes," came a woman's voice from somewhere behind the curtain.

"I gotta run. Don't move. Don't wander. Anyone asks, say you're just a critic."

Clarence left by the same route they had come, and Sterling watched him go, standing in the darkness. The only light came from the peephole, and he put his eye to it again and looked out.

The actors began assembling on stage, some up in a hayloft, others perched on the wagon or posed on a ladder. A trio of banjo players tuned up.

The curtains at the front of the stage swung open to loud applause from the audience, as the trio strummed a lilting country tune.

Five actors dressed as plantation workers called greetings to each other. Their faces were even more darkened by black crayon, and they talked through white-painted mouths.

"I hear o'ny the whites can git into heaven. Iz zat true? Cain't we all get into heaven?" asked one.

"'Course we can. Who else gonna open de golden gates for dem?"

There came roars of approval from the audience. Clarence strutted onto the stage. As he passed the peephole, he winked broadly in Sterling's direction, then turned to swing his cane and lift his top hat. He performed a graceful shuffle step into the center of the stage. His jokes flew so fast, Sterling could hardly keep up.

"Ladies and Gentlemen!" he said at last, getting down to business with a voice that carried to the rafters. There came a drum roll. "I present to you the one, the only, the great, Billy KERSANDS!"

Billy rode on stage on a tiny bicycle, his long body folded around it, his big feet pumping the pedals. From his perch, Sterling saw he was painted the same way as the other actors, but he had one facial feature that was extraordinary—a mouth to beat all mouths for size. The white paint that outlined it traveled right around the chasm on the lower half of his face, and stretched almost to his ear lobes.

Billy flipped the bike into the wings, sang and danced on his long legs, and the jokes zinged one after another. He twisted that mouth into all kinds of shapes as he talked; the slightest curl of his lips set the audience laughing. He opened his mouth as wide as a canyon and put a saucer inside. He sat a teacup on top along with a golf ball, all the while talking easily as though there was nothing but a peppermint in there.

The show was over all too soon for Sterling. To loud applause and one curtain call, the actors left the stage and the lights went out. Sterling stayed where he was in the dark, sitting on the crate, and listened to the comings and goings of the stagehands as he waited for Clarence. His thoughts turned to that poor man in the soda shop, and the rope. There were pictures in his mind he wished he could not see.

"Hey, Sterling. You there?" Clarence's voice called from the other end of the long curtain.

"Yessir, just waitin' for you to come git me."

"C'mon out, follow my voice and come through the curtains. Your brother is here, waitin' outside. Did ya enjoy the show?"

"I laughed real hard—I 'bout pissed my pants," said Sterling, as he made his way along. "You got a bucket? An' I'm real thirsty."

"I can fix both them things," said Clarence.

He was as good as his word, and then he led Sterling back through the passageways and up the stairs to the street.

"Clarence take good care of ya?" said Syl, who was waiting outside. "I'm takin' you back to the party with me. Gotta go finish up there. They good people, Suzie and Lou. They havin' a lawn picnic right outside their house. You gonna like 'em, an' they say to bring you along. They payin' me extra for a couple more hours with the band."

"You find Laura?"

"No, but I know where she live now. Suzie tole me she just along the railway track, other end of town, so we gonna go there right after. Got your bag?"

"I hope we all will meet again, for sure," said Clarence. "I aim to get back to Nawlins straight after this show closes for the last time tonight."

"Well, we gonna be real glad a-see you there. Be sure an' look me up," said Syl. "Thanks for takin' care of my brother."

Sterling liked this gentle-natured boy and hoped he would see him again. Little did he know how soon that would be.

TWELVE

"Make yourself at home," said Suzie to Sterling, as he and Syl walked into her back garden. Though she was Black Benny's cousin, Sterling could see no family resemblance. She was slender, petite, and graceful in her fashionable white dress and sunbonnet. Her straightened hair fell in soft waves around her face.

She lived with her family in a frame house on the bayou at the edge of town. He knew from Syl that her husband Lou was a dentist who did his practice from home.

Suzy gestured to the buffet table laden with good food. "You hungry, Sterling? Help yourself," she invited.

His mouth watered at the aroma of chickens roasting over a firepit.

"I'm gonna be another hour, I guess," said Syl. "Get some food and sit by the band."

The other four band members were set up to play, and Syl joined them to sit in on drum for Benny, who Sterling knew was still serving time in jail.

The guests danced to the music, or sat on rugs spread out on the grass, to talk and enjoy their food. Sterling noticed a group of white guests who did not mix in but stayed close to the band. Syl had told him they were musicians who had come to hear the music. They were looking to borrow some musical licks for their own performances at a club in Plaquemine.

Sterling put a chicken leg on his plate along with some potato salad, and settled on the grass nearby to eat. A white man came around the side of the house and walked by him to join his friends, waving a greeting.

Sterling's mouth stopped in mid-chew. It was one of the men from the soda shop. He was sure of it. Sterling looked over at Syl, but his brother was absorbed in his drumming. He stayed where he was till the band took a break to get some refreshments. Sterling called to his brother in a low voice. "Syl, over here."

Syl came over to sit beside him.

"That man there, the white fella," he said, pointing that way. "He one of them men from the store. I know it."

Syl glanced at the men. "Which one?"

"Blue shirt, black hair."

"He see ya?"

"Don't know if'n he look at me proper at the store. Maybe we better go soon?"

"You ain't done nothin' bad. You done what the man ask. Just keep your head down. Don't look at 'im. Stay a-ways off. We got another hour yet, then we can leave. Jus' a li'l walk down the railway track an' about half a mile to Cousin Laura."

"I jus' don't like bein' here," Sterling said. "I hope Laura gonna be home. Seem like nothin' goin' right today."

"I know where she live. Suzie tole me how to get there along the track. Might be cousin Laura ain't got our letter in time and don't know when we comin'. Stop worryin'. If you go lookin' for trouble, it be sure an' find you."

"Sometime it find us anyway."

The band played a few more numbers, some ragtime and then some waltzes. The dusk was fading into night as it played the last waltz, but Sterling was dismayed to hear the revellers call for even more music.

Syl came over. "The band gonna collect some extra cash and play till midnight, but I ain't stayin' here no longer. We got a curfew, and it ain't safe to be out after ten. We gotta go now. Got your things?"

"I can walk along, make sure you get home safe," said a man nearby. He moved closer, and Sterling saw it was the white man from the soda shop. His eyes glistened in the gathering dark.

Sterling looked nervously at Syl. "We won't be needin' that, thank you, sir," said his brother. "We all can make it jus' fine."

Syl turned to lead Sterling away, but the man followed along. "No problem for me. Police is mighty strict if they catch you after curfew. Right, Suzie?" he called.

Suzie hurried over.

"These boys need someone to walk along with 'em, don't you think?" the man said.

"Sure, walk along with Danny, jus' in case," Suzie said. She knew they could be in a barrel of trouble, but Sterling could tell by the nervous way she spoke, that she didn't dare disagree. "He a respected musician in town. If you get stop by the law, you need someone a-talk for you."

"There you go. It's all fixed," said Danny, drinking the dregs from his cup of beer. "We can take a short cut. Track is that way. You ready?"

"Okay. Thank you, sir," said Syl, his grip tightening on Sterling's arm in a warning that danger was hovering.

Suzy's husband walked over to give Syl some bills for payment, and the three called out their goodbyes as they turned to leave. They followed Danny onto the street alongside the bayou and toward the tracks.

"Good thing you got me along," Danny said. "It ain't too safe around here for boys like you."

There was a little light from the crescent moon, and they walked in silence for a while, till their feet met the rails. Cane fields covered the land on one side of the track. A black shape loomed up ahead. As they passed, Sterling saw it was a pile of railway ties, dark and sinister against the flat landscape. Danny swayed and lost his balance for a moment as he walked along in front.

"Sshh! Gotta all be quiet." Danny giggled foolishly and looked back at Sterling. "Could be the rougarou is out tonight, lookin' for li'l boys like you." He began to sing in a tuneless voice. "The rougarou is out to get you."

"Stay close to me," whispered Syl. "We gotta get away from this donkey."

Danny picked up speed, all of a sudden walking without swaying, as though the drunkenness had been a pretence. He disappeared out of sight.

"Where that devil go?" muttered Syl.

The silver track stretched ahead of them, and they could see the glow of lights from the town far ahead. The cicadas chanted in the trees and a bachelor mockingbird called for a mate. More shapes loomed blackly. These proved to be piles of rusting metal.

"Hooo! Hooo!' Danny leaped out at the boys from behind a hill of pilings, jumping this way and that, seeming disjointed and grotesque in the dark shadows. The two brothers stepped back in alarm. "Hooo Hooo! I'm the rougarou," he wailed, then cackled with high-pitched laughter.

Syl and Sterling dodged around him. Syl held onto Sterling's hand as they began to trot faster down the track. "He crazy?" whispered Sterling. "Here he come again!" A dark form sprinted alongside the line ahead of them, toward the next pile of metal. Syl bent to pick up something from the side of the track.

"Get ready a-run fast, Sterl. Next time he come at us, he gonna get this the side o' his head," he muttered. He held a narrow board at the ready. He dropped their bag by the track and went on, but Sterling turned back to it.

"Leave it," hissed Syl, but Sterling took out his trumpet. He would not go on without it. All was still for a few minutes, as they quickened their steps. Sterling heard the faint whisper of a footfall up ahead.

"Look out. He comin' at us again," he warned.

"Hoooo! Hoooo!" Danny jumped out. Sterling saw that Syl was at the ready with his weapon.

"Get away," said Syl. "Leave us be!"

"Here I come. Better run!" sang Danny, jumping and gesturing and crowing with laughter. He made a sudden leap their way.

Sterling heard a crack as Syl swung the board. He was right on target. Danny gave an "oomph" and dropped to his knees. Syl waited a minute, his weapon poised. Danny stumbled up, cursing and swearing.

"I'm gonna kill you," he grunted, rubbing the side of his head, and Sterling knew the pretend game of fun was over; now it was all about hatred. Danny reached for Syl. Sterling heard another crack as Syl swung again. The man crumpled down beside the rails. This time he did not get up but lay there moaning.

"Come on. We gotta run for it!" Syl grabbed Sterling's hand and the two turned and ran down the track toward town, as though the rougarou really was after them.

They did not stop until Sterling tripped on a rail tie and fell. Syl pulled him up and bent over to catch his breath. The two listened for steps behind them. Not a whisper of sound broke the stillness. They jumped as a night owl hooted. Sterling clutched his horn. Not even a rougarou could make him drop that.

"Think you done kill 'im?"

"We all gonna hide somewhere near the line," Syl panted, "an' hop a freight train goin' back home, jus' in case that man go for the police and they come lookin' for me."

"Why don't we go back to Suzie? Maybe she help us."

"Them whites all there. Bes' we get a ways out o' town. Come on now, keep up, and we gonna run some more."

Syl ran off down the track and Sterling tried to keep close behind. Alert to every sound, he glanced back often. They crossed a trestle bridge over the bayou, and the lights of a few scattered houses shone in the dark.

Up ahead, they saw a railroad siding where tracks met, then parted to lead off in different directions. Syl led him down into the gully alongside.

"Bes' we keep off the rail till a freight train come," he murmured. "Stay quiet now. I'ma look aroun' in case any guard keepin' watch."

He motioned for Sterling to sit down in the grasses. "Stay here. Keep quiet. Be right back."

Sterling listened to Syl's soft footfalls as he walked on. He stood up to look back the way they had come. If Danny was able, he would be moving up the track toward them. Maybe he was creeping up on them this very minute, revenge on his mind, and no more jokes. The minutes seemed to stretch too long till Syl returned.

"There's a shed for storin' things up ahead, all lock up, but we can hide behind it and wait for a freight to go by. C'mon this way."

He led Sterling through the high grass beside the track until a square shape loomed up ahead.

"Right here," said Syl, and the two sat behind the shed, their backs up against the wooden wall.

"Whyn't we jus' buy a ticket, get on the first train that come by?"

"'Cause if'n he dead or injured real bad, the police sure gon' be watchin' out for me at the station."

Syl was silent for a moment, then he gave a low

chuckle. "An' all we done was go to a picnic an' maybe a birthday party." He shook his head. "Well, now we got the Klan after us, an' maybe the police, not that they ain't all jus' the same thing."

He thought for a minute, then turned to Sterling. "I'm gonna change the plan. 'Stead of stayin' together, we all gonna go our own way, Sterl. Only thing for it. We sleep for a while. At sun-up, you gonna walk into Plaquemine, buy your ticket, git on the train, and git back home. I'ma make my way, somehow. It gonna be better if we separate. They mos' likely lookin' for two of us together."

"I ain't leavin' you!" Sterling reached into Syl's pocket. "Gimme that tie! I'm gonna tie myself to you, just like Momma say."

Syl wrestled the tie away. "Won't ya listen to sense? They lookin' for me and you—the both of us, together. Bes' we jus' go our own way, Sterl, first thing come sun-up."

"You ain't leavin' me here alone!"

"You ain't gonna be alone, not for long. Jus' get on that train to Nawlins, is all. You soon gon' be home again."

"I ain't doin' it alone! I'ma come with you. Happen Danny still layin' there."

"Okay, okay. You can come. Git some sleep now, Sterl."

"What if'n our train don't stop in Nawlins?"

"Don't matter. We just get out o' here first, then we worry 'bout where we goin'."

The minutes crawled by and Sterling fell into a half-doze. He wondered what his friends were doing now. Safe in bed, he guessed. In his sleepy state, he asked a question he had long wanted to ask Syl.

"You 'member when you took my money an' I done look for it every place? You sure you ain't usin' that cocaine in your drawer?"

"Nah. What ya take me for? You might as well get some sleep an' stop talkin'."

"But why you got it in your drawer?" he persisted.

"I tole ya, I don't never use it. Paulo gave me money to buy it an' give to the dock workers, keep 'em goin' all night—that way they never get tired."

Sterling knew it took strength and endurance to unload crates of fruit at the docks. Rats would jump out, it might be pouring rain, but the work had to be done. Poor blacks from Back o' Town were willing to do it, as long as they had cocaine to keep them working around the clock. Then ships could turn around and leave harbor as fast as they came in.

"But why you got so much?"

"Drop it," said his brother.

There were more minutes of silence.

"Hey, how come you tell folk here that we brother?" asked Sterling. "Why you ain't never tell folk at home, like you passin' or somethin'?"

"I'm always your brother, Sterl, an' proud a-be," said Syl.

At this, Sterling felt a fierce happiness. It was rare for his brother to speak so gently.

"I ain't passin' for white," he continued. "Well, sometime I do, but it ain't about that. I done some bad thing, not jus' tonight. That coke, I stole it from Paulo an' sell it on the street a-pay my gamblin' debt. I done stole their money, too. I ain't gon' let Paulo thugs get at you 'cause o' me. That why I kep' it secret that you my brother."

"How come you steal like that, Syl?"

"If I knowed, I'd tell ya. I got a gamblin' habit is all. I can't rid me of it. Now get some sleep. I'ma stay awake an' keep watch."

"I can't sleep. I feel scared."

"I'm gonna get us out o' this. No worry," said Syl. "Close your eyes. Here, put this on and stay warm." He took off his jacket and gave it to Sterling. "Least we eat good tonight, and right now we safe."

Sterling put on the jacket and lay curled into himself, his horn tucked beside him.

His eyes began to close and there came a troubled sleep and visions of running away into the night, a long track up ahead, and the echo of footsteps behind, always keeping pace with his own.

He awoke under a lightening sky to the gentle pressure of Syl's hand on his shoulder. "Take this," said Syl, handing Sterling some money. "This all I owe you and more."

Sterling took the bills and shoved them down into his pocket. "You ain't goin' without me!"

"No. That's just in case somethin' happen a-separate us. A train comin'," said Syl. "Come on, we gonna try catch it."

He pulled Sterling up as the rumble sounded a long distance away.

"See the bend right here?" Syl gestured up ahead. "If the train goin' along slow aroun' that bend, we can catch it easy. Do what I do. You gotta run fast behind it and grab onto the ladder. Jus' watch me and do the same. Understand?"

Sterling nodded yes and followed his brother up the embankment.

"Don't stand up till the train pass us. Don't want nobody a-see us."

The two crouched at the side of the track, waiting.

"Damn! You gotta leave your horn behind, you need both your hands!" said Syl, making a sudden grab for it.

"No!" Sterling thrust it behind his back.

"Give it here!" said Syl. "I'ma buy you another."

"I ain't leavin' my horn! I'ma tuck it in my pants."

"Hush! Keep still! Tuck it inside, then."

Sterling tucked it away. He felt its cold metal as he held it partly under his arm to keep it in place.

The rumble grew louder. A light penetrated the early morning gloom, and shone brighter as the vibration along the track shook the ground; it became a large monster's eye, hurling shafts of light at every shadow, seeking them out, and the monster's lungs puffing smoke.

The freight train was upon them now. Sparks flew as metal hit metal, screeching as the wheels slowed at the bend in the tracks. Sterling's hand was in Syl's and his grip was tight.

"Get ready."

The engine car chugged by in a cloud of smoke and cinders. Sterling felt his arm jerked as Syl pulled him closer. They watched the freight cars pass, waiting for the caboose with a ladder up its side. Here it came, Syl ran along behind. He let go of Sterling's hand and reached for the ladder. So close. The train was beginning to pick up speed and Syl leaped and grabbed on, his feet finding purchase on the rungs, his hand reaching for Sterling.

"Faster, run fast," breathed Syl. "Gi' me your hand."

Sterling pumped his arms and willed his legs to move faster, till he felt his hand caught and then his feet lifted off the ground, and he was clinging to Syl on the ladder. The two huddled there to catch their breath, Syl hugging him close to his body, their breaths coming in gasps and heaves. But there came a sudden lifting of weight where his horn should be, the dull shine of it as it clanged against the ladder and down onto the rails, and then Sterling pulled himself away from Syl, snatching back his hand, turning and making a leap after it, and the track coming up at him, the smack against his cheek, the bite of gravel in his mouth, the rolling over and over, tumbling down, down, and the grass and weeds rising up to meet him, then a spinning whirl until something stopped his forward motion and he lay still.

THIRTEEN

Sterling opened his eyes to the dawn sky and stumbled upright on bruised knees. A pain, swift and merciless, clutched his head, then let go. The rumble of the freight train faded into silence. The early light showed an empty track.

"Syl?"

Only stillness answered him, but he could almost hear his brother's voice.

You such a damn fool! Jumpin' off for that ole horn, it might a-kill ya! Why ya do it?

He spat small stones from his mouth, touched his cheek. Embedded dirt dug into his cuts and scrapes. He winced. Deep loneliness. Syl was gone.

A metallic shine in the gully revealed the trumpet, half buried in the tall grass. A few scratches marred its surface. He picked it up and found a small dent on the bell of the horn. It was still good to play, but what use was it, anyway? For all the times he had tried for that golden note, it was Sydney who created the notes that shone. The only encouraging words he ever heard were never aimed his way.

You got some chops. The King better watch out, Willie Cornish had said. But to Sydney, not to him.

One day I'ma come lookin' for you when I need a second horn in my band, the King had said—words that Sterling sorely wished were for him. But the King never called him anything except "kid," or "Mirror Shine." *He* already knew the truth: shoeshine boy was all Sterling Crawford was ever going to be. He remembered other words, as well. *You can be a two-bit musician if you work at it,* Armand said. *Playin' for pennies on your tin horn?* Syl had sneered.

The fact was staring him in the face, and he had been too dumb to know it: if he could not even play like Sydney, how could he ever play like the King? His trumpet had landed him here on this lonely track. Well, goodbye to it. Time to throw away his Kid Sterling dreams. He was done trying.

"Damn! I'm such a donkey!" he said out loud. His words hung in the silence, mocking.

He hurled the horn as hard as he could, and his dream along with it. The trumpet glinted in the pale sun, as it turned slowly in a wide arc across the rails and landed with a thud at the edge of the cane field. A startled crow rose, squawking over his head and away. He patted his pocket. The money was still there. He brushed the dirt from his clothes and hair, picked the gravel out of the cuts on his face, then turned without a backward glance and began to jog along to the station.

When he approached a hill of pilings, he ran faster. Danny might be hiding behind it, waiting to pounce. He reached Railway Street. The station was closed up tight. Only a few people loitered, waiting for the metal gate to open.

A shoeshine boy was setting up his stool and polishes nearby. Sterling felt a pang of envy. Would he ever have his old life back? Beside the shuttered ticket window, a board listed the train schedule and Sterling went up to read it. There was a train to New Orleans at eight o'clock. The station clock read six-twenty. He needed to stay hidden for a while.

"Beignets, fritters, come buy your beignets, fritters," called a seller from his wagon nearby.

"Get your shine right here. Best shine in Plaquemine," the shoeshine boy called out.

Sterling's mouth watered at the sweet aroma of fried pastries so close, but he kept near to the station and went up to the ticket window to wait. An hour passed as other passengers drifted in.

A tired-looking woman and her three young boys were making their way into the loose line forming by the window. The smallest child stuck out his tongue at Sterling. Maybe he could latch on behind them in line, look as if he were part of their family. More people ambled up and Sterling studied each one. Then his blood froze. A dark-haired white man walked onto the concourse with a purpose to his step, a blue-uniformed policeman at his side. A purple bruise on the man's face blazed against his skin, an ugly reminder that violence was never far away. His gaze was focused on the faces around him, searching.

It was happening just like Syl predicted. He'd been right after all. Sterling stepped closer to the family at the ticket window. Then he noticed something so frightening, he gasped in shock. The policeman was carrying a familiar woven straw bag. Syl's bag. Sterling tried to remember its contents. What was inside that would identify them? Syl's drumsticks, a piece of embroidery his mother had made for Cousin Laura's birthday present. Nothing there. But wait! Cousin Laura!

He remembered his mother saying goodbye to them, telling them, "Wait a minute," turning back to take the envelope with his cousin's birthday invitation inside. "You maybe gonna need Laura address," she had said, showing them the return address on the envelope. "Laura gonna meet you, but better take it jus' in case." And that envelope was addressed to their Aunt Ruth's store as usual, since there was no mail delivery on Sterling's street. Had his mother put it inside the bag, or had Syl shoved it in his pocket? Sterling tried to remember. In the excitement of leaving, he had not paid any attention.

But he had other worries. He wished he could camouflage himself, like that chameleon he learned about in school. He would like to change his color right about now. At least he was not carrying his horn. Danny might have recognized him as the little trumpet-toting brother.

There came a commotion of noise and activity some-where beyond his view.

"Yes, sirs. Happy to oblige."

He knew that voice. Clarence Williams! He was walking in from the street, managing to keep a spring in his step as he dragged a small trunk behind him, and looking good in a natty suit and tie. The shoeshine boy perked up. "Need a shine, sir?"

The passengers waiting by the ticket window all turned to look, attracted to the sudden energy that sparked off Clarence.

"Hey, Clarence," shouted one. "Le's see ya dance!"

Others called out to him. "Billy with ya? Give us a song."

Clarence beamed at them all, comfortable in the spotlight. "Certainly, ladies and gents." He stopped at the edge of the concourse, opened the trunk, and whipped out his top hat and a silver-tipped cane. He spun his hat on one finger, tossed it into the crowd, and bowed low. "Gather round and please pass the hat. A man can't live on dance alone!"

His feet moved in a rhythmic soft shoe as he sang the Maple Leaf Rag in a fine tenor voice.

I can do the country hoedown, I can buck and wing to show down ...

The crowd began to swell as more people moved

closer. One of the three children standing in front of him tugged on his mother's arm. "Le's go see. I wanna see the dancin' man." The other two did not wait for permission, but danced toward Clarence, their feet picking up his tapping steps. Sterling followed along behind. Keeping the bystanders between Danny and himself, he crept up close till he was standing among the crowd. People formed a loose circle as they passed the top hat from hand to hand, amused and entertained. Their coins clinked inside the hat.

Sterling was struck by a bold idea. Whenever he played with his band at the park, it was natural to hustle for coins. As the top hat came to him, he held onto it and pushed into the middle of the circle, only steps away from Clarence. He moved around as the boy danced, and he proffered the hat as though it was his job to hustle them all. Clarence noticed him and paused, then carried on with his routine.

And while I'm in the notion, just step back and watch my motion, he sang, stooping to mutter to Sterling, "Where'd you come from?"

"That policeman after me," Sterling said as Clarence spun away into his tap dance.

He held out the hat to the men and women and their coins dropped inside. "Thank you, sir. Thank you, ma'am."

Danny and the policeman stood at the edge of the crowd, their eyes on Clarence.

"Move along now," the policeman called out to the crowd. "No loitering. Move right along."

Sterling collected a few more coins before the crowd broke up. Danny turned away to scan the faces of the people around him. His profile exposed that livid bruise.

Syl had hit him hard.

Clarence soft-shoed over to Sterling, took the hat, and poured the money into his palm, then placed the hat on Sterling's head.

"Thank you, ladies and gentlemen," he called.

"I gotta get home." Sterling jerked his head at the policeman. "Syl in trouble. They lookin' for him."

Clarence's eyes widened. He glanced at the policeman. "They after Syl?"

"He done hit that white man and hop a freight train."

Clarence hesitated a moment, as if considering the danger. Then he bent to his trunk. "Syl is goin' to owe me big. Take one end of the trunk, and we are goin' to carry it through. You got a train ticket?"

Sterling shook his head.

"We can go through on my ticket. You act like my assistant and I'll buy your ticket on the train. Here, put this on, you look kinda raggedy." He opened the lid, reached inside the trunk, and took out a red waistcoat. "Keep that hat on. Your face looks beat up. Now, let's go."

These were welcome words to Sterling. Good to have Clarence take charge. The boys lifted the trunk and walked with it toward the platform. The early train pulled in, and the two lined up at the Jim Crow car to board.

"Don't turn around, look straight ahead," murmured Clarence. "That policeman ain't done, yet."

Sterling did as he was told. "It ain't only the policeman. It that white man with 'im. He still there?"

"Seem like that man is very interested in finding you," said Clarence.

Their turn came to board. Clarence stepped up first, bending to pick up one end of the trunk. Sterling kept his back to the platform and took the other end, and they hoisted it aboard. The two carried it down the narrow aisle to the luggage rack.

"Next stop, New Orleans, hoo-hah! We are on our way!" beamed Clarence.

But there was a ten-minute wait at the station. Passengers boarded the car, and the sight of Clarence brought bright smiles and cheerful greetings.

"Hey, Clarence! Where ya headin' now? Billy with ya?"

They ambled over to shake his hand. Through the crowd of admirers, Sterling saw Danny suddenly appear at the doorway to their car. Sterling played with the top hat, punching it down, opening it up, a crawling sensation on his skin. He felt the man's gaze as he walked by, looking to left and right of him. Sterling did not dare look up. He turned his head to stare out the window till he saw Danny outside again, walking back toward the street. Unaware, Clarence joked with the passengers and spread his cheer around the car. His good spirits were catching, thought Sterling, as he watched people's faces light up at sight of him.

Not till the train pulled out did he breathe easy again. Clarence sat back in his chair. "So, tell me all about it," he said, lighting a stogie.

The words were flying around in Sterling's head, but his tongue did not know where to begin.

"Start at the beginning," said Clarence, exhaling a cloud of smoke. "Keep your voice low, now."

Sterling told him about the rope, and how Syl had come to hit a white man with that board.

Clarence whistled under his breath. "A colored got a lynchin' in Plaquemine yesterday, hung from a tree. They all talkin' about it this mornin'. Good thing Syl got away."

Sterling went quiet. It was his rope that had hung that man. He swallowed a lump in his throat.

"Would've happened anyway, with or without your help." Clarence said, guessing his thoughts.

"Syl, he jus' stay on that freight. He ain't jump off after me!"

"He did right! You two should've split up, first thing. Imagine the both of you on that platform together just now? Give the game away. You would not have a chance. The two of you might of been hangin' from a tree by sundown. This way, least one of you is safe, likely both of you, if I know your brother. He always one lucky man. I bet he ain't never been shot, cut, stabbed, or hoodooed, and never will, neither."

Clarence was right, but Sterling felt a part of him was gone. "So, you gonna come live back in Nawlins now?"

"I'm tired of theater and tired of all the yessuh, nossuh," Clarence muttered. Sterling leaned in to hear him better. "And the whiteface and all of that patter so the whites can feel good about themselves." Clarence loosened his tie as if his frustration was choking him. "I heard Buddy Bolden play in Plaquemine a while ago. Soon as I heard him, I knew it was time to go back to the city. That is the music I wanna get next to. The way he embellish with them notes ..." Clarence hummed a bluesy tune and snapped his fingers in time, "... that is somethin' else! You ever hear him play?"

"Everybody in the city hear the King, no matter where they is. He play so loud. He take me up on stage with him one time. An' I shine his shoes. I got a stand at the station."

"That right? I aim to get close to him, write some music, learn all I can, start over new."

"The King ain't doin' so good," said Sterling. "They say he drinkin' too much. Everybody say he finish."

"Hah! Bolden ain't never gonna be finish. We still talkin' about him over in Plaquemine. Musicians aim to sound like him, best they can. And where is that horn you was carrying last time I saw you?"

Sterling shrugged. "I give it up. I ain't never gonna play like the King."

"You ain't got to. You find your own style. I never took you for a quitter."

"Don't matter now. I done throw it."

Clarence shook his head. "Throwin' away a good horn? Well, so what is your plan now?"

All at once, an idea came into Sterling's head, one that could not be clearer if it stood up and danced the buck and wing up and down the carriage.

"Armand Piron, he teached me a-write music on paper. That's what I'm aimin' a-do—write down all them tunes I hear in my head, and sell 'em to the big bands that come to the city."

"Armand? Creole boy? Armand J. Piron?" The boy's voice rose in excitement. "I run into him a few times. He's the first friend I intend to see, soon as I get there. We always spoke about goin' into the business, together, A.J. and me. Writin', composin' tunes."

"Armand don't like the King music. He like dicty tunes you can't dance. An' that Mozart feller. You won't git nowhere with him."

"I can make Armand see sense. Seem we all gotta get together, learn from each other, for sure. Or we are not ever gonna get ahead of the white man."

He stubbed out his stogie. "So, you make up tunes? Maybe you and me, we gonna collaborate some day. Now, I am gonna take a nap. Next stop, Nawlins." Clarence leaned back and closed his eyes.

Sterling gazed at the passing landscape. This time yesterday morning, he had set out with his brother, eager for new experiences. Now he was returning alone. His mother always saw right through him. If Syl was not waiting for him at home, he had better have a good story ready to tell her why.

FOURTEEN

Sterling never could lie to his mother.

"You back early! Syl ain't with you?" she asked as soon as he walked in the door.

A little while ago, Sterling had looked eagerly out the train window, asking himself that very question. He had scanned the crowd at the New Orleans station, hoping Syl would be there waiting. He and Clarence stepped onto the platform and looked around; then Clarence shook his hand and said goodbye for now. He told Sterling that he would come and call on them when he was settled.

"Keep the hat," he said when Sterling moved to give it back. "I am done with it an' it saved your skin."

He hailed a horse and cab. "Can I take you along, let you off at your door?"

Sterling told him he would wait at the station a while longer, have a last look around for his brother.

He hoped Syl was playing a joke and was about to jump out and surprise him. He wished with all his might that Syl would be leaning up against the street entrance, his body in its familiar slouch, or lazily waving to him from across the station. At last, he turned for home, hoping to find him there.

But Syl was not home yet, and his mother did not believe Sterling's story, no matter how sincere he tried to sound.

"He done stay on for another job in Plaquemine."

"What happen to your face?" His mother's warm hands touched his cheek, tilted his head as she stared at the cuts. "You tell the truth, now," she chided. "I can tell you lyin'. What happen? Where is Syl?"

"I tole ya ..."

"Stop that lyin' and tell me!" she said, tears in her eyes.

"He got in some trouble," he began. There was nothing else for it. When she heard about the freight train, she clutched him and hugged him tightly.

"Oh, mercy me," she moaned. "You might a-been kilt!"

She took some pork fat from the shelf. "I'ma make a poultice for you, and a physic."

"No, you ain't gonna do that. Leave it, Momma."

"What we gonna do? Will they catch 'im? All alone with no one to help 'im."

"I tell ya what I aim a-do," said Sterling. "If'n Syl don' come back, I'ma quit school and earn some money for us all. I gotta be the man o' the house now."

His mother raised her hand to slap his face, but stopped, remembering his cuts and scratches. "Don't talk like that, please! Syl gonna come back. An' you need school. I ain't never gonna send you out workin' only ten year old. Why ever I let you go? An' jumpin' on a freight train! I might a-lost the both o' ya." She began to cry in earnest.

Sterling paced the room, waiting for his mother to calm herself.

They heard a rustling outside the front door. Aunt Ruthie pushed through into the parlor. "Maria! Whatever ...?"

His mother sobbed out the story and, at the end of it, his aunt hugged him to her till his shirt was wet with her tears. They asked Sterling to tell his story again, throwing questions at him, and giving each other horrified looks at his answers.

Ruthie made some tea and the two women sipped in silence finally, deep in thought. His mother occasionally uttered a moan and wiped away fresh tears. She took a lady's fine lace handkerchief from the basket of laundry she had pressed that morning and blew her nose into it.

"I gotta tell you, Maria, Syl got some people lookin' for him," said his aunt, hesitant, a look of pain on her face. "A loan shark come around Rampart Street, up and down, askin' after 'im—one o' them Italian men that take our protection money. I know Syl all mix up in that. He collect from us one time. I ain't never tole you 'cause he beg me don't say nothin'."

"Ruthie, I wish you done tole me! I never guess he so bad that he steal off'n his own family."

They turned as one to look at Sterling in silent accusation.

"No. I never knowed nothin' 'bout that," Sterling protested. "It ain't fair, blamin' me."

"I jus' don't know what to do, anymore," sobbed his mother. "We all gotta see the pastor today, start prayin' for Syl—maybe Pastor Robert gon' know what to do."

"I ain't seein' no pastor. Two more month an' I'ma be eleven. You can't make me go to school nor church nor nothin'."

"Do you hear that boy? The way he talkin'?" His mother pointed her finger at him. "Get to your room and stay there till you ready to say sorry."

"I ain't goin' to my room." Sterling felt himself shaking with rage—seized with a need to smash and shout and stomp. "I'ma go out a while."

Before his mother could respond, he darted out the door and away. Pastor Robert? How was he going to help when there were men in chains, or hanging at the end of ropes? Pastor Robert preached about hell and damnation in the next world, but he talked very little about the evil in this one.

He ran through the streets in turmoil, his feet taking him as always to the riverside. A ferry horn moaned, caught on the tide of city sounds that drifted toward him—the chants and shouts of dock workers, vendors singing their wares, and the music of the river.

Yesterday, he had glimpsed this same river through the train window. Sometimes hidden, always present, it had sung its melodies to him, and now its music flowed once again into his mind. He remembered Clarence's words on the train, how he wanted to write music with Armand. Maybe Clarence was at Armand's house right this minute.

He got up and hurried toward Columbus Street. If Clarence was there, it was a good time to talk to them together. His feet broke into a run as he dodged around pedestrians, almost knocking over a fruit stall in his haste to reach Armand's house. The front door stood open to let the breeze through, and he heard the strains of a piano tune from the open window. He knocked and hurried inside, almost too breathless to speak. Armand was playing a waltz, probably music by that Mozart fellow that he liked so much, and Sterling waited for him to finish.

"Armand? You seen Clarence today?"

Armand raised his eyes from the keyboard to glance at him. "Did we have an appointment today, Sterling?"

"No. I'm jus' lookin' for Clarence. We gonna c'llaborate together an' I wanna git started."

"Who is this Clarence?"

"Clarence Williams from Plaquemine! He come down on the train with me and say he gonna come see you."

"I remember him. I haven't seen him for years. I'm working now. Close the door on your way out."

Armand turned back to the keyboard.

Sterling tried again. "Clarence say we maybe gon' c'llaborate an' write tunes. That's why I'm here. We gotta get started. I got the tunes. You know how to write 'em."

"An interesting idea. But Clarence always did speak a lot of nonsense." Armand began to play a gentle melody.

"My brother Syl, he in trouble, Armand. He gone and left town."

"Bad news, but I'm busy, Sterling."

Sterling tried again. "When I'ma get another lesson? I need a-learn fast an' write my tunes, so I can c'llaborate with Clarence. Ain't no one gonna bring money in now, 'cept my ma, but she don't make much, not cleanin' an' washin'."

"I am sorry your brother is gone," Armand said in a voice that showed he was not. "I can give you a notation lesson another time, but it takes countless hours to learn what you believe you can accomplish so quickly."

He stood up to show Sterling out, then paused to look closely at him. "Have you been fighting?"

"That don't matter none." Sterling shielded the cuts

on his face and moved in front of Armand to block him from the doorway. "When I'm gonna start? I got money to pay ya."

He dug into his pocket and pulled out the ten dollars that Syl had given him. Some of the bills floated to the floor around his feet, and he tried to thrust the remaining bills at Armand.

Armand stared. "Put those away. Come and sit at the keyboard. I can see you will not listen to reason any other way."

Sterling stuffed the bills in his pocket and sat down on the bench with Armand. He felt as if he were going to burst if he did not persuade Armand to help him.

"I got another tune," he said. "It got a beginning, an' a middle, an' I'm fixin' to write an end, like you teach me. Can you write it down? The train to Plaquemine done put it in my head, an' it start with a raggedy *chugga chugga* beat. I call it 'Plaquemine Blues.' Wish I had my horn, but I'm gonna hum it best I can."

Sterling hummed the bright quick melody, his foot tapping the beat, his fingers snapping in time. "It a happy tune, 'cause the train goin' places it ain't never seen before.

"Then the river start talkin'.." He hummed the river's slow yearning song. "See, the river, it sing a different tune, slower and sadder 'cause of the bad *it* seen—it so very old. Both them songs, they all fit together like one song in the end, like they belong together, see? One gotta have the other."

He hummed the river's song again and Armand nodded. His fingers on the keyboard, he softly echoed Sterling's notes, adding notes with his left hand, just the way Sterling could hear it in his head.

Sterling remembered all the times he sat by the river, to watch and listen, and draw from its strength. That river had been catching every drop of music, every golden note that ever was played in New Orleans. It was all there beneath its rippled surface, King Bolden's notes most of all.

"The river carry all them tune. Jus' like a horse tied to a wagon. Without it, jus' nothin' gonna move. An' it carry my tune. There is like a tie between us, me an' that river, an' you can't see it, but it always there."

A new thought struck Sterling. "Kinda like my brother and me. He wanna tie me to him one time, I wanna tie him to me another time, so he won't leave me, back when we was waitin' by that track in the dark, an' that white man try an' hurt us. But Syl, his tune so different than mine.

"Maybe his'n be sad 'n slow, 'cause he seen more 'n me. Maybe mine be quick 'n laughin'. Even if Syl ain't never gon' come back, we always tied, him to me, rope or no, and playin' our two different song that all fit together."

He looked at Armand through blurred vision, surprised to feel a wetness on his cheek. "Our music, it jus' gonna *always* fit together like one tune, no matter we far or near, him and me. Ain't that so, Armand? Ain't it?"

Armand rose from the bench. "Stay there. I'm going to fetch Rose."

Sterling placed his fingers on the keys, sounding the notes he could hear in his head, waiting for Armand to come back.

"Sterling, whatever happened to you?" Rose's soft voice offered comfort as she sat beside him and turned his face to hers. "Armand, pour a little brandy for this boy," she called. A moment later, she held out a small glass of amber liquid, and Sterling smelled a sharp tang that reminded him of the physic his mother gave him every week.

"I believe sleep is what you need right now," said Rose. "Swallow this first," she urged, "then go and lie down on that chaise."

She held the cup to Sterling's lips and tipped it gently. The liquid tasted bitter like a physic, yet it was sweet at the same time, and fumes tickled the inside of his nose as he swallowed. Rose gently pulled him up from the bench and led him over to the couch.

"I got more tunes," protested Sterling.

"Armand is going to help you with your music. Now take off your shoes. Lie down. Stop thinking and let yourself sleep. Everything will be well again when you wake up."

Sterling did as he was told, a cushion soft under his head. He felt his eyes closing. When he opened them again, he was looking into Rose's eyes, and her cool hand was stroking his head. But things looked no better to him now than they did before.

No better at all.

FIFTEEN

Sterling soon learned something about silence—it carried its own sound.

When he walked into the house that day, it was almost suppertime. His mother looked up from her ironing but barely spoke. Only her heavy sighs echoed inside the quiet, along with the thump of his plate when she put down his supper, and the scrape of his chair on the boards.

She had no blues to sing tonight.

He finished eating, then broke the silence with the words he needed to say.

"Momma, Syl gonna come back. I'm sorry for what I done say to you and Auntie Ruth."

He took out the bills Syl had given him. "This from Syl. Rent money."

She turned to him with a sad smile and accepted the money. "You better get to bed now. You need your sleep. School tomorrow."

In their room, Syl's bed covers lay rumpled, just the way he had left them yesterday morning. His brother's high-top shoes peeked out from underneath the bed, and his second shirt and pants hung on the wall beside it.

Was Syl sleeping rough tonight? Maybe hiding in a gully? He remembered the rope and shivered.

When Monday dawned, Sterling got up, ate some bread and molasses, and left the house before his mother awoke. He planned to search for Clarence Williams, and would not give up till he found him. He stopped by Armand's house and knocked. Maybe Clarence had come by at last to say hello to his old friend.

"Door's open," called Armand.

He found him at the piano, playing chords, a pencil and paper on the bench beside him.

"How ya doin', Armand? That my music you playin?" Sterling asked.

Armand turned to him with a smile. "You look much better today. You come for a lesson? I've been writing some harmony for your river song. It's a very promising little composition."

"Can you teach me again today? You seen Clarence Williams?"

"Not yet. Don't you have school today?"

"I ain't goin' no more. I gotta go out an' work."

"Not wise, Sterling. You need your education. Sit down a while and listen."

Sterling sat beside him on the bench, looking at the black and white keys. There must be so many tunes in the air, just waiting for their sounds to be played on this keyboard.

"Here's what we have so far." Armand played the lively train music Sterling had hummed out to him yesterday. His left hand played the train's cheerful steady rhythm, his right took on the singing melody.

Sterling watched and learned, as Armand stopped playing every now and then to ask Sterling what came next. Sterling hummed his tune, while Armand took the pencil from behind his ear and showed him how to write each note on lined paper. At first, Sterling's head was too full of his own worries to concentrate. But the lesson Armand was teaching began to make sense and settled his troubled mind. He watched his hands on the keyboard and listened to the flow of music, magically changing from the clear notes in his head to these notes on lined paper. But when Armand began the river's song, Sterling interrupted.

"An' this note you jus' play, it sound different on a horn, it slide up more, kinda like how Buddy Bolden play. How ya gonna write that?"

"We will round it up to its proper place on the chromatic scale." Armand penciled the note firmly onto a line, so firmly that the tip of his lead pencil broke. "What you do with it after that is up to you. We'll hear no more talk of Bolden."

Sterling noticed the tight line of disapproval on Armand's mouth when he spoke about the King. But, as the lesson continued, he began to understand teamwork and felt a happiness new to him. He was collaborating, sharing ideas, creating a musical story. His story! Armand knew how to rope in all those wild notes dancing in Sterling's head, fix them on ruled lines, hold them steady—or they might fly away and never return. Sterling learned how every note had its own time value and how to write that. Immersed in the work, he had no awareness of time flowing by. When Armand's mantel clock chimed noon, Sterling jumped up.

"I gotta get home. My momma maybe waitin' for me."

"She know you quit school, Sterling?"

"Yes. She want me a-learn all this so I can sell my music, bring in some money," he lied.

Armand looked steadily at him and Sterling dropped his eyes. He figured Armand knew the truth, that he'd skipped school and his mother didn't know. Before Armand could say another word about it, Sterling thanked him, and they arranged to meet again tomorrow. He hurried home for a meal, worried that Mr. Trask might have already reported his absence. But his mother had only a few words to say.

"Ruth got a note from your cousin Laura. She say she ain't pick you up at the station 'cause Syl letter come late."

She turned back to her ironing. Sterling knew he would have to tell his mother some time real soon that he'd quit school.

Just not today.

Sterling's days abruptly took on a new rhythm. Plaquemine had drawn a line down the middle of his life. Before Plaquemine, he had played horn in the park with his friends, but now, he rarely saw them. Before, whenever a parade marched by, he always jumped joyfully into the Second Line. Now, he only stood and gazed after it, remembering how it was to blow his horn and march along with the best.

One day, he walked by his old spot across from the station where the King used to stop for a shine. Another boy had since claimed his place, his tools spread out around him on the pavement, as he called out to customers. He likely shined the King's shoes, now. Sterling's own toolbox lay unused in Paulo's store. Useless to go for it. Paulo would question him about Syl. That job was gone and lost forever.

Each day, Sterling awoke early before his mother, skipped school, and left for a lesson with Armand. The rest of the morning, he searched the streets for Clarence, and stopped at grocery stores to ask if there was any work for him. He could stack shelves or sweep floors, anything to bring in something extra. So far, no one needed any help. His mother seemed too worried and distracted to notice he was skipping school. Soon as he found work, she would have to accept it. He was taking Syl's place, no argument.

His new life was full of dodging and ducking and hiding. He felt ashamed of lying to his mother. Today after breakfast, his feet took him in a different direction, toward Tulane Avenue. He scarcely noticed anything around him, till the sight of someone up ahead got his attention. There was no mistaking that jaunty stride, the large head and fashionable clothes. Clarence Williams!

"Hey, Clarence!" Sterling called, but the boy had already turned the corner out of sight. Sterling hurried after him through the strollers and street merchants. He stood for a moment, looking this way and that. Chinese laundries and chop shops lined the wide avenue. Down the street, the door to a laundry swung open, and Clarence stepped out with a load of suits folded over each arm.

"Clarence!" Sterling called, but Clarence had set off, already halfway along the street. His long strides parted the crowds around him, head and shoulders above the sea of people along the avenue. Though Sterling shouted loudly, the cries of a hot dog vendor drowned out his voice. But the vendor brought Clarence to a halt, and he reached into his pocket, juggling the load of clothing as he fished for some coins.

"Clarence!" Sterling reached him at last. The boy was nattily dressed in striped pants, a blue waistcoat, and a jaunty bow tie. "What ya doin' with all them suits?"

"Here, hold 'em a minute." Clarence dumped the load in Sterling's arms and did business with the vendor. "Never have time to eat no more. But I sure am making my rent money."

He took a hot dog from the seller and bit off a large mouthful. The savory aroma of the dogs and sausages hit Sterling's nostrils, and his stomach rumbled.

"You want a dog?" He paid the vendor and handed a hot dog to Sterling. "I got my own business," he continued, spewing bits of bun and meat as he talked, "takin' musicians' suits to the laundry and back in time for weekend dances. They are mighty glad to wear 'em clean and pressed. Takes a load off 'em, and they pay me good for my trouble. Don't take much out o' my precious time, neither. Got a night job playin' piano."

He crammed the last morsel into his mouth. "How you doing? Syl come back okay?"

Sterling chewed his hot dog and shook his head, feeling the usual heavy sadness. "No. Ain't seen 'im. But I been lookin' for ya a long time. You gonna start work with Armand and me? I got lots of tune. He helpin' me write 'em down on paper."

Clarence looked confused.

"You forgot?" asked Sterling. "That time you say we gotta write music together?"

"Right! I remember. I'm learnin' all the current hot tunes myself, from Chicago way, so's I can play 'em on the piano, print 'em, and sell 'em to music shops. Cleanin' suits is just somethin' to tide me over. I plan on going to visit Armand, soon as I got more tunes under my belt and learn how to play them." He smiled. "Give him my regards. Tell him to expect me soon. Hope your brother is okay."

He took the suits from Sterling and turned to go, but Sterling grabbed his arm to slow him down. "I need some work. Maybe I can help fetchin' suits?"

Clarence's face lit up. "Good idea, Sterl! Your brother asked me to look out for you, and I guess I'll keep at it. We're gonna work together after all, you and me, startin' Monday. Free me up to learn them songs and put some cash in your own pocket. Tell you what. I'm gonna give you the list, starting next Monday. Give you a cut. That gives me space to work at my night job and learn some new tunes as well. I play piano in a spaghetti joint."

"I can start work today! I ain't goin' a-school no more." Sterling felt proud to say it. He was one of them now. A working man.

Clarence considered for a moment. "Whyn't you come along with me now and I'll show you the ropes. Then they're gonna know your face and know to give you their suits next week."

Clarence pulled out a piece of paper with a list of names and addresses scribbled down. He showed Sterling how each customer's name was pinned inside the suit collar. "You just gotta match each suit to its address on this paper. Can you handle that?"

"Sure, I know them streets real well."

"They're gonna pay you two dollars for every suit with shirt, delivery included. One hundred percent profit for me 'cause I get a special rate at the laundry. Don't let 'em cheat you. If you can't find 'em home, or they don't have no cash, just hang onto that suit and try again later. No money, no suit. Say that after me."

"No money, no suit," said Sterling.

"I'll pay you twenty-five cents for each delivery."

Sterling estimated that Clarence was carrying at least fifteen suits. The money would be a good start to tide him over and help pay the rent. He trotted along beside him, hurrying to keep up with the boy as he hugged his load of suits. Clarence took half of them back as they walked along.

"Bet I can bring in more customers," said Sterling. It would be easy to spread the word. "Soon we gonna need a cart to carry 'em in."

"Give you a dollar for every new customer you get," said Clarence. "We are sure gonna do good with you on board."

The two stopped in dank little cottages, and in saloons and tonks, finding each musician on the list and delivering his suit. Some men were snoring on their cots, some raising a glass of beer on their stoops or inside saloons, some blowing their clarinets or horns in alleyways, practicing for their next job.

"Pay ya tomorrow," said a few, but Clarence was having none of that.

"Then you get your suit tomorrow, plus a dime fee for storage overnight."

Right away, the coins clinked into Clarence's out-stretched palm, the profits growing larger as the load of suits grew lighter.

As they hurried along, Clarence chattered non-stop to Sterling about his expectations, a cheerful whistle filling the spaces in between his words.

"An' we all gonna c'llaborate, right?" asked Sterling for the second and third time, and whenever he could get a word in. "I got some good tunes. You can ask Armand. He helpin' me write 'em down."

"Sure. I'm gonna see Armand one day soon, work with him and you. If he's writing your music, Sterling, that's a sign you are on the way to fame and fortune. You got it, for sure."

The sound of a horn met their ears. As they turned the corner and walked along Perdido Street, the notes drifted toward them, unmistakeable in their brilliance.

"Why, is that King Bolden there?" said Clarence, but Sterling was already running toward the musician, who sat outside the entrance of Union Hall. The King played a soft melody, his eyes closed.

"Hey, Buddy. You playin' here tonight?"

But the King had lost his shine. Gone were the smart

threads. His white shirt was soiled and grubby, his shoes unpolished, and stubble lay on his chin. The only thing unchanged was the bluesy melody he played, the notes singing out mournfully. He stopped playing but did not give Sterling a glance. He stared down at his horn, turning it this way and that in his hands, as though looking for some message hidden within its sheen. He muttered to himself.

Sterling felt Clarence's warning hand on his arm, tugging him back to put some space between them.

"Pleased to meet you, Buddy. My name is Clarence Williams. This is my friend, Sterling Crawford, also a friend of yours, I believe. I heard you play in Plaquemine a while ago. Sure like your sound."

Buddy did not look up. He gazed at the horn and muttered words in a steady stream—till panic crossed his face. He got to his feet to hurry away from them down the sidewalk. They watched him gesturing and arguing, as though someone walked alongside.

"Well, ain't that a sorry human being," said Clarence, scratching his head in wonder. "Never would've guessed it. Whatever become of him?"

"He gonna be okay. He maybe jus' sick, is all."

But Sterling's heart felt sore. With Syl gone, it seemed everything familiar had left with him. The old routines were finished— the spasm band, his shoeshine stand, now Buddy. He no longer looked like a King. They watched the musician walk away, gesturing and mumbling; then Clarence moved quickly on.

"Come on, one more suit left," he called.

When the job was finished, Sterling pocketed the laundry list and arranged to meet Clarence at the spaghetti restaurant the following Monday. Sterling would begin work on that day, and pick up all the suits again for cleaning. He hoped to find even more customers during the week. Every little bit helped and there was rent to pay.

He figured he would talk Clarence into buying a cart to carry the load. Maybe he would paint a sign on it like the sign he had seen on that picture-palace cart in Plaquemine.

Things were looking good! Now, at last, he could tell his mother he had found a job. For sure, she would understand why he quit school!

Full of plans, he ran up his street, past a Black Maria waiting outside his house.

Can't wait a-tell her I got me a job, tell her the truth, stop all the lyin' and sneakin'.

He ran into the house, noting too late the sound of men's voices coming from inside, and of his mother's soft crying. He saw Mr. Trask sitting at the kitchen table. Beside him sat a white policeman.

"Here he is, at last," said his teacher as all eyes turned on him.

His mother's eyes were fearful. Mr. Trask's eyes showed worry. And the policeman's, they told him the worst of all.

In the policeman's eyes, he saw victory.

Part 3

LOCK AND KEY

SIXTEEN

Run! Run! Git away!

Sterling lunged for the door. A hand grabbed his shirt and yanked him back, and he squirmed and wriggled to get free, like a possum in a trap. There came a ripping sound as the seam of his shirt tore at the shoulder, but the hands held him with a steel grip and shoved him down into a chair.

"I can put the cuffs on ya, or you can sit there and be still," said the policeman. He had narrow eyes in a square-shaped head and a bull neck. His clenched fists looked ready to punch out at Sterling. His skin was slack and pale, the color of Momma's raw dough before she baked it in the oven.

"Okay, okay! I ain't done nothin'." Sterling wriggled free and sat still, his body tense with fear.

The policeman tossed a straw bag onto the middle of the table.

Syl's bag.

"This your bag, boy?" The officer leaned over him, contempt plain on his face.

Sterling kept mum.

"Answer him, Sterling," urged Mr. Trask.

He glanced at his mother's face for guidance, and she gave a slight shake of her head.

Don't give 'em nothin'.

"Ain't mine," breathed Sterling.

"We found this bag on the railway track where Daniel Turner was assaulted and left for dead."

The policeman turned the bag upside down. Its contents spilled out—drum sticks, his mother's embroidery, Syl's spare shirt, and the birthday invitation from his cousin Laura, addressed to his Aunt Ruthie. The man picked up the drum sticks and held them up to Sterling's face.

"These belong to you?"

"No, suh."

"They belong to your brother?"

Sterling did not answer.

"Where is he now?"

Sterling shrugged. "He done got on a freight train. I ain't seen 'im since."

"We got a warrant out for his arrest. You are gonna come on down to the station for questioning."

His mother gave a low wail. "He jus' a boy."

"I'll go with him, Maria." Mr. Trask patted her hand. "I can attest to his good character."

"I'm gonna put the cuffs on 'im," said the officer.

"He's no criminal. Surely there's no need for handcuffs," protested his teacher.

"Ain't he just try an' run for it?" The policeman hauled him up and slipped on the cuffs, linking one wrist to the other.

There was no escape.

"Where you takin' him?" asked his mother.

"Parish prison."

"But I ain't done nothin' wrong," said Sterling, over and over.

"Shut your mouth."

He shoved Sterling out the door to the waiting Black Maria.

"Don't be afraid, boy. I'll be right behind you," called his teacher.

Sterling looked back at them. His mother sobbed against Mr. Trask's chest, and he had his arms around her. The policeman shoved him up into the wagon and climbed in after him. The door slammed. As the wagon drew away, Sterling stared out the barred window for a last look at his street, scared he might never be back. The horses broke into a trot.

"Take a good look," taunted the policeman. "You won't be seein' your momma again for a long time."

Down the street, he saw his Aunt Ruth, running as fast as she could to try and warn them. Too late. As the wagon passed her, their eyes met. He saw a look of cold terror on her face. Suddenly weak with fright, he slid down to the floor and hugged his knees, bracing himself for whatever was to come.

The wagon drew up at the Criminal Court, and the policeman encouraged him out with a shove and a push. He lost his balance and fell into the sewage ditch that ran alongside the boardwalk. He scrambled up out of the filth, helped along by the policeman's grip on his shoulder. A dark stain covered his pants, just freshly laundered and pressed by his mother's loving hands that very morning.

As he was hustled up the steps, Sterling glimpsed the red brick fortress he was about to enter. Its green rooftop thrust skyward. A clock tower chimed the hour. A state flag fluttered at its peak. He had walked by the prison many times with Barrel, making up stories about the evil murderers and robbers within its cells. Would he end up sharing a barred cell with one of them?

A white man roughly pushed ahead of Sterling through the double doors. Sterling and the policeman followed closely behind. Inside, noise and bustle, shouting voices, and the clang of metal doors rang in his ears. The two faced a long hallway flooded with crowds of people. Some of these wore tailcoats, or black robes. Important-looking white men in fine suits hurried past him to important offices along the corridors. Doors opened and closed with urgent swiftness. Ordinary citizens in working clothes sat waiting on benches that lined the hallways.

"Need a lawyer?" a white man called out to someone walking up ahead of Sterling and the policeman. "I can give you legal representation for a small fee, get you out on bail, guaranteed." The man leaned by the entrance, his suit shiny in places from being washed and pressed too many times. He darted a glance Sterling's way, his pinched sallow face seeming to consider, then reject him, within seconds.

"Keep movin'," snarled the policeman, pushing him forward. A well-dressed black man walking toward the exit stopped to watch Sterling's progress down the hall. As Sterling approached, he smiled and sent a look of encouragement his way. Sterling scarcely registered the glance, intent on staying upright as the policeman shoved him along. He flung open a door and pushed Sterling into a small room, empty except for a table and four chairs.

The policeman pulled out a chair and shoved Sterling into it. "You sit there till someone comes along to question you."

There came a tap on the door, and the tall black man he had seen seconds ago entered the room. Slope-shouldered and slightly stooped, he looked as if he were sorry to be tall, but hoped to lose a few inches to compensate. His head was bald, and his drooping eyelids gave him a sad and knowing look, like nothing could surprise him.

"I have the judge's permission to talk to this young man, sir," he drawled in a voice slow as molasses. "In private, sir, if you don't mind, sir."

The officer appeared to know the man. He nodded and walked to the door. "Five minutes, Jones."

When the door had closed behind him, the man sat down opposite Sterling.

"Seems like you got some trouble," he said. He had a way of talking low-down that put Sterling at ease. "My name is Cap'n Jones, and I aim to give you some help out of this situation. We don't have much time, so just tell me in your own way what happened to you."

Sterling looked into the man's face. His eyes were kind. He wanted to help. Sterling knew he had better tell the plain truth.

"We done went to Plaquemine," he began. He described the trouble there, his brother's actions on that black night by the train track. When he had finished, Captain Jones pushed back his chair.

"You don't want to be put in some prison cell with criminals, ain't that so?"

"No. I don't want it. They gonna put me in prison?"

"Not if I have a say. I'm goin' to talk to the judge and make sure they don't." He stood up to leave.

A yellow-haired man in a plain brown suit entered, glanced at Captain Jones, and nodded to him.

He pulled back a chair and sat down opposite Sterling, laid a file on the table, and opened it.

The Captain stood there for a moment. "This gentleman is goin' to question you, now. Just answer truthfully. I'll see you later."

He left and the room became suddenly colder.

The policeman walked in and took up a position directly behind the man, his eyes on Sterling as he slid a slim wooden club out of the holster in his belt. He bounced it lightly on the palm of his hand. Tap. Tap. Tap.

The seated man looked down at his file papers.

"Name?"

"Sterling Crawford."

"Says here you are a half-orphan, indigent, and keeping bad company."

"I ain't keepin' bad company." Sterling guessed indigent was not a good thing to be. "Nor indigent, neither."

The policeman stepped up. "No one said to talk! Keep it shut till you're asked, 'less you want a taste of this." He tap-tapped the club against the palm of his hand.

"Says here your school attendance is poor and your mother can't account for your whereabouts on any given day," said the man in the suit.

"She don' want me goin' out to work. I been lookin' for work, help pay the rent."

The man looked at Sterling for the first time, his gray eyes holding Sterling's in an unblinking stare. "Where were you on the third day of March?"

Sterling had no idea of dates. He kept quiet.

"Look at that. Guilty for sure," taunted the policeman.

"Do you remember the day in question?"

"If tha's when we in Plaquemine, I 'members it good."

"What were you doing there?"

"I jus' keepin' company with Clarence Williams. He let me watch Billy Kersand minstrel show."

The policeman's club slammed onto the table. Sterling started back in alarm and his questioner flinched.

"Minstrel show! Tell the truth or this club is gonna land on yo' head," snarled the policeman. "Then we are gonna throw you in a cell, boy."

The officer held the club in Sterling's face to make him take a good look. Sterling felt tendrils of fear at this close-up view. A red-brown mark stained its tip.

Sweat rose on his forehead. *I ain't gonna let 'em scare me. I ain't never rattin' on Syl. Never!*

"Did you witness your brother's assault on Danny

Turner?" The man spoke in a mild and friendly way.

"No, suh." His voice sounded thin to his ears, and his stomach twisted. The hot dog was not sitting well in his belly.

"Tell me what happened that night on the tracks."

"That man, he done try an' hurt us on that railroad, jumpin' at us. It real dark. Syl, he say stop, but he kep' on. Syl done grab me and we run away."

"Your brother took a weapon and tried to kill Danny. True?"

"No, suh. He ain't never done nothin'. Danny done jump out on us, but he done trip an' fall, an' me and Syl, we run away fast. We ain't want no trouble."

"You swear your brother did not assault Mr. Turner with intent to kill him?"

"I ain't seen nothin' like that. My brother only takin' care o' me, lookin' out for me."

"Your brother is facing a serious charge. Where is he now?"

"I ain't seen 'im since he got on a train and done left me behind. Honest, Mister."

The man turned to the police officer. "Put him in the bullpen. He will go before the magistrate."

"Get up, boy." The policeman yanked Sterling by the collar, across the room and out the door. Sterling heard himself whimper as the man shoved him down a hallway, then tapped his keys against a green metal door. It swung open from the inside. A burly guard filled the doorway. Beyond him, a narrow corridor led the way between rows of cells,

"Watch out for this one," he said to the guard. With a smirk, the policeman unlocked Sterling's cuffs and pushed him through. The clang of the door closing behind them brought the prisoners to life. Shouts and laughter rang out.

"He a scary lookin' criminal."

"Better watch out, keep them cuffs on 'im. He look real fierce."

"Where ya takin' me?" Sterling rubbed his wrists and followed close behind the guard, his eyes on the pistol holstered in his wide leather belt. He dodged hands that reached through the bars, fearing the prisoners wanted to grab him and take a bite.

"Shut your mouths," commanded a familiar voice.

A spark of hope rose in Sterling. The clamor died in an instant.

SEVENTEEN

"Sterl! What ya doin' *here?*" Black Benny looked out through his cell bars.

"I ain't done *nothin',*" cried Sterling. "I dunno why they brung me here."

"Ain't no one gonna hurt you. I make sure of that," called Benny.

How he gonna help me, all lock up in that cell?

Benny scared everyone on the streets. But on the inside, barefoot, his striped prison uniform shrank his power, took it all away.

The guard unlocked a metal door at the end of the corridor. Foul air greeted them, heavy with the stink of unwashed bodies. Men sat hunched on low benches or paced back and forth. They glanced his way without interest. The guard shoved him through, and Sterling gazed around him. He saw a heap of rags on the floor. It moved, moaning, and a bloody face poked out. "Gimme water."

"I gotta stay here?" he asked, but the guard had left, and the cell door slammed shut behind him for answer. It seemed like Sterling's luck had taken one look at that room and given up.

A hatch in the door swung open. The guard looked through. "This the bullpen. Ain't no hotel. You got a bucket to piss in, an' a bucket for drinkin'. Don't get 'em wrong way round. Someone is gonna come and get you in time for court. Or you sleep on a bench and, come mornin', you speak to the magistrate."

Sterling let his eyes adjust to the gloom. A narrow barred window high above his head allowed neither light nor air into the room. Only a faint gas lamp flickered above, making shadows dance on the walls.

"Come sit beside me, boy," called a voice. Sterling crept away to the furthest corner and slid down to the floor.

He noticed lettering scratched into the brick wall beside him and looked closely at the line of script.

No no no no no

He read another.

VINCENT P LIVED 21 YEARS HANGED JUNE 1902

Four years ago, and only this one message on a prison wall to remember him by, thought Sterling. As his eyes adjusted to the gloom, he saw that the walls were full of scrawled messages. He remembered that colored man hung in Plaquemine. What were the chances they wouldn't hang him, too? Sterling hunched into the shadows, still and quiet. Barrel and Clancy must be just getting out of school now, on their way to play music in the park and collect some coins. He wished he could be there with them. He felt fear, like a live thing crawling over his body, prickling the hairs on his arms. The hatch in the door opened and a face appeared—the white pinch-faced lawyer.

"Sterling Crawford! I wanna talk to you."

Catcalls and harsh laughter came from the prisoners.

"Git outta here, Sawbuck!"

"Don't listen to him, kid. He a ten-dollar crook and a thief."

Sawbuck spoke above the noise. "You need legal representation, boy. Tell me where you live and I'm gonna ask your father to hire me."

"I'm gonna twist your neck and cut out your tongue if you don't get away," muttered a prisoner.

Sawbuck acted like he didn't hear. He kept his eyes fastened on Sterling. They glistened whitely in his face. "For ten dollars I can get you released, and you can be back with your momma by bedtime."

Sterling stood up and moved toward the door. "My momma don't got no ten dollar."

He remembered how Syl gave him the only ten dollars he ever had, and he had passed that to his mother for rent. If he had that ten dollars now, he would gladly pay it to get out of here.

"No matter. I can take a dollar on account."

Sterling shook his head no.

Curses, taunts, and threats drowned him out, but the lawyer raised his voice. "Think about it, boy! Your poor mother is missing you, crying over you. Tell the guard to fetch me if you want to be with her again. Ask for Jasper Fellowes."

The hatch closed and Sterling slunk back to his corner. He never prayed, not even in church, except sometimes when he hoped that the preacher might finish his sermon quick, so his own sorry butt could get up off the hard bench.

He prayed now.

God, let me out o' prison and I'ma do anythin' for ya. Obey Momma, go to school. Jus' le' me out!

A rattle of keys in the lock. Sterling huddled deeper into the corner.

The same guard stepped back in. "Sterling Crawford, git over here. You comin' with me."

That quick? This praying maybe work real good. "Where we goin?"

Sterling followed the guard back down the cell-lined passageway. Keys jangled as the man unlocked a cell door.

"In you go. You got a new roommate."

He pushed Sterling inside.

Black Benny got up to seize Sterling's hand and shake it, stooping a little, his head almost shaving the ceiling. With his hand enveloped in Benny's big paw, Sterling felt the man's strength flood into him.

"How ya' doin', kid? Hadda git you out o' there. Only cost me a dollar." Benny called after the guard. "Thanks, Mr. Morgan. Who the judge today?"

"Judge Wickham."

Benny nodded, satisfied with this answer. "Now, Ringlets! He a good judge! Tell me what brung you here, boy?"

"I ain't done nothin'."

Benny shook his head. "You done somethin'. Don't never say you ain't done nothin' or they put you away for years!"

Sterling told him about Syl and that fellow in Plaquemine.

Benny listened intently. "That's real bad luck," he said when Sterling had finished. "Sound like nothin' goin' right for you in Plaquemine." Benny's expression turned ferocious. "So why you tellin' me all this time Syl Crawford ain't your brother? Why you lyin?!"

"He say never tell folk he my brother. I jus' do like he say."

Benny nodded to show that was okay by him. "Now, I gotta tell yuh a few things. First, you know about talkin' to a judge?"

Sterling shook his head.

"You gotta say, 'Yes, Suh, Your Honor. No, Suh, Your Honor,' and stand up when he talkin' to you. Gotta show the judge you a upright citizen. Now let's hear it. Stand up straight, now."

Sterling threw his shoulders back and chin up, made his voice strong. "Yes, Suh, Your Honor."

Benny frowned. "You gotta look sad an' sorry both. Old Ringlets a good man if'n you git on his good side. Look 'im right in the eye, but look sorry. Try again."

Sterling did not have to practice looking sad. He only had to think of all his sorrows. He looked up at Benny. "Yes, Suh, Your Honor."

In the safety of Benny's cell, he felt his body, taut and compressed till now, suddenly give way. His head drooped to his chest, his knees gave out, and he sank to the floor.

"You lookin' tired," observed Benny as he perched on the sleeping bench. "Whyn't you git some rest. Take that straw tick, put it down there." He gestured to the thin covering of straw wrapped in burlap on the raised platform. "I'm gonna sleep on the plank. Got some more hard labor tomorrow, early."

But Sterling's legs felt too heavy to move. Benny separated the tick from the wood planks to make a pallet for Sterling and placed it on the stone floor. Sterling lay down on the thin straw, scarcely noticing the hard, cold floor beneath his back. Benny took out some tobacco and papers from a crack in the brick wall behind him and fashioned a cigarette, struck a match against the wall to light it, then lay on the planks to smoke.

Somewhere along the row of cells, a prisoner broke into song, and other voices blended in to sing a deep, guttural blues, unlike any Sterling had ever known. The music felt like a cloak of sorrow that came down to wrap him in all its dark and heavy hopelessness. The men sang out stories of loves lost, of wrongful punishments, of chains and ropes and gallows. He heard the rattle of shackles beat in time. As he listened, Sterling's own sorrows came to haunt him—the pain of parting with his brother, of being torn from his home, his mother's tears, even the terror of that poor man hanged in Plaquemine with Sterling's rope, and the suffering of his great grandfather, sold as a slave inside a fancy hotel on Canal Street. But inside the music, he could feel a lightness. He remembered that time at the Globe Hall, when King Bolden's horn had hit a note of hope that stopped everyone cold. He could almost hear that same golden note right now, as if the King were there among them, his tune weaving that hope in and out of the prisoners' song. Lulled, he drifted to sleep.

It might have been hours later, or only minutes, but he awoke suddenly at the rattle of keys in the lock. The guard named Morgan opened the cell door and beckoned.

"You, boy, come on this way."

Sterling scrambled up.

"Where ya' takin' him, Mr. Morgan, suh?" asked Benny in a sleep-filled voice.

"Afternoon court. The judge is waitin'."

At the doorway, Sterling looked back at his friend. Benny sat up, yawning. "Don't be a'feard. You gonna be fine. Remember what I tole ya."

EIGHTEEN

"Name?" asked the clerk

"Sterling Crawford, Suh, Your Honor."

Sterling trembled as though an unwieldy engine pulsed and thrummed inside him. Along the walls on either side of the court hung portraits of white men in black silk. Each pair of eyes glared down at him from its gold frame.

Earlier, Sterling had sat, cuffed and watching the proceedings from a barred cell overlooking the courtroom, along with other prisoners, some in shackles. He was comforted to see his teacher, Mr. Trask, sitting in the seats for coloreds, at the back of the court. Sterling had some time to notice a common pattern. The clerk would call each prisoner to stand before the judge. After a few questions, the judge barked his sentence with a bang of his gavel—"One year hard labor," or "One month solitary confinement."

Each poor prisoner's head sank lower, and a policeman led him out by a side door. However, if any well-dressed white man stood before him, the judge allowed him to pay a fine, go free, and leave by the front exit.

Sterling guessed that the side door was not the door he wanted to go through. When his turn came, the guard opened the cage door and let him out. It seemed to take him a hundred steps to reach the front of the court. He looked around at his teacher. Mr. Trask nodded encouragement, but Sterling took no comfort.

He stood behind the wooden railing near the raised dais, and kept his eyes fastened on the state flag above them, too afraid to look into the eyes of the silver-haired judge sitting beneath. The flag pictured a mother pelican bent toward three baby birds.

"Age?"

"Ten, goin' on eleven, Suh, Your Honor."

He willed himself to look away from the pelicans and into the eyes of the plump, robed judge who sat on the raised bench. His silver hair sprang over his head in curls and wavelets. The mouth beneath his handlebar mustache looked small and pinched with disapproval. The judge scribbled on some papers with an ink quill. The clerk took those papers, then set more down, and the judge scanned them. He set the quill in its holder and peered down at Sterling, his gaze sharp and inquisitive.

"Now, Sterling," he began in a kindly voice that belied his fierce expression. "You are accused of a serious crime, boy. But this ain't a trial. This is a hearing to help us decide whether you are to be tried for aiding and abetting the attempted murder of Mr. Daniel Turner."

At the word, "murder," an excited murmur rose from the spectators.

The judged glared and banged his gavel.

"Silence in the court," commanded the clerk.

"Do you know what truth means?"

"Yessuh, Your Honor."

"Kindly explain it."

Sterling groped for an answer. Truth changed to fit the situation, didn't it? Truth in one person's mouth might be lies in another. He knew he would never tell the truth if it hurt his brother. Protecting his family, earning their trust, that was a kind of truth all on its own.

"It mean not tellin' no lie."

"Then, without telling any lie, I want you to describe the events of the night in question, the third day of March this year."

Sterling took a breath and began, trying to still the tremor in his voice. "Well, that gentleman, Danny, he was scarin' us and jumpin' at us, till we never knowed which way to turn. Syl, he beg 'im to stop, but that Danny, he jus' kep' tryin' a-hurt us—then Syl done grab me an' we run an' we hide till sun-up. Syl done hop a freight train an' I ain't never seen 'im again."

"Did you witness your brother's assault on Mr. Turner? By that I mean, did you see him beat Mr. Turner about the head?"

"No, Suh, Your Honor, I jus' run away down the track."

I ain't truly lyin', thought Sterling. *It were too dark to see much. I jus' heared the crack that board made on Danny head. But that judge ain't ask me if'n I "hear" somethin'.*

"Do we have a character witness present for this boy?"

Mr. Trask stood up. "Yes, Your Honor."

"Come forward."

Mr. Trask stood beside Sterling as he addressed the judge.

"He is a reliable, hard-working boy, your Honor. Honest. Never any trouble, and very musical. Talented."

"Thank you, Mr. Trask. You may sit down. Cap'n Jones. You may approach."

Sterling had not noticed Captain Jones among the crowd of spectators. The Captain bowed and walked through the gate in the partition and up to the dais. The judge leaned toward him and the two spoke in low voices. After a moment, the Captain returned to his seat, giving Sterling an encouraging pat on the shoulder as he walked by.

Judge Wickham leaned over to look down at him. "Sterling, I am a forward thinker. Unlike some, I do not believe any child should be put in prison among hard-core criminals. However ..." His pale blue eyes gazed into Sterling's, his gavel poised in his hand.

"You need discipline! Cap'n Jones here has talked with me and is convinced you are worthy of rehabilitating. I am sentencing you to the Colored Waifs Home for Boys. There, you will stay under his guardianship for a period of no less than three months, and no greater than one year. The length of your sentence will depend upon your good behavior. I have confidence that Cap'n Jones will set you on the straight and narrow once again."

The judge paused. The spectators waited in silence for the gavel to come down.

"Heed my words. I do NOT expect to see you in my court again. Your sentence begins now."

Bang went the gavel.

"Next!"

The bailiff beckoned Sterling toward the side door.

But, but ...!

Sterling stayed in place. Judge Wickham needed to know more. There were some important questions he had not even asked.

"But, Suh, Your Honor, I gotta work and help my ma. She don't got Syl no more a-pay the rent. What's she gon' do?"

The judge possessed a pair of thick white eyebrows. They met in one long frown over glaring eyes that frightened Sterling, who was wishing he'd kept his mouth shut. The man's voice turned suddenly cold and clipped.

"Are you questioning my decision, boy?"

Sterling shrank back and whispered to him. "No, Suh, Your Honor."

"Take him away, Officer."

Sterling turned for a last glimpse of his teacher. The man's face spoke worry and dismay. The bailiff led him toward the barred door. Sterling had a moment to reflect that Mr. Trask was a good sort of fellow. Then he followed the guard through the side door.

NINETEEN

The door slammed. The wagon lurched forward.

"Well, lookit here!" said a voice. "Ya brung a horn? Gonna play some tunes for us all?"

Sterling looked up from the floor of the police wagon where the guard had tossed him. A boy stood cuffed to a bar in the window. A thin white scar curved over one eyebrow. Sterling knew him. Scarface—that time a gang had chased him and Clancy down Sydney's street and the two had jumped on a streetcar to escape a beating. He still felt the sharp sting of the rock on his back, mixed with the slow burn of shame for running away. But this time, Scarface was cuffed to the barred window.

"So, they finally brung you in." Sterling's pent-up anger spilled out. "'Bout time, ain't it?" He began to get up, but the boy's kick caught him in the ribs.

Sterling scrabbled out of the way, but Scarface moved as far as his cuffs allowed and kicked again. His foot hit its mark, right in Sterling's kneecap. Through the pain, Sterling managed to grab the foot and twist it till the boy yelped. In the struggle, its sole flapped open, exposing grimy toes.

"Leave 'im be," came another voice beside him.

Sterling let go. He stayed on the floor and rubbed his knee as his eyes traveled upwards from a pair of smart trainers, white linen pants, good cotton shirt, on to the face—fine-boned and proud looking. A pair of brown eyes stared back. No one he knew—a slim boy about fourteen, sitting sprawled on the seat, one arm resting along the back like a sightseer out for a day in the country. Sterling got up from the floor and perched alongside him, away from the other boy's reach.

"What do we call you?" the boy asked, as though meeting him on a street corner. "This here is Jack. My name's Alphonse."

"Sterling."

"What you in for?"

"Nothin'. They aimin' a-punish me for what my brother done, hit a white man."

"Hope he got in a few licks before they lynched him," answered Alphonse in a matter-of-fact manner.

"He got away."

"Some brother," mocked Jack. "Leavin' you to pay for what *he* done."

Sterling lunged at him. Alphonse got up and stood between them, balancing himself expertly as the cart swayed. "I don't wanna hear no more. Shut up, the both of ya." He spoke as though he didn't care either way, but his stance carried weight.

Jack opened his mouth for a retort, but seemed to think better of it, and turned away to stare out the window. Sterling studied Alphonse. The hands at the end of his long thin arms looked like they could just about wring a chicken's neck. Even so, a person would think twice about challenging him. There was tension in his body, coiled up and ready to spring. His clothes could have been laundered by Sterling's own mother. They were spotless—his laces new, his trainers unscuffed, his linen pants pressed, his white shirt boasting not a smudge of grime.

"What *you* done?" asked Sterling.

Alphonse's mouth curved in a smile too faint to reach

his eyes. "About killed my mother's boyfriend. But don't neither of you say nothin' or I will cut your throats some night when you are fast asleep." The tone was casual, and Sterling felt a chill.

The three settled back in silence, thinking their private thoughts, as the wagon headed toward the city's edge. After a while, it approached the gate of a farm where dairy cows grazed in a field. Through the barred window, Sterling saw a cluster of white two-story buildings and, among them, a small white church, its steeple rising toward a cloudy sky. Barbed-wire fences edged the property. A boy saluted at the open gate as their wagon rolled through.

The driver climbed down to unlock the door. He uncuffed Jack, his mouth curled in contempt. "Out you git, now. You soon gonna learn some manners here."

A bugle sounded from some distance away. A tall man walked across the field toward them. He was dressed in a blue serge sack suit. Captain Jones! Sterling felt a comfort to see the man again. The driver handed over some papers to the Captain and climbed back onto the wagon.

"Reckon you can whup it outta them and teach 'em a lesson," the driver called. He shook the reins and departed, carriage wheels rumbling over the stony road. Sterling looked around at grazing cattle, a white horse standing in a paddock beside a barn, and, in the distance, a field where a group of boys bent over a patch of ground. A whiff of manure mixed with the sweet smell of hay.

"Names?" Captain Jones asked in a gruff voice, very different from the slow drawl Sterling knew from their first meeting. He tried to catch the man's eye, but he acted like they'd never met. Jack looked at his feet. Alphonse gazed coolly at the Captain.

"Stand up straight and answer quick!"

"Jack Higgins."

"Sterling Crawford."

"Alphonse Bernier."

"Okay, Higgins, Crawford, Bernier, my name is Cap'n Joseph Jones. You will soon learn the ropes and thank the courts for sending you here."

A bugle called again. Boys raced from every direction across the fields to form a straight line in front of the main building—feet together, arms straight at their sides, as though a hand had come down from the sky to arrange some toy soldiers.

"Now, march right over there and take your place

at the end of that line, when I say so," the Captain commanded. "Now then. Quick, MARCH! *Hup,* two, three, four! *Hup,* two, three, four!"

Sterling stood in place, confused. Alphonse looked away, bored, but Jack stepped toward the building, his feet moving in time.

"MOVE! *HUP, TWO, THREE, FOUR!*" bellowed the Captain.

Sterling stepped back in alarm at this new Captain. What had happened to the gentle man with the slow drawling way of speech? His feet fell into step with the Captain's prompt. Alphonse followed, out of step. As they approached the lineup, all eyes were on them. The boys were of various shapes and sizes, some young, some older, many barefoot, all neatly dressed in loose blue overalls. An older boy tooted on a tin bugle in time with their march. Sterling and the two others joined the lineup and faced the front.

"At ease, men," said the Captain. The line of boys smartly moved their feet apart, arms behind their backs, and the three new boys copied them.

Captain Jones looked at each boy down the line, and all eyes fastened on him. "I want you to welcome these newcomers and show 'em the ropes. Remember when *you* first came here, *you* got help, and now you are gonna help *them* through their first night here."

He turned to the bugler, a tall, slender boy of about fourteen, with a pleasant, open face. "Merrit, take 'em to Miz Jones. The rest of you get along inside, get washed and scrubbed for supper. DIS-MISSED!"

The boys scattered like catkins in a wind, till only Merrit stood with them, bugle in hand. He looked them over in a friendly way and his eyes rested on Jack. "Miz Jones, she gonna have some scrubbin'—cleanin' *you* up."

He led the way to a large white shed at one side of the building. He stared at Alphonse with open curiosity as they walked along. A slender, middle-aged woman stood at the shed door, veins strung roughly over strong arms, her gaze sharp. A long apron covered her skirt and her hair was braided in corn rows and swept up in a blue rag.

As they reached her, Sterling felt her eyes assessing him from head to toe. He looked at the rip in his shirt seam, and down at the dark stain of sewage on his pants. His momma would be ashamed.

"I'm gonna take it from here, Merrit." She turned and strode inside. "Come in here, boys."

Inside, through a fog of steam and heat, laundry tubs and kettles perched on rickety tables. A coal fire burned in the grate. A tub of water stood ready on the floor. Baskets of clothing lined the wall, and above them, lists of names were nailed. The woman turned to Jack and picked up a long wooden laundry paddle, holding it like a weapon.

"Just call me Miz Jones." She looked at Jack. "Seem like you could use a scrub. Take off them clothes and in you get."

Jack's eyes darted from the paddle to the hard look in her eye. Keeping his back to her, he hunched over and stepped out of his rags. He tested the temperature with his foot, then climbed into the tub. Sterling got a look at his thin body before he submerged. He felt a surge of pity to see scabby stripes and long scars across his back.

"Tsk tsk, who done this?" Miz Jones gently pushed him forward to examine the scars, then handed him a sponge and a bar of lye soap. "Scrub your head with that and don't forget behind your ears."

When Jack finished and climbed out to dry himself, she tossed some clothes to him. "This here shirt and pants gonna fit you, boy."

Jack dressed in a hurry. His new clothes were in better shape than the rags he had come in with.

She turned to Sterling. "In you get."

Sterling looked at the now dirty water. "I ain't gettin' in that!"

Miz Jones picked up the paddle with a warning look. Sterling knew she meant business. He turned his back, undressed, and lowered himself gingerly into the tub, its water dark with Jack's filth. He found the soap and washed himself quickly, climbed out, and took the shirt and overalls that Miz Jones handed to him.

"You ain't puttin' me in that tub," said Alphonse matter-of-factly. He crossed his arms and turned away from her. Miz Jones' sharp eyes took in his neatly pressed cambric shirt and pants. She did not order him in but picked up some clothes from a pile of folded laundry.

"You, come on over here—these might do for you. Put your own clothes on that shelf over there."

Sterling watched, interested. Miz Jones and the Captain seemed to believe the boys were to be trained and bugled at and commanded into some kind of order. Sterling figured it might not work on Alphonse. The boy stared coolly at her, his chin jutted out, but he was no match for Miz Jones. She stared right back, then pretended to take his challenging look for modesty.

"No need for shyness here," she chortled. "Get them clothes off an' put these on. Hurry now, or you gonna miss supper."

Alphonse took the easy road. He turned his back, undressed, and folded his clothes carefully before placing them on the top shelf. He looked closely at the overalls and shirt she handed him and shook out each piece, as though vermin were hiding among its folds.

She picked up Jack's discarded clothes with laundry tongs and held them away from her body. "Only one place for them." Her mouth set in a grimace, she dropped them into the fire and the flames flared and crackled, greedy for the grime of Jack's life on the streets. His shoes followed.

"If Cap'n Jones asks, tell 'im I put you in Squad D," she said, studying the list of names on the wall. "You be off, now—go on over to the mess hall for supper."

Sterling's skin itched from the rough cotton. He looked the other boys over. Except for Alphonse's cold stare, they looked like all the rest at this jail—loose blue shirts and overalls. He and Alphonse still wore their good trainers, but Jack walked barefoot. The boys trailed across the yard after Merrit. Around them in the late afternoon, fields stretched into the distance. The soft mooing of cows and the bittersweet smell of cut grass added a peaceable and quiet note to a day full of humiliation and uncertainty. Sterling let his exhaustion sink into his muscles and bones. He had a heavy feeling that this place was the end of the road for him. He remembered the times when his mother threw up her hands in defeat. He understood how that felt—to just give up. It felt freeing to stop resisting. He imagined all the terrors of today drifting away on the gentle evening breeze. He had run a gauntlet of misery and felt lulled into submission. But he had been wrongly accused! White men had humiliated and imprisoned him. He looked at the wrought-iron fencing. It was not too high. How easy would it be to start running right now?

"Thinkin' about leavin' so soon?" Merrit laughed at him. "You like a good whuppin'? Go right ahead. Let's see how far you get."

"How long you been here?" Sterling asked.

"Few months, but I aim to get out in a couple weeks. They settin' me free. But you gon' find it easier inside here than out there. Mos' of us do, even with the hard work."

"What you in for?" Sterling asked.

"I done fire a gun on the street. Jus' at the sky."

They entered the largest building, slender columns flanking its front entrance, and heard a gabble of voices from a room down the hallway. There, in the mess hall, boys sat bent over their meals, on benches at rough plank tables, or waited, spoons clutched in their fists, as Captain Jones ladled out white beans. There came a hush as fifty pairs of eyes turned to stare at them, then the talking and eating resumed.

"Take your places over there." The Captain gestured to three filled plates at one end of a table.

The boys sat where he pointed. In an instant, Jack was shoveling the beans into his mouth, his head down close to the plate, one arm encircling his bowl. Alphonse wrinkled his brow at the sight of him, then picked up his spoon. Sterling looked at his bowl but kept his hands in his lap. Not once today had anyone given him a choice. But now he did have a choice—to eat or not. Well, he chose *not*. He would starve himself till they let him go. And he would start right now, this minute.

I ain't gonna eat. Not never, till they le' me go. He noticed bits of sausage and onion in the bowl and his stomach rumbled in protest, but he clutched his hands even tighter in his lap. He remembered his last meal—the hot dog Clarence had bought him. That seemed a long time ago. Since then, he'd eaten only a dry crust at the prison.

"Gimme that. You ain't eatin' it." Jack had already finished his meal and reached for Sterling's bowl.

Sterling shoved his hand away. "You ain't, neither. Get away." His belly felt so empty, he could resist no longer, and dug his spoon into the meal to eat. When all the plates were emptied, the Captain gave the three their orders. "You're on mess hall duty with Squad D. Get on over to the kitchen, boys. Make a clean job of it."

The boys at Sterling's table mopped up their bowls with crusts of bread, as they stood up and filed into the kitchen to pile their bowls into a cast-iron sink.

Sterling took a close look at the boys in his squad. They looked about his age, some a couple of years older. They laughed and jostled, sharing private jokes, and shooting glances at the three new boys. Under Merrit's command, Sterling took his turn washing plates, spoons, and pots. Other boys dried and stacked or swept the kitchen and cleaned the tables. Merrit had an easy manner, and the boys in his squad did their work in good cheer.

Now and again, curious boys approached the newcomers. "Where ya from? How long ya in for?"

"Three month," said Sterling.

"Dunno," said Jack.

The boys turned to Alphonse. "How 'bout you?"

"Five years."

The boys fell silent and turned away. Their faces mirrored their thoughts—pity mixed with admiration—but no one asked what he had done. They seemed to follow rules of their own about that. Sterling guessed that a long sentence demanded respect. Merrit bugled some quick notes and Squad D stood in formation, then marched outside toward the dormitory, a two-story building next door. In the gathering night, squads of boys moved toward the dorm building from all directions to join them. One group of about ten came from the fields; a second marched from the stable and paddock where the white horse grazed. A third came from the vegetable patch, its rows of plants stretching out in formation, straight as the rows of boys who lined up in front of the dormitory.

The smaller, younger boys filed upstairs to the second floor, the stairs creaking as they trod lightly up. On the main floor, a long narrow room held three rows of cots, and two barred windows let in the evening light.

"We got three empty cots over yonder." Merrit pointed to a few beds at the far end, beneath the windows and the cool night air.

Them look like the best place. How come we get 'em? wondered Sterling.

"Hang your shirt and pants there." Merrit pointed to a nail in the wall. "Sleep in your skivvies."

Sterling and Alphonse took the cots closest to the window. Sterling lay down on the straw tick and felt his body fighting weariness.

"You know about the ghos'?" asked a boy from the cot next to his. "Some boy jump out a window up above this'n, kilt right down there on the ground—ya dasn't look out that window in the night, 'less'n ya wanna see a hant lookin' back at ya."

"He gonna come and git you, fly right in, take you to hell with 'im," said another. "Las' boy a-slep in that bed, he gone next mornin', ain't never seen 'im again."

"No more talkin'. Goodnight, boys," the Captain

called from the door before closing and locking it.

"G'night, Cap'n," they murmured.

The building rustled with whispers, yawns, and the creak of cots, like an animal settling to sleep in the darkness. But Sterling lay awake. Ghosts did not scare him, but questions clamored in his head.

Where Syl at right now?

Clarence still waitin' on me to work come Monday?

A distant bugle sounded the end of the day. He figured his whole life was just like that bugle—out of tune. All his young life, his mother had sung to him, called him in to supper, to chores, to his bedtime. As he waited for sleep, he conjured the sound of her rich voice, humming those bluesy tunes to wrap him in safety and love. But memories brought him no comfort. Tonight, he had only loneliness and sour notes to call him to slumber.

In his dreams that night, he stood with King Bolden, trumpeting the same four notes over and over. But Bolden's horn must need tuning—his notes sounded like a wounded bullfrog. Then Sterling's eyes sprang open as the bugler blasted more notes. Wake up, wake up, called the sour music.

A new day had begun.

TWENTY

"Up and at 'em!" With a rattle of keys in the lock, Captain Jones entered the dormitory. "Last one out o' bed gets the bucket."

Sterling caught the urgency and scrambled out of bed. The barred window above showed pitch blackness. Boys flung off their covers in a flurry, yawning and stepping into their pants. Jack lay snoring. The Captain bent over the sleeping boy. "Higgins! That means you! Get dressed and take the bucket down to the cesspit. Merrit, show him."

The Captain walked on down the hallway.

"Haw haw!" laughed the boys, as Jack sleepily threw on his overalls and gingerly picked up the smelly latrine bucket. When Sterling joined in the laughter, Jack flashed him a look. While Higgins and Merrit were gone, Sterling and the rest shook out their straw ticks, neatly folded their

covers at the foot of the cots, and lined up. Jack returned
from his latrine duty, a mean look in his eye.

"Teacher say to come outside. You got a visitor," he
said to Sterling.

Sterling did not stop to think twice. Could be his
momma had come to see him! Down the passageway he
hurried, looking in the rooms as he passed. Empty. No
one waited for him anywhere, and the front door was
bolted shut.

"What you doin' there?"

A middle-aged lady with graying hair and a severe
expression hurried down the hallway toward him. She
peered at him through small round glasses.

"Ain't my momma come a-visit?"

As she came closer, he saw that her eyes were kind.
Her voice softened. "Whoever told you that is mistaken,
boy. You don't get visitors for a month."

So, Jack had played a trick. *Might a-knowed it.*

"Which one are you?" She carried a folder and
opened it. "Sterling Crawford?"

He swallowed his disappointment and nodded yes.

"Musical, it says here. You might like to join the
school band? We got a good one."

Sterling looked toward the dorm. What was Jack up to next?

"I give all that up, ma'am," he said. "I jus' wan' a-learn a-write music down on paper. I know how to write music a little." He turned to hurry away. He would be late for inspection. But she called after him.

"What kinda music?"

He turned back to her. "I make up tunes, raggy tunes, bluesy ... some day, I'm gonna sell 'em to bands that come in town."

"So, you got a dream. Gonna make a deal with you. Join the school band, then you come to me for help, learn how to write it. Okay?"

Sterling looked closely at the woman. How much did she know about music? He had not heard of many colored women musicians. But any help was better than none. Armand had taught him a little, but he needed to learn more.

"Okay, I guess."

"You gonna meet Mr. Davis soon—our bandleader. Come see me in the band room before breakfast tomorrow. I'll make it right with Cap'n Jones. Run along, now."

On his way back to the dorm, he met Captain Jones coming down the stairs.

"Where you been, Crawford?" He walked into the room where the boys stood to attention. All the beds were neat and orderly, covers folded. All but his own. His cover and tick lay in a heap on the floor. Jack's smirking face told the story.

"Bed all in a mess, absent without leave. You can take bucket duty, rest of the week."

Sterling glared at Jack. The boy wore a grin on his face that begged to be knocked off, but Sterling clenched his fists and held his temper. He could not risk getting a bad report.

He found bread and molasses on his plate for breakfast. The sweet molasses on fresh warm bread was heaven. As dawn brushed the sky, the boys filed into one of two classrooms, and sat in rows on the floor in front of their teacher. Down the hall, Sterling had a glimpse of a pretty young woman who taught the younger boys. But his own teacher turned out to be the lady he had met that morning. Her name was Miss Vine.

"New boys, come up here to the front," she said.

She opened a primer and Bernier stepped up to read.

His voice, smooth and colorless, glided along with no stumbles, and Miss Vine nodded. "Practice reading with feeling," she told him. "Give the words the meaning intended."

She seemed satisfied with Sterling when it came his turn. Jack could not read at all.

"By the time you leave here, you will be a reader and a writer, Jack," she told him. "Reading opens your mind and opens a door to the world."

Jack smirked. "Then I'm gonna run through that door real quick and get out o' here," he responded to loud laughter from his classmates.

"The Cap'n!" someone hissed as Captain Jones walked in.

The boys stood up smartly. Sterling, Bernier, and Jack followed their lead. "You newcomers need to keep your record clean," he said to the three. "You misbehave— you gotta work that off, wipe the slate clean again, or that mark stays in your record. Collect three demerits and the judge gets to know about it."

Sterling remembered what the judge had told him. Keep a clean record and he could be out sooner. Miss Vine was firm but patient, and the boys worked hard for her. But Jack was lost. Letters and numbers were a new language to him. After five minutes of it, he tossed his slate and chalk across the room in a fit of temper, and Miss Vine made him stand in the corner.

"You waste time in here, you make it up after school," she told him.

Jack muttered, "Ain't doin' that."

Miss Vine had sharp hearing. In seconds, he was writing, "I will not waste time in class," on the chalkboard, copying Miss Vine's letters over and over.

When the teaching was done, Captain Jones gave the orders for the day—weed the vegetable patch, feed the hens, collect eggs, repair the fences. Merrit led his team toward the field and on into a barn, to muck out steaming cow dung and lay new straw. Sterling had never been this close to a cow. As they worked, Captain Jones rode the Colonel, his prize white horse, around the land, keeping a sharp eye out for disobedience.

Halfway through the morning, Merrit was called away to attend to something across the field. As Sterling wheeled a barrow full of steaming cow dung outside, a push from behind sent him headfirst into the muck.

"Haw haw," laughed Jack. "Hope it taste good!"

Sterling righted himself and brushed the filth from his face and shirt, a stink in his nostrils.

He went for Jack. The others stopped their work to watch the fun. Jack ran fast, dodging left and right as Sterling tried to catch him.

"Ha, ha, Stupid! Can't get me!" Jack taunted, always just out of reach, sneering and calling insults.

Merrit was returning across the field. Sterling gave up. "I'm gonna get you. You better look out!" he shouted as he went over to the water tap to wash himself. His shirt was stained, and a bad smell enveloped him. He flung it off and dunked it in the trough. Jack laughed all the more and gave him the finger.

"Take your time," said Bernier in his calm way. "You got lots of days to get him back. And nights."

Work, supper, more work, then bed. Sterling felt like a crawfish caught in a bucket. He had so much to do on the outside, his music with Armand, his new job with Clarence, but he was stuck in here, helpless to change things.

Next morning before sunrise, and after Sterling emptied the latrine bucket, he made his way to the music room to wait for Miss Vine. A raised platform across the back of the room held rows of chairs, and band instruments were arranged neatly on shelves at one side. An upright piano stood in the corner. He sat down on the bench and softly sounded the notes, wishing he could let loose all the tunes those keys might play. He felt eager to learn more about how to match the black and white keys to those dancing musical notes printed on paper, how to measure them and give each note its special due.

Miss Vine bustled in. "Good. You're on time."

She placed some printed music on the stand and pulled up a chair to sit beside him.

He looked at the cover and pushed back on the bench. "Not that white guy. That Mozart don't know nothin' 'bout music."

Miss Vine stared at him, astonished. "My boy! Mozart learned all the rules of music, then he pushed it where no one had ever taken it! A musical genius."

Sterling shook his head. "The King do that easy. He play like no one ever can play. He the best! An' people, they dance to Bolden an' his horn. Can't dance to no Mozart."

"Huh! You need to know the rules of music before you make such judgments, Sterling. Bolden never did learn the rules. No training—just some shooting star, burning out in the sky. He won't last. Mozart's music is still bein' played today. Will Bolden's music last a hundred years?" Miss Vine sat up, stiff and proud. "Some day, with the right teaching, you will know the difference."

Sterling shut his mouth and got down to work, studying the Mozart piece. But he couldn't help thinking that the King knew everything about music. Why, he could take it to a level no one else in New Orleans ever had before. That dicty Mozart had no place in a dance hall. But Bolden! Now that was music!

The bandleader, Mr. Davis, taught at the Home one day every week. Sterling came late to his first band class. Squad D had been working with Miz Jones, hanging out the clothes to dry. He hurried into the music room and stood a moment at the doorway to watch. Mr. Davis sat on the raised platform while the boys sat at his feet, listening with rapt attention. Sterling heard the names of famous musicians—Joe Oliver, Bunk Johnson. The man's body, long and loose-limbed, looked as though it had curved itself around to mimic the curve of the saxophone he held. His neck and shoulders hunched forward over the instrument, sheltering it as he talked, occasionally blowing some notes to illustrate a point. His voice came low and gentle. The boys leaned in to catch every soft word he spoke. He looked up to welcome Sterling and then dismissed the others. The boys placed their instruments on the shelves and filed out, talking excitedly.

"So, what do you play?" Mr. Davis gestured to his selection of saxophones, trombones and clarinets, trumpets, and a drum.

"I know trumpet."

His teacher placed one in his hands. "Let's hear you."

The last boy left the room as Sterling raised the horn to his lips and played his own composition, "Bouncy Feet." The notes sounded sure and sweet to his ears. Holding the horn, pushing the valves, made him feel like a missing piece was back in place—like a broken engine that only needed a tiny component to make it hum again.

"Pretty good," said Mr. Davis. "I can tell you had lots of practice."

"That my own tune. Armand done help me write it on paper."

"Armand?" asked Mr. Davis.

"Sure. Armand Piron."

"You got some fine friends, Sterling."

Sterling looked at him closely and saw doubt in his eyes.

"Honest, I ain't lyin'. Armand, he been teachin' me music, an' he tryin' a-teach me them Mozart tunes, same as Miss Vine. I never like 'em. But I sure like Bolden. Clarence Williams say we gonna collaborate, him an' me an' Armand. Buddy Bolden, he a friend of mine," added Sterling.

Mr. Davis shook his head, whether in disbelief or wonderment, Sterling couldn't tell, but figured the man did not believe him.

Sterling drew himself up, feeling angry. "I ain't lyin'!"

Pictures flashed in his mind like the images in a kinetoscope—the trouble in Plaquemine that had brought Clarence into his life; Rose Piron, the girl he had loved till Syl stole her away. But Rose had led him to her brother, Armand, who had sneered at Bolden and tried to teach him about Mozart. As for Bolden, so many times he had asked the King to show him some licks, but he never had time. Impossible to explain all this to Mr. Davis. Sterling didn't even try.

"Bolden is crazy good," said Mr. Davis. "I done played with him a few times. Ain't no one can touch him when he feelin' right. He ain't feel so good this last little while. Not playin' so much."

"Just goin' through a bad patch," replied Sterling. "He gonna be okay."

Mr. Davis shrugged and turned away to pick up a piece of paper.

"You learn these songs quick enough, you can come with us to a concert we gonna give near the city for some white folk. We gotta play real good. They give money to the Home and want to see good results for it."

Sterling looked at the list. On it was written "Swipesy Cake Walk," "In the Good Old Summer Time," and others he already knew—even "Didn't He Ramble." He felt sure it would be easy catching up.

Days turned into a week full of hard work, of rising before dawn, of lessons with Miss Vine, band practice and more hard work to follow, the weary falling into bed, and the waking and sleeping framed by the blast of the bugle. The routines were numbing. He wished he could be back on the outside. There were possibilities out there.

Miss Vine proved to be a good teacher. She taught him the keyboard, the sharps and flats, the crotchets and quavers. Soon, it all began to make sense, and he could write a simple tune in the lines and spaces of the manuscript paper. It felt just like the first time he learned to read and write. It had opened up a whole new world for him back then. This was no different. But still he longed to get back to the city, where there must be a thousand more chances to learn.

While Sterling only wished for freedom, Jack grabbed at it. He hated school. His letters did not look like any letter of the alphabet. As for arithmetic, he counted on his fingers and toes, his mouth moving in a constant mumble that invited ridicule from his classmates. He tried to run away the second day, a wild light in his eyes as he charged across the field fast as he could.

"Git away, Jack! Run!" shouted the boys. But the Captain was riding his horse, the Colonel, and galloped across the field, cutting him off before Jack reached the fence. For punishment, Jack had to help Miz Jones for a week in the hot, steaming laundry shed.

As the days, then weeks, passed, Sterling noticed Bernier falling into step with Merrit as they crossed the fields or headed to the mess hall. They had become fast friends—an unlikely pair—Merrit open and cheerful, Bernier closed and cool. He had made himself the unofficial second-in-command, stepping in for Merrit if the other boy was called away.

Bernier helped his friend take care of the Colonel, brushing and feeding him, leading him to the field to graze. Soon the grooming became his task alone. Merrit had never enjoyed the work and was happy for him to take over. And although Bernier maintained his cool exterior, it was easy to see his special fondness for the horse. He brushed the Colonel's mane carefully, and fed him carrots that he had slipped into his pocket from the vegetable garden.

Whenever he entered the barn, the horse whinnied a greeting to Bernier and tilted his head for a carrot. Once or twice, Sterling saw Bernier up on the Colonel's back, riding around the paddock, leaning forward to speak gently to him. One morning at breakfast, Sterling noticed that Merrit was not with them. He soon found out why. The Captain called them to attention.

"Time to choose your new Lieutenant," he said. "Merrit has shown exemplary behavior and is going home today."

At this news, the boys groaned and sighed and whispered to each other. Sterling and the others had known Merrit would be leaving soon, but they were disappointed the event had come so quickly. They liked and respected him. He dealt with every boy fairly. The Captain acknowledged their sadness.

"May he be an example to you all. You got time to wish him well. But now, think about his good habits, and choose a leader good enough to take his place. I'll leave you boys to make a wise decision. You have ten minutes."

The Captain left the room. There came a gabble of noise. The boys' voices were low at first, but rose as some called out names that others rejected.

"Bechet," shouted one.

"No, he get demerits all the time," protested another.

"Smith," shouted another over the growing din.

"He too young!"

"Rogers!"

"He ain't never done nothin' for no one!"

"You crazy? That don't make no sense!"

The noise of disagreement had reached a peak, but a shrill whistle sounded that hushed the boys. They looked up to see Bernier standing at the front of the room.

"Vote for me, boys. I'll do a good job. I can get you special privileges, and keep things in line, so that you all are never gonna get demerits," he said.

The boys looked at one another, their eyes flashing unspoken doubts. They knew he was telling the truth. Bernier was always as good as his word. Whenever he spoke out, he made sense and the others listened. But they also feared that he could make their lives difficult if they did not vote for him. A dark mystery surrounded him that put them on guard. Sterling had kept his promise to Bernier not to tell, and he guessed Jack had not spoken of it. But the boys knew he must have committed a serious crime. So they were careful.

Like the others, Sterling sensed that one wrong step would put him on the boy's bad side. Bernier had a gift for speaking clearly and sensibly, but if something did not agree with him, he had a way of narrowing his eyes, tightening his mouth, and conveying a threat of physical harm as good as any words. And he was in for five years. That fact alone made them scared of him for whatever he had done wrong. The boys did not want any trouble. They voted for Bernier, but when the Captain heard their decision, Sterling saw doubt on his face. Then he shrugged.

"Bernier. You're on trial for now. Do a good job."

Merrit came into the mess hall smiling, dressed in his regular clothes, and the boys rushed to surround him and say their goodbyes. He had a good wish for every boy as he shook their hands.

"Stay out o' trouble," he said to Sterling. "You done real good so far."

"See you on the outside," he called to them all.

Sterling and the boys followed him down the hallway, and would have followed him out the door if the Captain had allowed it.

"Goodbye, goodbye. See you on the outside. Goodbye."

The door closed behind him, and they turned away to begin life under Bernier's rule.

The days went by as quickly as pages ripped from a calendar. Bernier was proving as good as his word. He kept the boys in line, using their fear of him to good purpose, seeming to read their thoughts, always one step ahead. He managed to keep Jack from his tricks, and no demerit points were given on his watch.

Bernier had a gift for storytelling. But the stories he told frightened the boys. At lights out, Bernier told tales of Jean Lafitte, a pirate killer who haunted a blacksmith's shop in Frenchtown. He followed up with a tale about the La Prete mansion in New Orleans, and the boys hung on his every word. "Someone walked by one morning and saw a river of blood flowing out under the front door," he recounted. "The police went inside and found ..."

"What? What he done find?" whispered one of the boys.

"... a room full of murdered folk, all cut into pieces!"

Some of the boys were enthralled, but many more suffered disquieting dreams. One night, Tony woke them all with screams and cries.

"Help! I seen it at the window!" he called out.

The boys sat up in fright. "What? What ya see?" they asked, dreading the answer.

"The hant at the window! It tongue all hangin' out, them eyes all poppin'!"

In the darkness, the boys gabbled with fear. "It comin' in, Bernier? Don't let it!"

"Ain't here now," said Bernier. "Go back to sleep."

Sterling spoke to Tony. "I ain't seen nothin'. You jus' dreamin'."

He reached out to pat the trembling boy's shoulder, and his assurances seemed to calm him. The rest of that night was filled with tossing and turning. Next morning, the boys looked tired and drawn. Bernier's stories were beginning to frighten them all out of a good night's rest.

One of the lieutenant's responsibilities was to bugle out the measure of their days, but Bernier's bugling voice was not as polished as his speaking voice. He had no ear for music. It sounded even worse than Merrit's bugling.

Even the Captain complained. "You got a tin ear, Bernier."

One day, as they were pulling weeds in the vegetable patch, Bernier spoke to Sterling. "If anyone can make this bugle tuneful," he said, "it's you. Here, take it."

Sterling began to rise earlier than the rest, already awake and dressed in the darkness when Captain Jones, keys jingling, unlocked the dormitory door to let him out. He picked up the bugle from under his bed and stepped quickly down the hallway. At first, the Captain kept watch, as Sterling walked outside into the fresh morning air, but he gradually loosened his control and let him out without supervision. Sterling felt proud to be trusted with this important job.

The bugle allowed him only four notes, but he put all four to good use, amazed at the number of tunes he created. After waking everyone, he would slip into the music room and play his tunes at the piano, as he waited for his lesson with Miss Vine. He was working on the piece he called "Plaquemine Blues," the one he'd worked on with Armand. There were so many tunes that made up the composition—the train journey, the escape, the river's song—he had a plan for all these stories in music.

"Yep—the piano is the place to go when you need to work somethin' out," Mr. Davis said to him as he passed by the room one morning. "Your tunes or your troubles. Once you master it, the keyboard is always there for you. Keep at it, kid. You got a gift for composition," he said. "Don't let it go to waste."

A few weeks later, the twelve band members set out in a wagon hitched to the Colonel. They were on their way to perform for some rich white folks. Mr. Davis told the boys that these whites liked to help out Captain Jones with donations of money. He said that Captain Jones sorely needed this money to operate the Home and pay the teachers, so the boys must play as good as they ever had before.

Sterling respected the boys in the band. They each had a natural talent that kept Sterling on his toes. He had worked hard to keep up with them and to finesse the pieces. Today, the boys wore special white shirts and black short pants. The words "Colored Waifs Home Band" was printed on a board nailed to the side of the wagon. They were traveling in style!

Captain Jones stood at the gate to see them off. "Make us proud!" he called.

The boys sat or lay sprawled beside their instruments, enjoying the lazy sway of the wagon as it rolled along. They were headed to a riverside sugar cane plantation beyond the city. Sterling gazed eagerly around him, and soon the view he'd been seeking appeared—the sparkling Mississippi! It wound alongside fields of young cane, singing to Sterling as it flowed on its way to the sea. Phrases of his own composition, "Plaquemine Blues," drifted into his mind as the wagon rumbled along. Maybe his momma was walking somewhere beside the river this very moment. He sent his love to her as he gazed at the quiet water.

They pulled into a long curving driveway that wound through moss-draped oak trees. Glimpses of a white mansion made the boys lean forward in excitement. Being this close to white men filled Sterling with dread. He took little comfort from being with the band, and being able to blend in with the other boys as one unit. He remembered his momma's story about his great grandfather Ned, sold as a slave on Canal Street. "Fifteen hundred dollars they done pay for him. Muscles like iron," she'd described. White men had shackled Ned and auctioned him off to the highest bidder, then taken him for hard labor on a plantation. "Just like a cow or a horse," his mother said. He'd come through that misery and died a free man. She had told Sterling about slavery many times, those evenings after supper when he sat with her by the glow of the lamp. He loved to hear the sweet cadence of her voice, rising and falling as the iron sizzled against linens. He now felt the hurt of missing her.

They crested the top of the hill, and there stood the graceful home, slender pillars flanking it on three sides, ornate balconies overlooking gardens that swept down to the riverbank. In the distance, sharecroppers toiled in the cane fields that spread out behind the house and gardens. The wagon rolled to a stop, and the band set up on the lush green lawn. Members of the family and several guests rested on lounge chairs, or lay in hammocks among shade trees. They sipped drinks from silver cups and fanned themselves, as white-jacketed servants carrying trays crossed the lawn.

The boys took their positions. Mr. Davis bowed to his audience and began the concert with "Maple Leaf Rag." Sterling blew his horn, letting his notes shine, enjoying the good sound they were making together. The white folk seemed to enjoy the music and clapped lazily after each piece. At break, the boys drank lemonade and ate cakes set up on a table.

The sun beat down and the boys had little shade where they sat. Mr. Davis was talking to a white-haired gentleman up near the house.

"I'ma go for a swim," said Tony.

He looked around to make sure none of the grown-ups could see him, then ran down to the riverbank where he stripped naked and jumped in. The others watched him splashing. It looked so cool that they all decided to jump in, too. But before they could act on it, the elderly white man heard the splashes and hurried, wheezing and puffing, down to the riverside.

"That is a federal offense for coloreds to swim naked, boy. Get outta there! I'm calling the sheriff on ya."

Tony stopped in mid-stroke and began to sink. He came up spluttering, but his panic made him sink again, and his head disappeared beneath the surface. The water roiled

as he struggled up but then managed to right himself.
His arms sliced through the water like the paddle wheel
on a steamer, as he swam toward shore as fast as he could.
Sterling started down the riverbank, ready to jump in and
save him. He knew how to swim, and felt overwhelmed
with fright that Tony might drown. *Ain't that jus' like a white
man. Always makin' trouble for us—out to get us.*

"Haw haw, just jokin'," wheezed the man, coughing
and spitting a wad in his direction.

Mr. Davis walked down the hill and apologized to
the man.

*For what? Always gotta bow and scrape, just like Benny
say.*

His teacher helped Tony out of the water. "You s'pose
a-make us proud, Tony," he said as he gave him his
clothes. "Behave yourself."

Sterling almost choked on his anger. Whites! The
cause of all Sterling's misery, from Danny Turner all the
way to Judge Wickham. He feared and hated them for
hurting him—him and Tony and the boys, Syl and all
the rest. Was there to be no end to it?

But Mr. Davis and the Captain were pleased with
their work that day. The family had put an envelope

into Mr. Davis's hand as they were leaving. There was chicken gumbo for supper.

One late afternoon, Sterling was stooped over the vegetable patch, picking ripe tomatoes off the vine, and placing them carefully in the straw basket beside him. They were for canning and would be sold at market. He chose the largest, reddest ones he could find, his fingers gently cupping the fruit to lift them away from their stems. Now and again he brought one to his nose and sniffed its fragrance.

"Crawford, get over to the chapel," called the Captain. "You got a visitor."

Sterling took off at a run. His momma was visiting, at last! He would give her such a hug, he could hardly wait.

He stopped a moment outside the chapel to wipe the dirt from his hands and brush off his overalls, then he pushed open the heavy door and gazed around inside. In the gloom, a tall figure dressed in white caught his eye.

He looked closer.

There, in a fine linen suit, his leather shoes polished, a red scarf at his neck, stood his brother, Syl.

TWENTY-ONE

"Syl! Where you b—"

"Hush!" Syl put a finger to his lips. "I'm your cousin, Jim," he hissed as the chapel door opened behind them. "Ya gotta call me Jim!"

Captain Jones stepped inside. Syl shook hands with Sterling, a warning look in his eye. "How ya doin', cousin?"

Sterling gazed up into his brother's face. If Buddy Bolden had walked in playing his horn, he couldn't have felt more astonished, or more joyful, than he was this minute. But Syl frowned and gave a faint shake of his head. *Play along.*

"So, Jim, what do you think of young Sterling?" asked the Captain. "I think he's settling in real well here. Learning some manners."

Syl gripped Sterling's arm hard. "Well, he sure grown

some—feel them muscles! I'd say you been doin' a mighty fine job takin' care of 'im, settin' 'im straight. Lost all his puppy fat. Growin' up fast, ain't he?"

"Hard work keeps 'em out of trouble. Take your cousin around the place, boy," the Captain said to Sterling and pulled out his pocket watch. "You got thirty minutes before supper. I'll take care of your bugling."

He held the door open and ushered them outside.

"Thanks, Cap'n."

"Thirty minutes," the Captain reminded him.

"Come on, I'll show ya the stable," said Sterling, proud to be seen with Syl, but feeling some anger rise that Syl's actions had put him in this place. He soon forgot his resentment when he noticed the other boys were looking their way. Sterling hoped they felt impressed to see him with someone so smart and good looking. He led Syl outside and across the fields to the paddock. The Colonel ambled over to the fence, looking for a treat.

Syl peered around to make sure they were alone, then put both hands on Sterling's shoulders to look at him closely. "Ya lookin' good, Sterl! They takin' good care of ya? You really grown, ain't ya!"

"Where you been all this time!" said Sterling. "You ain't never write nor nothin'!" He looked up at his brother and figured he must have grown a little. The top of his own head came right to Syl's shoulder, instead of only halfway there.

His brother looked as slim as ever, but there were some changes—the way he held himself with sureness, looked strong, as though nothing could scare him. A mustache on his upper lip added a few years.

"Jackson. I only come back a-see if you was okay. I wrote to Momma, done sent her some money. She wrote back an' tole me you was in prison. I know you took the punishment for what I done." He reached inside his jacket. "Here." He handed Sterling a little package tied with string. "Momma's beignets. She gonna come visit soon, but you maybe gon' be movin' on before then."

"No. I still got one month."

Sterling tore open the package and crammed a pastry into his mouth, enjoying the sweetness that linked him to her.

"So, you back in New Orleans?" he asked between bites.

"Nah. Jus' visitin'. Too many folk lookin' for me here."

"Where ya livin' now?"

Syl leaned against the paddock fence. "You ain't never gonna believe it. That day when you jump off the train, little fool, I kep' on, hid in a boxcar. Well, that train, don't it end up back in Nawlins! I peek out and damn! There I was, back in the same damn city I'm tryin' a-get away from. Know it ain't safe there no more, and decide I'm gonna wait till night, then sneak onto another freight. This time, I got all the way to Jackson, done find me some work there, and hear Chicago the place to be, and that's where I aim to go. Now. Tonight, Sterl. Gon' get me a job in a club an' a place to stay."

The Colonel pushed his nose gently toward the pastry. Syl held out a piece and the horse's soft mouth closed around it. "You know, you bein' punish—jus' can't abide you bein' in prison for what I done." He shook his head. "That white bastard sure deserve a beatin'. Jus' lucky I ain't kill 'im. But we gotta stick together, you an' me."

Sterling felt another surge of resentment. He shoved the last piece of beignet in his mouth and spoke through the sugary bite. "You never tole me you ain't never comin' back, that time when we all by the track."

"I jus' got thinkin' about it on that freight. They

surely was lookin' for me. Ain't seem wise a-go back home, least not for a time."

Syl took Sterling's arm, turned him to look into his face, his voice low and urgent. "Look here, I'ma take ya to Chicago, set us up real good. I hear things much better for folk up Chicago way. Why, white chillen and black, they all go to school together."

"You lyin'," said Sterling. "That can't be."

"Look, now! I'm tellin' ya, in Chicago everythin' different. Black folk mix together with white folk— waitin' rooms, streetcars, ain't no line down the middle. You gotta come see it with me. An' we gotta see The Stroll, Sterl! That's a street on the South Side, an' they got musicians from every damn place in America, black folk and white, they all come to The Stroll. I'm aimin' a-find work there. We jus' gotta see it, you an' me."

"Momma gon' be real sad if'n I jus' up an' run."

Syl's voice rose with impatience. "Sterl, Momma don't need us no more! She all close with that teacher fella. Once you start makin' good money, she gon' be real proud of you. When this all over and done ... maybe *she* come to Chicago."

He lowered his voice again, glancing around him.

"Listen now, here's what we gonna do. You sneak out tonight when everybody sleepin'." He looked over the fields that stretched around them and the long fence line. "I can get back in, easy—be out here waitin' near them trees, maybe."

Syl gestured toward a stand of tall cypress at the far end of the property. "Soon as it get dark, you slip out, find me there, an' I'ma get us away. Here." Syl took a paper out of his pocket. "Got you a train ticket leavin' midnight tonight, see? Chicago, Sterl! An' this time, you gonna travel in style."

The doubt Sterling felt must have shown on his face. Syl's expression suddenly hardened. "Don't waste your life followin' *rules,* Sterl. Take your freedom! I'ma fix you up fine. You can be a musicianer or anythin' you want in Chicago. Us folk, we all leavin' a-get free."

Syl thrust the ticket at him, but Sterling hesitated, his fists clenched at his side.

Syl snorted. "You gonna meet me or no? Say now! I ain't risking my ass for nothin'. Why, you ain't no yella belly, is ya? The risk I take comin' a-get you, and you ain't got the guts to start anew?"

The beignet tasted like dust in Sterling's mouth.

"We all lock up come nightfall. Bars an' everythin'. Ain't no way to leave once them door lock."

"You can find a way. You comin' or ain't ya?"

Sterling opened his mouth to answer, but no words came. Out of the corner of his eye, he glimpsed a motion in the stable. He glanced toward the open door.

"Fine. Run along, now. Obey yo' damn rules," Syl sneered. The temper that simmered beneath flashed out. He began to stalk away, then turned back.

"Here. Happen you change yo' mind." Syl thrust the ticket at him and took a dollar bill out of his pocket. "Put 'em all in your pocket. Quick now! Keep it hid. I'ma be at the station. Train leavin' aroun' midnight."

Sterling shoved the ticket and bill into his pocket.

Syl placed a hand on Sterling's shoulder, giving him a shake. "See some sense, Sterl!"

He pointed toward the road behind the fence line. His voice softened. "If'n ya change yo' mind, walk down that road there, City Park Avenue, 'bout a mile, you gonna find a streetcar stop. Listen now, you gotta keep out o' sight till the car come by. Maybe I see you at the station, come midnight."

He held out his hand. "Shake hands now so's I know

we still friends. If you ain't on the train, we ain't likely gonna meet again in a long time."

Sterling felt his brother's strong grip, and a bolt of borrowed strength coursed through him. Syl turned without another word and hurried away, back along the fence toward the gate in the distance. He could see the Captain walking across the field to let his brother out. There came a tug on Sterling's heart—an invisible string pulling on him to follow. He watched till Syl was gone through the gate and out of sight.

He took out the ticket and dollar bill and stared at them, thinking hard. It had come all too sudden, this chance to change his life. He remembered that day last summer when a team of horses, startled by a gunshot, had set off on a wild gallop through uptown New Orleans, careening this way and that, the carriage pulled along behind, its passengers screaming with panic. That's how it felt for him now—the terror that a sudden change in direction might be the wrong one, might sink his dreams forever. How would that be— saying goodbye to New Orleans, to his mother, his friends? He held the choice right here in his hand. Go or stay.

The bugle sounded. Supper time. A footfall sounded from behind.

"Gi' me that!" A grimy hand snatched his ticket and money.

Jack, his face full of spite, dodged out of reach and ran off. "I'ma take it to the Cap'n."

Sterling stood frozen till boiling anger kicked in. He pounded after Jack, and his hands reached to grab him by the collar. Jack was fast but Sterling got a good grip on his shirt. He held on tight and jerked him off balance till Jack, arms flailing, stumbled. Sterling brought him down and straddled him, then drove his fist into Jack's face. Jack turned his head away and Sterling's punch glanced off his cheek, just missing his nose.

"Git off or I'm gonna kill ya!" roared Jack, his face a mixture of surprise and fury at being hit. He struggled to get up but Sterling had the advantage. He held down the struggling boy, his anger poured into every punch.

"You little bastard!" he panted as Jack wriggled and squirmed and hollered.

How he hated that smirking, bullying, taunting grin. He had endured it for too long and he didn't hold back. It felt good to let loose at his tormentor. Blood streamed from Jack's nose. A hand gripped Sterling by the shoulder and hauled him up and away from Jack, even as his fists kept swinging. A backward shove sent him sprawling. He glimpsed Bernier through hot anger that clouded his vision, but he jumped up to get back into the fight, fists at the ready. He still had lots of punches left.

Bernier reached down and yanked Jack to his feet. He gripped the boy with one hand and held Sterling back with the other. The ticket and bill lay crumpled on the ground.

"What's this?" he asked Jack.

Jack screamed in Bernier's face. "I'ma take 'em to the Cap'n. He ain't s'posed to have 'em."

Bernier held onto Jack and picked up the ticket and dollar bill. Sterling stood poised and ready for Bernier to get out of the way, so he could swing again.

Jack wiped his nose, then looked down at the blood on his hand. "I'ma tell the Cap'n!"

"Just shut your mouth and git." Bernier shoved him away. "I don't want to see your face till supper. And if you tell, I'll kick your butt into the swamp and no one ever gonna see you again."

"I'm gonna tell, don' you worry," threatened Jack.

But he turned tail and slunk toward the vegetable plots, glancing behind him now and then, and once or twice stopping to turn and stare back at them.

"Git!" yelled Bernier.

When Jack was gone from sight, Bernier turned to Sterling. "You plan on runnin?" he asked, studying the train ticket.

"Dunno," gasped Sterling as he tried to catch his breath. "Maybe."

"Look, you maybe better hide these. For sure, Jack is gonna rat on you. Keep them safe, out o' sight. I know a good place." Bernier walked toward the barn and gestured for Sterling to follow. Sterling tailed him into the gloom and, as his eyes adjusted, he saw a couple of saddles hung on pegs inside the entrance.

"The Cap'n only uses this new one on the Colonel," Bernier said, pointing to the polished leather saddle on the first peg. "This other one here, he never uses that, 'cause some of the stitchin' broke. See here?" He pointed to the frayed threads in the leather seat of the older saddle. "Slip your ticket in there, and the dollar. No one will find it there."

Sterling did as Bernier told him, and tucked the ticket and folded bill inside the small space, pushing it down till not a corner showed above the worn leather.

Bernier's eyes glinted in the shadowy barn. "Now, I got a deal for you. You give me that dollar and I will let you keep the ticket."

Sterling shook his head. "Or what? You gonna tell? Never took you for a rat."

"Hold on, now. You keep the ticket. I help you get free and I'm goin' with you. You can't do it less'n you get help from me. I know how to get away."

"How?"

"I been thinkin' and plannin' a long time. I got it all figured out and we can do it, no problem. But once we get free, we ain't staying together. You get to your train, keep the ticket. I go my way and I keep the money. We go tonight. Deal?"

Although Bernier never lied, his plan might take some magic to work. But Sterling trusted him. If the boy said he could get them to freedom, then his word was gold. The long road outside the gate beckoned.

"Okay, deal." They shook hands.

"Jack is maybe gonna squeal. We gotta move fast. Here's what we do. Tonight, you are gonna find a slab of grease under your bed. When the light's out, you rub it all over, especially your shoulders and arms. That's all you need. Then you wait for my signal. We are goin' out the window."

"But them bars ..."

"I already took care of 'em. Been sawing them bars for weeks, little by little. Clean cuts. Greased and ready to slip out. No one ever looks at them bars. Mostly, they just look away from 'em, and the scaredy ones don't wanna see a ghost. Why'd you think I'm always tellin' them stories? To scare them, o' course. Make them too scared to sleep one night, so they sleep tight the next."

Sterling remembered that just last night, Bernier had entertained them with a story about Madame La Laurie, a murderess in New Orleans, who kept a torture chamber in her attic for her servants, gouged out their brains, even. The boys had tossed and turned in their beds after that one.

"I guess they'll sleep good tonight," Bernier said, as though guessing Sterling's thoughts. "I've just been biding my time, make sure I'm ready. But heard the Cap'n say he is putting iron bars in all the windows, heard him talking to a workman the other day. Can't wait no longer. I'll go tonight. That dollar will help me on my way. I got just one more thing to take care of."

"What you gotta do?" Sterling had Jack on his mind. Maybe Bernier did, too.

The Captain blew the bugle across the fields a second time. Sterling's job. His absence had been noticed.

"I'm gonna fix that gate to open. Let's get in line now."

They ran back to the main building to line up for roll call. Jack stood among them. He glared at Sterling but kept his mouth shut. A darkening bruise decorated his cheek.

At supper time, Sterling watched Bernier talking intently to Jack in a corner of the mess hall. Jack hung his head as Bernier moved in closer, a hand on Jack's shoulder. Bernier wore his usual cold expression, but Jack's eyes darted about like a frightened rabbit's. He backed away as Bernier spoke softly. Sterling felt a twinge of sympathy for Jack, but he thought back to all his tricks. He deserved whatever Bernier was threatening. *I bet he sayin' somethin' real bad. Make him think again afore he tell on me.*

After supper, Sterling and the boys went outside to work an extra hour, weeding the runner beans. Bernier had kitchen supervision, but he spoke to Sterling as he led the boys to the vegetable patch.

"You're gonna find the grease under your bed," he said quietly. "Wait for my signal. Leave your clothes behind. When we get out, I'm goin' to the wash house to get back our own clothes, but you go right to the barn. Wait there for me."

He walked away and Sterling bent to his weeding. Doubts filled his mind.

Stay or go? Stay or go? The question tormented him with each tug on every weed he pulled. He had done nothing wrong. He should be on the outside right now, but that Judge Wickham had put him in here like a criminal. And Syl *wanted* him to come with him and start a new life! Chicago beckoned, all glittering and sparkling new. It promised excitement and musical possibilities, wrapped together in one package. He'd get to the train station. There his brother would be, sitting in the waiting room, not even expecting to see him. He would sneak up on Syl and surprise him. Syl would be so proud. He swallowed his doubts.

The Captain signaled it was time to go inside. Sterling picked up the bugle to sound the evening call, a tuneful song he had composed to sing out a calming message before bedtime.

Day is done, boys. Day is done.

Time to rest now. Time to rest.

Rest,

Boys,

Rest.

Inside the dorm, the boys filled the room with chatter. Jack was usually the loudest, bragging about how he had sneaked an extra piece of chicken or cake from the pantry, or made a younger boy do his latrine duty. Tonight, he was quiet, watchful, his eyes darting from Bernier to Sterling. When Bernier had turned the other way, Jack glared at Sterling and made a slicing motion across his throat. Just before lights out, Sterling looked over at Bernier for a signal. Bernier gave him a quick nod. Sterling bent to untie his shoes, feeling a prickle of excitement. He took a look under the bed as he placed the bugle there. Sure enough, a slab of pork fat lay on the floor. So, it was happening tonight, for certain sure! Sterling took off his shirt and pants and hung them on the nail.

Captain Jones came to the doorway, his keys in hand, and checked that every bed was occupied. He blew out the lamp, wished them goodnight, then shut and locked the door behind him. The room was plunged into darkness. There was no moon tonight.

"Tell us a story?" asked a boy, but Bernier ignored him and pretended to settle for sleep. In the darkness, Sterling lay listening to soft breathing. He looked over at Jack's cot and heard a faint snore. The boys grabbed their sleep quickly after a hard day's labor. Dawn arrived too fast for their tired bodies.

Was Bernier asleep, too?

He reached over the side of his bed for the grease and got to work smearing, stopping now and then to listen for any change in breathing from the sleeping boys. His shoulders and arms soon felt sticky as molasses. When he was finished, he lay waiting for the hours to creep by, dozing now and again, then startling to wakefulness. It felt late enough to leave. Around him, the boys' deep breathing signaled all were fast asleep. Right about now, Syl would be waiting at the station.

A hand touched his shoulder. Bernier stood beside his cot. He gestured to the window. Sterling's heart pounded as he quietly pushed back his cover. He picked up his shoes and followed the boy to the window. Bernier slid a wooden bar out of the frame. It made barely a sound and he dropped it to the ground outside. Two more bars followed the first, leaving an ever-widening space.

Bernier glanced back at Sterling, then slithered through, head first. Sterling watched him wriggle out and heard a faint thud as he landed not far below. The space in the window seemed just wide enough. Sterling looked out. He caught a movement in the dark as Bernier began running toward the wash house.

Now it was his turn. An image of his mother appeared in his mind, her sad eyes reproaching him. He drew back a moment, hesitant. Around him, the boys slept on peacefully. As he stood there, weighing his chances, he could hear his brother's voice taunting him. *Ya ain't no yella belly, is ya? Don't spend your life followin' rules, Sterl! Take your freedom!*

He dropped his shoes out the window, then shoved his head through the space and pushed off. He felt the few remaining bars scrape against his shoulder, holding him back, and he pushed harder. Bernier had slipped through with ease. His shoulders were narrow. But Sterling had more muscle since he had left the city. When he wasn't at his lessons, his body had done nothing but pull and push, lift and carry, bend and reach, walk and run. He pushed again, but he could not get through! Not even the grease was working. One more heave and there came a loud crack. Sterling froze in place.

"The ghos'! I see the ghos' out the window!" called Tony's trembling voice. "Help! The ghos' comin' a-take us with 'im!"

Boys began waking, some whining with fear, some yelling with excitement. In the rising confusion, Sterling threw caution away. Might as well get caught running than just standing here, bent over like a fool. He pushed with all his might. Snap! The last wooden bar broke in half. Gravity took over as he hurtled downward to hit the ground in an awkward sprawl, a sharp pain in his elbows and knees. He got to his feet, hunted for his shoes, found them, and paused to look back at the dorm window. A face peered out, and Sterling took off in a dash toward the barn. He heard voices calling from the window.

"You see 'im? You see the ghos'?" called a boy, his voice wavering.

"Don' git too close, it gonna take us all!"

Jack's voice shouted louder than the rest. "Ain't no ghos'. It Crawford!"

Sterling stumbled a few times in the field, slid on some cow droppings, but kept his balance, gulping air as he raced onward. He heard Jack's voice calling out. "Cap'n Jones! Cap'n Jones! They gittin' free! Crawford and Bernier gittin' free!"

Sterling gathered speed as he peered ahead into the darkness, looking for Bernier. He could see the stable looming ahead, a mass of shadows in the gloom. He crossed the paddock and reached its doors, then stood for a second, gasping, catching his breath. "Bernier?"

No answer. Only the cicadas singing. How long did they have? Could be just seconds. The bugle sounded—ragged, tuneless, and loud. Lights shone out. Sterling picked up some straw to wipe the muck from his feet and put on his shoes. He paced outside the barn, peering into the darkness for Bernier. Had he broken his promise? Was he already running away down the road with the ticket and money? Sterling ducked into the barn to check. A whiff of dry straw and warm air greeted him. The Colonel whinnied. Sterling's fingers scrabbled in the old saddle. They met the paper ticket and the bill that Bernier had shoved inside. Still there.

He hurried outside again. A shadow came swiftly across the pasture and Bernier raced past him and burst through the barn doors, a bundle in his arms.

"Get in here. That damn bugle. Wish I took it with me. We gotta move." He shoved a bundle of clothes into Sterling's arms. "Maybe they all will fit. No time to put 'em on now."

Bernier was already dressed. The boy opened the Colonel's pen, gently stroked the horse's nose, and whispered a greeting. He grabbed for the bridle that hung on the post, pushed the bit between the Colonel's teeth, and led him out of the barn. He paused to feel for the ticket and money in the old saddle, tugged them out, and shoved them into his pants pocket. He pulled himself up onto the Colonel's back and reached down to help Sterling. His hand slid along Sterling's greasy arm, losing its grip.

The night became filled with shouts, some distance away. Sterling tried to scramble up onto the horse. He felt despairing. All was lost.

"We ain't got no chance. They comin' for us."

"Get up here." With a firmer grip, Bernier hauled Sterling up to sit behind him. "We ain't dead yet."

Sterling perched on the Colonel's wide strong back

and clutched the creature's flanks with knees and feet. Bernier urged the horse onward. Sterling held his bundle of clothes in one arm and hung onto Bernier's shirttails with his free hand. The shirt fabric he clutched had the feel of fine linen. Bernier had taken his own good clothes from the wash house, where Miz Jones had stored them, and used precious seconds to dress.

Seconds that had counted dearly.

Bernier urged the Colonel to a trot. "Come on, boy," he called and, for the first time, Sterling noticed laughter in his voice. Laughter combined with something else.

Happiness! Bernier is maybe gon' get killed, but he happy!

"You're our freedom ride!" called Bernier to the horse, not bothering to speak softly, his joyful laughter bubbling like a creek in springtime. "Step up, now! Move along, my beauty!"

Responding to Bernier's voice, the horse began to step lively along the fence line. Sterling clung to Bernier's shirt as he bounced along behind. More shouts echoed in the distance. The searchers were hunting over at the far end of the property, where a work team had been repairing fences. *Still time, maybe.*

Sterling could see lamps that bobbed and shed light

among the shadows. The faint shouts grew louder as the crowd of boys and teachers came closer, moving along the fence line, like dogs after a coon. Sterling heard the Captain shouting commands over a babble of voices. The Colonel reached the gate.

"Get down and open it," said Bernier, his voice light and easy. "I already jimmied the lock. Just lift the latch." He took the bundle of clothes from Sterling.

Sterling looked toward their pursuers, closer now, their lanterns creating dancing shadows. In the moving lamplight, he could make out the tall figure of the Captain. He slid down from the horse and hurried to the gate. The padlock opened with ease. He swung the gate wide. Bernier dug his heels in the Colonel's flanks and the horse obligingly trotted through, then, at a tug on the reins, stopped on the other side.

"Get up here, quick."

As Bernier leaned down to haul him back up, Sterling looked into his eyes and thought he saw fire there, but maybe it was a reflection from the glowing lamps of their pursuers, ever closer. Once again, he clung to Bernier's shirttail as the Colonel moved forward into a trot. The hunters let out a roar.

"Over there, Cap'n!" Jack's voice. During his time at the Home, Jack had made friends with a few rebellious boys and won them over to torment Sterling, just as much as he did.

"I see 'em!" his friends called to one another with rising excitement.

"They on the Colonel!"

In the darkness, the crowd transformed into one menacing creature with one voice, growing ever louder and fiercer as it closed in for the kill. A rifle shot split the night wide open. Sterling felt cold terror. The Colonel pranced and snorted and tossed his head, eyes wild. Bernier clung to the animal's neck and spoke soothing words. The Colonel was not in the mood to listen. He rose up on his back legs and Sterling lost his grip on Bernier's shirttails. He grabbed at air, arms flailing as he slid backward and down.

For a moment, he found himself floating, his head strangely empty, his very name forgotten, the stars wheeling above, the white horse in a slow dance, its powerful body rising upward in sharp relief against the black sky. But in a sudden reversal, motion became cruel and harsh and swift.

The hard road to freedom rose up to meet Sterling, and knocked the breath clear out of him. A thundering pain swept through his head. Sterling heard the sound of galloping hooves fading away and, ever nearer, the shouts of the hunters closing in.

TWENTY-TWO

Some musical chords sound unpleasant—like a problem needing to be solved, or a question waiting for an answer. But in the language of music, tension is good. A melody flows onward to find a solution that is pleasing to the ear and creates a sound of beauty. These lessons Miss Vine taught Sterling in the days following Bernier's escape.

That terrible night, he had lain there on the ground as voices called out to him.

"You okay?"

"Wake up, Crawford!"

"He look dead."

Sterling kept still, eyes closed, filled with shame. He felt a hand on his shoulder as someone gently shook him.

"He ain't dead, Cap'n?"

"Maybe you done kill 'im!"

Sterling almost wished he were dead. Better than taking the punishment that was sure to come.

"Stand back!" Captain Jones pushed through the boys. "Get on back to bed, boys!"

Sterling opened his eyes a crack. The boys stayed put to gape, and weigh Sterling's chances of being dead or alive.

That shotgun blast had set their imaginations going.

"Go on, git!"

Sterling heard them move away.

The Captain raised his lantern to look down at him, the shotgun in the crook of his arm. Sterling closed his eyes tight against the brightness, the ache in his head, the shame he felt for being caught half-naked in the road.

The Captain laid down the weapon and held the lantern steady as he felt Sterling's arms and legs.

"Nothin' broke. Get up." His voice came clipped, gruff.

He carefully pulled Sterling upright and steered him back through the gate. The lantern illuminated the shadows, as it bobbed and swung to his long stride. Sterling stayed in the circle of light as best he could. His unsteady steps numbered several to each one of the Captain's, as they walked into the building, then up the stairs. The Captain's silence was full of accusation. Inside the sickroom, he put the gun down, then paused to light a wall sconce that cast a flickering light and illuminated his own face. Sterling could scarcely look in the Captain's eyes for the coldness he saw there.

The Captain pointed to a cot. "Sit. We'll talk first thing tomorrow." He took the gun and left, his footsteps echoing down the hallway.

Sterling slumped down onto the cot and rested his head in his hands. All this time, he never once figured on getting caught. Bernier had been so confident they could do it together, and now he had escaped with the ticket and money all for himself! How did that happen?

Miss Vine hurried in, barefoot, wearing a robe over her night dress. She carried a nightshirt and bowl of water. She looked him over and tutted, as she put the bowl down and held up the shirt.

"Put this on." She pulled it over his head then examined his face. "You made some bad choices this night," she told him, as she cleaned the dirt from his cheek and treated the cuts.

He winced as she dabbed at a tender spot on his arm.

"The judge ain't goin' to like hearin' about this," she said, almost to herself. "Looks like you gonna have a lot more time here to make somethin' good of it all."

"Wish I never done it," he muttered. "Now I ain't never gonna be free."

She spread some liniment over the cuts and bandaged the wound on his arm. "Feelin' sorry for yourself ain't the answer. Tomorrow, you come to the music room, first thing. We are gonna use whatever you feelin' right now, make some harmony out of the sour."

She tied the knot on the bandage, closed the lid of the first aid box with a snap, and stood to leave. "I think harmony, in one way or another, bin missin' from your life."

She blew out the lamp, and Sterling pulled his legs up onto the cot and lay down, trying to make sense of the swirling images in his head, feeling his eyes grow heavy. A dull weight pressed on him and numbed him into a downward slide, deeper and deeper. He heard Miss Vine's voice speaking faintly, as though from far away.

"Yes, best sleep in here tonight. The boys gonna be all fired up—won't none of you get a moment's rest."

There was not much left of this night and, when he startled awake to the bugle call, aches and soreness pummeled his arms and body. Flashes of memory came to him like the flickering images in a nickelodeon—the Colonel's lively strides along the fence line, the clutch of fabric in his hands as he held on tight, a carefree voice ringing through the night, the downward slide as the hunters closed in. He remembered how the horse had picked up speed after the gunshot, the sound of his hooves pounding the road, growing fainter and fainter as the voices came louder—no way they would ever catch Bernier now. He must be far, far away.

Some clothes lay at the bottom of the bed. He reached for them and dragged them on. The Captain wanted to see him first thing. Maybe the police wagon was waiting outside, come to take him back to prison. He trod carefully down the steps to the main floor. As he passed the music room, he heard piano music drifting through the open door and stopped to listen.

"Come inside," Miss Vine called to him. She sat at the piano, playing a pretty piece, her back straight, the notes flowing like the gentle currents in a river. She paused a moment to look him over. "Guess you're feelin' sore," she said. "But I want you to sit down here and listen."

Sterling went inside, sat beside her on the bench, and

wondered how Miss Vine could be thinking of lessons at a time like this. A book of printed music sat on the stand. Miss Vine leaned forward to play a series of rippling notes, blending one into the other, as she carried the melody from left hand to right. One hand came up to turn the page as the other kept playing, till the music came to a quiet finish that lingered in the silence of the room. She sat still for a moment, then lifted her hands from the keyboard.

"You playin' Mozart, Miss Vine?" asked Sterling, interested in spite of himself.

"This a piece by Bach, another dicty white composer." She smiled to show him she remembered his words about Mozart. "You like it?"

"I guess ..."

"... but it ain't no Bolden? It called *Prelude in C Major*. Listen again to the notes that Bach uses, but this time I'ma play those separate sounds as chords."

Sterling shifted, feeling impatient. Why ever was she teaching him now? He was finished at this place, likely going back to prison. But she acted as though nothing unusual had happened. She played two chords, combining the notes into bunches of sound.

"Which one sounds prettier, this one or that one?"

What did it matter? But she played them again, insistent. The first chord sounded wrong.

"That second one sound good," said Sterling, as he tore his thoughts away from the punishment to come.

"Listen again, now."

She layered some simple notes one above the other to make another sound, harsh and unpleasant. She held it there for a while, so the vibration lingered in the room. "We call this a dissonant chord. If you listen, seem like it askin' a question and hopin' for an answer."

She played it again, holding the sound as before. To his ears, the chord seemed like it was in trouble, lost, and maybe waiting to get home again. She played a different chord that seemed to answer the first and bring it home from its lost place.

"See? I gave the first chord some space, so you can feel the tension. Then I found an answer to it with the second chord, and don't it feel good to get it back into a beautiful sound again! The tension all gone. If you create a dissonant chord, it lookin' for an answer—gotta give it space to find one. Let it hang. It gonna make the findin' all the better."

Miss Vine stood up to leave. "Writin' a tune is just like tellin' life's story. Music ain't all pretty. And stories ain't all good. I know you bin writin' your own story with music. Your hard times are just like these dissonant chords. They waitin' on an answer, is all. Give 'em space to find it. Put all that in your music, Sterling. Stay here. Practice awhile."

She placed a pencil beside him and the sheet of manuscript paper that contained some of his Plaquemine composition, then paused at the door.

"The Cap'n say I gotta go see him," he told her.

"Do as I say. Cap'n Jones gonna call you when he ready."

She left him alone. He began to play the notes he had written for his River piece, that music he had first heard in his head when he was on the train to Plaquemine. The melody filled his senses till there was no room left for his troubles. It flowed from his fingertips onto the keyboard till he was scarcely aware of the room, the passing minutes, or the ivory keys yellowed with age.

Now and then, he snatched up the pencil and transcribed his notes onto the lined paper, as both Armand and Miss Vine had taught. His fingers explored the black and white keys as he played the bluesy dissonant notes of the prisoners' song, remembering the way it had twisted his insides. He heard Bolden's horn leading them to an answer. Sterling wove it all in, ache and fulfilment, hand in hand. He felt a presence in the room but, sunk so deeply into his melody, he scarcely registered it, as he let his mind roam into the sights and sounds of the past. As he replayed his composition from the beginning, he wished he could get at the special notes that Bolden knew, but it seemed no keyboard carried those. He would add a solo part for Bolden's horn, so he could take it where it was meant to go. The King's melody would give the piece just what it needed. Almost there.

"What music is that, Crawford?"

Sterling tore his attention away from the keyboard.

The Captain leaned against the doorway. His clothes were rumpled. His eyes seemed sunk in gloom, the lines in his face drawn downward in defeat. Miss Vine stood beside him. She nodded encouragement at Sterling, her eyes bright with something like anticipation. How long had they been there? Sterling hung his head, not daring to look in the Captain's eyes.

"This my river music. 'Plaquemine Blues.'"

"Where'd you learn to make tunes like that?"

The question stumped him. He glanced up at the Captain and dropped his eyes again. There was that look he hated to see. Distrust. "They just in my head, is all, Cap'n."

"His own music, Cap'n," said Miss Vine. A look passed between them.

Captain Jones stared at Sterling till the boy bent his head, wanting to escape, feeling judged. Shame welled up in his chest.

"Well, boy. Let's we have a talk," said the Captain, at last. "Come on with me."

Sterling pushed back from the bench and got up, but an unfinished note lingered in his head and his eyes went back to his notation paper. He wished he could pencil it in. He forced his attention back to the present and moved to the door. Miss Vine nodded encouragement, her eyes fierce and bright. Captain Jones led him into his office, a space just large enough for a desk and chair. On one side of the desk lay a pile of files, neatly stacked. One lay open. The Captain sat down and fastened tired eyes on Sterling as the boy stood, waiting for his punishment.

"Wasn't for Miss Vine, you'd be feeling my boot kicking your ass into the wagon and back to prison right now."

Sterling winced. The Captain's voice might as well have been that very boot.

"That's what you deserve. For vandalism, damage to property, criminal behavior, theft of one horse. How'd you come by that train ticket and money?"

Jack had squealed. *The rat!*

Sterling kept his eyes down, not daring to look into the Captain's face. "My cousin done give it me, so's when I get free, I'm aimin' a-visit him in Chicago."

"Look at me, boy. Your cousin say to leave last night?"

He would never rat on Syl. He looked the Captain in the eye. "No, sir, Cap'n. He jus' give me the ticket for when I get free agin."

"That was your first mistake. You know the rules. No gifts from family without they pass through this office. Where is the ticket now?"

"I guess Bernier done took it." And his money, too.

"This all Bernier's idea? Runnin' away?"

Sterling did not have an answer. He guessed he only ran away because of Bernier's confidence and his brother's scorn. Without them, Sterling would have been asleep till daybreak. He did not want Bernier to take all the blame. He looked down at his feet.

"All this, it ain't only about you. It makes our school look bad. People that teach you, take care of you, feed you. This is the gratitude you give back? Whose idea was it to cut the bars?"

Sterling kept silent.

"Seems like you tryin' to protect Bernier. That ain't goin' to help your case, boy. You are this close to goin' back to prison. Talk, dammit!"

"I didn't know nothin' 'bout that, Cap'n. I'm sorry for it, but I never knowed he done that. Least not till las' night."

The Captain leaned forward and pounded his fist on the desk to punctuate his words. "See, this is your *weakness*, Crawford. You are *easily led*. Plus, you think you are maybe *entitled* to get out o' here on the fast train. *Wrong*. You *pay* your *dues* in this world."

Behind him, shelves displayed rows of books, some new, some with the stains of age, their bindings frayed. The Captain reached behind him, slid out a book, opened it, and carefully turned the pages, searching the text.

"This here is a book written by Booker T. Washington." His finger followed a line of text. "Here it is ... *Nothing ever comes to me that is worth having except as a result of hard work.*" The Captain nodded to himself and closed the book. "I want you to think about that, Crawford. Hard work brings success. If you ain't willing to do the work, your lessons, your chores, you ain't gonna find success. All your victories are gonna come cheap. Worthless. Stolen."

His chair screeched angrily as he pushed it back and stood up.

Sterling gulped. "Sorry, Cap'n."

"Now, I got a report to write. This ain't all Bernier's fault. I took you out of that prison because I had faith in you. It'll take a long time for you to earn my trust again."

The Captain's words stung.

"But I ain't done nothin'. I dunno why they done send me here. It ain't fair! I never done nothin' a' nobody. I never deserve no prison!" He felt tears spring into his eyes, but he would not let them spill over. He would not. His breath came fast as he stood, waiting for his punishment.

The Captain became silent, slowly shaking his head. "I wondered why they put you there, boy. Knew somehow you didn't belong, no more does any child belong there, but look like you just in the wrong place with the wrong skin. I was just hopin' to ease the punishment, bringin' you here. Hope I was right to do so.

"After breakfast, you will write two apologies—one to me and one to your teacher. Explain why this was a bad idea, and that it will never happen again. You gotta convince us all you're worth a second chance.

"And thank Miss Vine. If not for her good word ... Now, get out."

Sterling had never felt so bad about himself, not even that time when he had punched Syl in the face and told him how much he hated him. He slunk back to the mess hall. The boys' voices came loud and excited from the open doorway.

"Crawford!" They jumped up and swarmed around him to fire questions, admiration clear in their voices.

"Bernier tell ya where he goin'?" they asked.

"I dunno. He never tole me." Sterling pushed through the boys to sit down at his place, but they followed to crowd around him.

"Maybe the ghos' git 'im. I maybe see 'im go out the window," said Tony, "but might I was dreamin' it. He done fly like a bird."

"You and Bernier some clever!"

"Where ya think he at now?"

"Far away if'n he lucky," said a boy.

"Guess you gonna plan another escape, Crawford?"

Sterling ducked his head. "Nah. I'm stayin' out o' trouble."

The boys groaned, not believing him. All became silent as Jack walked into the room, followed by the Captain.

"Get your breakfast," the Captain said to Jack.

As Jack walked to his place at the table, he stared at Sterling, triumph plain on his face. But the boys' eyes showed anger as they watched him. They hissed at him from under their breath.

"Snitch."

"Rat."

Jack squared his shoulders and sat down, reaching for a slice of bread. Someone's hand jerked the plate out of his reach.

The morning passed with no word about Sterling's punishment or Bernier's whereabouts. An ironsmith measured windows and placed temporary wooden bars in the dorm to replace the broken ones. Miss Vine taught her lesson as usual, in spite of the raised excitement in her classroom. Bernier's slate sat on the table, his spelling words from yesterday's lesson still chalked on it. One word stood out from the list of dictation words—*possibility*. Many pairs of eyes stared at it, as the boys wondered about its owner. Was he hiding, running, maybe caught?

That afternoon, the boys were at their work in the field when a shout arose. "Lookit that!" They all looked up from their field work to see a white horse at the gate, snorting and blowing and tossing his head.

"The Colonel!"

The boys raced across the field and the Captain hurried over to let him through. The Colonel trotted to the water trough. Sterling did not move from his work. He stayed put among the vegetables he was weeding. Across the field, he watched the boys crowding around the horse, and heard their raised voices asking questions, as though the Colonel might answer.

"Where was you, boy?"

"Where you take Bernier?"

As Sterling watched, Captain Jones pushed through the crowd and examined his horse from head to tail. He gestured to the boys to get back to work. Sterling pulled weeds in short jerks and flung them aside, stooping as low as he could, and wishing the earth could swallow him.

"Cap'n wanna talk to ya," said Tony. "He ain't too mad."

The boys fell silent and watched as Sterling stood up, took a breath, and walked over to the stable. He stood in front of the Captain, waiting for his punishment, head down, fingers crossed. The Captain stroked the horse's nose. "Wish you could talk, boy," he muttered. He led him over to the food trough and shoveled in some oats from the feed bin, scarcely glancing at Sterling.

"Lucky for you, my horse is in good shape. Had a talk with Miss Vine."

The Colonel bent his head to the trough and chomped his breakfast. The Captain laid down the shovel and turned to look at him. "Better get used to it here, Crawford. You're getting one year to learn your lesson. No more family visits. Starting now. Get back to work."

Homesickness welled up in Sterling as he walked back. The boys watched his progress across the field, calling out to him.

"What he say?"

"You gettin' a whuppin'?"

Sterling felt too sunk in misery to answer, his head full of the hundreds of days and nights before he could earn his freedom. The boys quietened.

"Must be real bad," someone murmured.

They left him alone.

That evening after supper, he felt drawn to the piano, and discovered it was just as Mr. Davis had told him—the keyboard was the place to go to work out his troubles, find the notes of sorrow, and the chords that sang out his yearning for what used to be.

Part 4

THE DEVIL'S
INTERVAL

TWENTY-THREE

"You! Come 'ere. I wanna talk to yuz."

Sterling turned, startled at the gruff voice.

Paulo di Christiano crossed the alley beside the train station, his short thick body grown rounder over the year. "Your brother owe me money."

More than a year ago, Sterling had stored his shoeshine stand inside this man's grocery. Syl had always kept it a secret from Paulo that he and Sterling were brothers. But now the man knew the truth.

Sterling stepped back, keeping his distance as Paulo's stout legs moved with lumbering slowness toward him. "I ain't got no brother."

"Your brother no pay—you gonna pay." Paulo, chest heaving with exertion, stopped and jabbed his finger at him to milk an imaginary trigger.

That parcel of cocaine Syl had stolen—how much did he owe?

"Get away from me. I ain't gotta pay nothin'." He slipped away into the crowd. That old man could never catch him.

But the man had friends. They could catch him.

Sterling's first day of freedom, but already he had trouble. Just this morning at the Colored Waifs Home, Miss Vine had handed him the bound pages of all his written music. Sterling felt proud to see his keyboard work captured this way, all his blues and ragtime pieces. His "Plaquemine Blues" was still a work in progress, but he felt no hurry to reach the end of that piece. He liked puzzling out the melody, plunging into that place of contentment each time he sat down at the keyboard.

"Make somethin' of your life, Sterling," Miss Vine said. "You got the tools. I 'spect to hear about you, lots of good harmony to come."

Mr. Davis shook his hand. "Look me up. I'ma be around." He shoved his hat at an angle on his head and sat down on the front steps. As the police wagon drew up, he called out. "Don't forget what I teach ya. Stay close to that keyboard."

"You exceeded our expectations, boy," said the Captain, his voice stern, a smile playing at the corners of his mouth. "You ain't deserve to come here, I know that, but you persevered. A lesson for you, next time you're in a tight spot—you know you got the right stuff. Now, stay out of trouble, boy. Don't come back."

Sterling saluted and the Captain returned the salute. He turned to climb up into the police wagon, glancing back to see their kind faces one last time. Three new boys had just climbed down from it, scared and uncertain, to start their lives in the Home. Like them, Sterling owned only the clothes on his back, except for a dollar in his pocket and his music in hand. He knew his teachers were sending him away with much more. Now he could write his own music.

The police wagon rattled along the city streets into town. He peered through the barred window, eager for glimpses of life outside, and for his feet to meet the city boardwalks at last. The driver delivered him to the courthouse, and he climbed out of the wagon and stepped lightly along. Joy swept over him. He'd been shut away a long time, and no one knew he was back. There were no expectations, no locked doors, no commands.

"Hell, today I ain't gotta do nothin', and no one gonna tell me different," he muttered.

He found the windows of his old home shuttered like eyes closed against the sun. A note was tacked to the door in his mother's hand, to come and find them at an address on Dumaine Street.

So, things were just like his brother had told him. How would it be, he wondered, living with his teacher? Would he have to call him "Uncle"? Go back to school?

All that aside, right now he was free. His feet took him back down the streets he knew. He soaked up their flavors, revisiting the old neighborhoods and greeting them again like lost friends. Their colors and sounds greeted him back and he sniffed at the hint of salt in the air, blended with the sweet and sour odors of the city. At the Globe Ballroom—that place of beginnings—he remembered how King Bolden had opened the door to invite him inside. How much older he felt now! Nearby, a new dance hall offered tango lessons, Brazilian style.

Musicians still lined up outside pawnshops, to put their instruments in hock or buy them back again.

Drunkards sat on stoops in back alleyways. Coal carts rumbled down avenues. The Mississippi River sent its silver winding ribbon through the city. But the streets and buildings looked different than he remembered— smaller, faded, as though he were looking at them through a backward lens. In his memories of them, they had seemed taller, larger, more vivid.

He passed the place where Joe Never Smile stabled his horses, but found boards nailed over the entrance and the sign torn down. Only a whiff of rotten straw remained to tell the tale. Here was the corner he'd chased down Clarence Williams, laden with suits from the Chinese laundry. The laundry had become a hock shop, and where once the hot dog seller stood, a row of empty fruit and vegetable crates waited for pickup.

He paused at Basin Street to soak up the noise and bustle, as passengers hurried from the train station, and his eyes found the place where he used to perch and give mirror shines. Nothing had changed there, except that a skinny white kid worked a stand on the sweet spot where Sterling used to sit.

"Get your shine! Nickel for a shine! Shine your shoes, Mister?" the boy called out to people hurrying by.

Mirror shine! Sterling would shout, watching for King Bolden to walk by. *Teach me some licks?* Where was Bolden now? Those carefree days were all gone. He could never go back there. The city had not changed so much as he had changed. This whole year, he'd been like a fish in an aquarium, opening and closing his mouth inside the glass, to gulp all the learning that Miss Vine and Professor Davis could teach him.

And he'd learned the art of biding his time.

When the Captain gave him latrine duty for six months, or he felt fierce pangs of homesickness, when the day's labor and the night's troubled dreams became more than he could stand, he'd take each new day as a step toward the next, and the next, ever on toward his release. Every evening, he sat at the keyboard and his fingers sketched a musical landscape of chords, like shades of color from an artist's pallet. Music became his freedom, comforting and lifting him.

There came six months of keeping himself in line and leading by example, until the boys elected Sterling as Lieutenant of his squad. His first order concerned Jack. The boy had paid heavily for his snitching. He could scarcely move for looking over his shoulder, waiting for the next nasty trick. Countless times, the latrine bucket somehow soaked his bed, the occasional shovels of manure were tossed at him in the barn, or he'd find a dead rodent in his chicken gumbo.

The time had come to make peace.

"Let Jack alone. I think he done learn his lesson."

So the boys let Jack be. To Sterling's surprise, a friendship sprang up between the two. Jack had shared with Sterling the bits and pieces of his life on the streets, with no parent to guide him. "Times my uncle done hit me with a buckle belt, times a switch. So I run off," he told him.

In turn, Sterling related his story of Plaquemine and his brother Syl.

"Them white folk hate us, but I hate 'em more, a hunner'd times more," Jack growled, as Sterling nodded agreement.

When Jack's term at the Home was up, the Captain apprenticed him to a plasterer in the city. Sterling had felt a surge of loss when the boy left for the last time.

He broke out of his reverie as a page of newsprint, propeled by the morning breeze, wrapped itself around his ankle. He picked it up and looked at it absently, then more closely. In bold print at the top of the page was the newspaper's name, *Chicago Defender,* and its date, April 2, 1907. A comic drawing caught his eye. It depicted a white man with a bullying stance, facing a colored man, eyes cast down. He folded the page, stuck it in his pocket to read later, and turned to walk away. That's when Paulo di Christiano had recognized him and called out, "You! Come 'ere."

For a second, the two of them seemed to be enacting that scene in the newspaper cartoon, Paulo with threat in his eyes, Sterling ready to run. Paulo was still a gangster, a fat spider who sat in a web of influence that lay over the city.

"I better watch my back," he thought, as he slipped into the crowd and out of reach. He hurried along, clutching his music, as he headed toward his mother and his new life.

Passing by a music shop, Sterling heard the tinkling notes of a piano. He stopped to peer through the window. A young man sat at the piano, and Sterling recognized the large head, the round glasses, and bow tie. Clarence Williams! He rushed inside, eager to say hello to his friend. A crowd of people surrounded Clarence as he bent over the keyboard, singing along with his tune.

If I should take a notion, to jump into the ocean,

'T ain't nobody's bizness if I do, do, do.

The crowd hummed along, and repeated the chorus, *If I do, do, do ...*

Sterling inched forward as Clarence swung into another ragtime tune, and a couple beside Sterling said, "Let's get that music from the shelf over there. Sure like that beat." People lined up at the cash counter and handed over their dimes, as Clarence played on. So, this was his new job, playing piano to encourage people to buy, buy, buy. Clarence came to the end of his last song and pushed back the bench, stretching his fingers and beaming at the audience.

"Lots more where that come from, folks. But I gotta get along now and write some more. This shop is runnin' out of sheet music!"

He ambled through the crowd and pushed past Sterling, humming a tune as he made for the door.

"Hey, Clarence! Clarence!"

Clarence stopped in mid-stride and stared down at him. "Well, if it ain't Sterling Crawford! You sure been gone a long time. You grown, some. Come on along, let's get out of here an' you can tell me about it."

"I done been livin' at the Colored Waifs a year. I'm aimin' to see Armand—you seen 'im?" said Sterling, hurrying to keep up with Clarence's long strides as he swung down the street.

"I tell you, A.J. and me are doin' pretty good. We both writin' music, composin', and we aim to start a publishing business, get into the recording business."

"You workin' with Armand Piron now?"

"That's right. I'm goin' back up to Chicago next month to look over the publishing business, see how it's done. How long was you in jail for?"

"One whole year. Jus' got free today!"

"You still writin' music? Me and Armand got a surprise for you."

"I can read and write music, and I done learn a-play piano, too. An' I write lotsa tunes. What surprise you got?"

"Ain't sayin' right now. But that's fine news, Sterling." Clarence took a half-smoked butt out of his jacket pocket and stopped to strike a match. "Piano is my meal ticket right now. I always had a yearnin' to play, since I was only eight year old. Pianos so scarce in Plaquemine, I had to walk five miles on foot to find one. Folk see me comin' they say, 'Lock up the piano! Here comes the music boy!'

"You want a dog?" Clarence paid some coins to a vendor. "Someone ask me, 'You know where to find a good piano player these days?' 'You talkin' to him,' says I. So I got me a job in that music store and play tunes on request." He took the hot dogs from the vendor and handed one to Sterling as they walked on.

"Could only play but five or six pieces when I started, and if they'd ask for a waltz, I'd just play 'em five ragtime tunes in three-quarter time. Asked a piano lady to teach me some new songs, but cost me a dollar for every song she teach. Figured I better just learn on my own and save myself some dollars. Now I can read music and write it, too, maybe not as good as you."

Clarence stopped in his tracks. "You lookin' for work? I got just the job for you."

"I should say so. What kinda work?"

"I go round knockin' on doors on a Sunday. Tell the folks I got a new song. It's only ten cents. They always say, 'Come on in!' I sit down at their piano and play and sing. Pretty soon the neighbors come in and I sell 'em plenty of my tunes."

"I read music easy. I gotta practice the tunes first," said Sterling.

"Folks love to see a kid playin' piano. You wanna come along this Sunday? I'll show you the ropes. Give you a chance to make some dimes."

"Yessir! I can do that."

"I can give you a few pieces now." Clarence finished chewing the last of his dog, opened his bag, and pulled out some printed music. "Practice these and meet me at A.J. Piron's house come Sunday. You remember where he live?"

"Sure, Columbus Street."

"I gotta get goin'. I see you at Armand's house Sunday after church. We got such a big surprise for you, too. You gonna like it. Just wait till Sunday. And practice them songs."

Sterling walked on to Dumaine Street, a dance in his step. He had a job lined up and only just come back! Mr. Trask's cottage sat back from the road and looked trim and tidy, just like its owner. The walls had a fresh coat of white paint and the windows sparkled clean in the sunlight. A fancy wrought-iron railing separated its tiny patch of lawn from the quiet street.

The front door flew open as Sterling swung the gate shut behind him. His mother rushed down the steps, arms held wide, skirts flying in a whirlwind of motion.

"Why, lookit my boy! Just look at 'im, Robert!"

Sterling stepped into her embrace, feeling encircled with love. She held him at arm's length to take him in from top to toe. The worry lines on her face had lifted, as though someone had taken a brush to her forehead and swept them away. Her body had grown rounder in a plump, satisfied way.

He glanced behind her at Mr. Trask, waiting on the steps. He was just as thin and bony as ever, but he looked more content than Sterling remembered. A pointed beard peppered with gray decorated his chin. It felt strange to see him in casual clothes and carpet slippers, his reading glasses slipping down on his nose.

"Don't squeeze him to death, Maria. Let me have a look at him."

"An' ain't he growed!" she said, pushing him toward his teacher. "Why, you gettin' taller than me!"

"Good to have you back, Sterling." Mr. Trask shook hands and guided him inside.

The cottage was larger than their former home. The furniture was finer, too, but he noticed his mother's knick-knacks in the china cabinet, the hen teapot that she liked so much, and a few of her vases. He wondered about Clancy and Barrel. And Sydney. He longed to ask but felt suddenly shy and awkward, being in such close quarters with his classroom teacher.

As if sensing Sterling's discomfort, Mr. Trask stepped out of his slippers into his shoes lying neatly inside the door. He brushed some biscuit crumbs from his shirt front and tapped the ashes from his pipe into a saucer.

"Well, I have some preparation work waiting for me at school. You two have a good visit. Good to have you with us, Sterling. What is that you got, there?"

He gestured to the ribbon-bound book and the sheet music Sterling held.

"Nothin'. Jus' some music, and this some tunes I done wrote. You wanna see 'em?"

He knew Mr. Trask loved music. "Yes, but no time now. Show it to me later. And when I get back, we'll talk about your future. Think about sending you on to junior college."

"Give the boy some time, Robert, get used to us all."

"We'll see." Mr. Trask gave him a meaningful look. "We'll make some plans, now you're back with us."

When his teacher had closed the front door behind him, Sterling spoke up. "What I gotta call 'im? Ain't callin' 'im Uncle, that's for sure. Nor Daddy, neither," he added.

"We gonna work that out, in time." His mother fingered the sleeve of his worn cotton shirt. Miz Jones had given him someone else's old street clothes to wear home. The clothes he had been wearing when he first came to the Home no longer fit.

"These worn old threads," she said. "Shoulda brung you new, soon as I heard you comin' home. I done forgot how much you likely growed. You taller'n me! Guess I'm gonna do some stitchin'. But I still got Syl clothes. They maybe gonna fit. I put 'em in your room." She gestured toward a narrow hallway, where doors opened off to three bedrooms. "Lot o' space here for you." She showed him his new room, with two cots inside, a colorful rag rug on the floor. A desk and chair stood in front of the window.

"Robert gave you that desk. He hope you gonna study an' all, finish school."

Sterling sidestepped the subject. "You hear from Syl?"

His mother nodded. "Some letters come at first. Been a little while since the last one. Tole me he done visit you? Hope he brung them beignets?"

"Yes! He still in Chicago?"

"Still there. Earnin' good money." She held out her hand for his music and looked through the pages. "Your

Uncle Ned, he real sick. Heart trouble. You and me gotta go visit soon."

"Barrel doin' good?"

"He about runnin' that store now, with your Aunt Ruthie."

"This here all my own music." Sterling showed her the bound booklet. "My teacher, Miss Vine, done teach me a-write my tunes."

"Well, that's really somethin', Sterling! You knowin' how to write your music. That's some fine teachin' they all givin' there." Her face showed a hint of sadness. "You still aimin' a-be a musicianer, like Bolden?"

"I ain't never gonna play like Bolden! But I can make a good livin' at composin', sellin' my music to musicianers."

"That way of livin' ..." She gave a slow shake of her head. "I seen musicianers ruin they own lives, end up drunk in gutters. Never did see no good end come of it."

"That ain't all of 'em. Some of 'em do fine. Lookit Bolden." Too late, he suddenly remembered the last time he had seen the King. It was like his mother said. Bolden had not been in good shape that time he and Clarence had stopped to talk.

His mother echoed his thoughts, sighing. "Bolden is

done. Burned out. Me and Robert want good things for you. Maybe college. We can do it now, Sterling. There gonna be lots of chances for a good life, for you and me."

"That why you with 'im?"

His mother's eyes flashed hurt. "Robert, he a good man. Schooled. I never got no money to send my boys to college. But now, we got that chance, Sterl. Best not turn away from it." She gazed at him, her eyes brimming. "Don't do nothin' bad, Sterling. Not like Syl done."

She waited for his assurances, but he kept silent. He needed to take in this new situation, think about his choices in his own time. "I'm so hungry," he said, to distract her. "You got some dinner for me?"

"I sure do!" his mother hurried into the kitchen, pleased to be taking care of him, humming and bustling about with pots and plates. Sterling followed her, sat down at the table to watch and let it all soak in—the sensation of being gathered in and no worries. There were no laundry baskets in the kitchen, he noticed, no lines of linen drying by the stove. She sure had a different life now. She opened the larder door, and a glimpse inside revealed molasses pie, real butter, and a ham hock. For a skinny fellow, Mr. Trask sure liked his eating.

Sterling ate his meal, while his mother sat at the kitchen table with him, content to watch.

"Barrel still in school?" he asked in mid-chew.

"He done quit. But you ain't gonna quit, Sterling."

Sterling wished he had not asked. "This sure is good!"

"Lots more if you hungry."

He had just taken the last mouthful of ham and grits when the sound of a marching band filtered into the room.

The sweet harmony of trombones and saxophones, drums and horns, pulled Sterling out of his chair and over to the front window, and from there to the door. He opened the door and stuck his head out to judge which direction the band was going, then hurried onto the stoop to hear better. Sounded like only a few streets away.

"I'm gonna be right back," he called to his mother. "Won't be but a minute."

"Where you goin'? I got pie!"

"Won't be long," he called, running down the steps, through the gate, along the street, and around the corner. Seemed like years ago that he and Barrel, Syd, and Clancy had stepped into the Second Line to dance and jive. It seemed like the clock had turned back and he was chasing that special horn, just the way he did when he used to hear it through the open classroom window.

For those were Bolden's notes! He felt certain of it!

At Johnson Street, he glimpsed the Second Liners rounding a corner, the horns blaring as his ear separated each instrument from the next, to find the singular threads of those dancing golden notes that aimed higher, louder, sweeter.

He dodged through the tail end of dancing people to the back row of drums, on around them to pass the trombones—must be ten of them—his feet splashed through gutter sewage, and he pushed into the crowd lining the boardwalks. "Watch it, kid. Little bastard, quit shovin'!"—stepped on a little girl's hand as she perched there in the front row, "Momma, that boy ...!"—found a narrow alley of space between the buildings and the crowd, dodged around the stray bystanders, unable to see the band through the mass of people lining the street, but trusting his ears to tell him he was getting closer; on past the wail of the saxophones—must be a dozen—and, at last, the horns, and his ear attuned to just one, its voice soaring higher than them all—*The King! Bolden still King!*—and Sterling ran behind the crowd alongside that horn, followed it, drawn and pulled by it, till it sounded from slightly behind him and he had just moments to shove through the crowd again. "Hey, watch yo'sel'! Git out o' here, boy!" and his feet met the gutter once more, and here came King Bolden marching toward him, pushing that sound, aiming it all the way to Plaquemine and beyond—"*I'M STILL THE KING! NO WAY YOU EVER GONNA PLAY HORN LIKE ME!*"

But something was wrong.

The King's gait looked lopsided, his feet stumbled, froth appeared at the mouth, and his eyes turned as gray as his face, as gray as the final notes that were fleeing his horn to land, limping and wounded, in a heap alongside the King's body as he went down, and the cornet hit the street at Sterling's feet. The band played on, its members stepping over the King—*Keep movin!*—as Sterling stooped to pick up the cornet, and a few bystanders exclaimed in disgust at the fallen musicianer, bent over him, yanked him out of the band's path till he lay full length in the gutter, shook him, slapped his face, but the King's eyes rolled back in his head till the whites showed, and the crowd, their attention drawn from the parade, reluctant to act, waited for someone to take charge so they could join the Second Liners and go on enjoying such a fine day, with the sun high in the blue sky.

Someone called out, "That's Buddy Bolden! Go fetch Cora. She gonna know what to do!"

Sterling tucked the cornet under his arm, his eyes fixed on Buddy's prone figure, much thinner than he remembered, the face ravaged and bony. He waited, not like the rest, not indifferent, but with a clawing dread that clamped down over his heart as the band's joyous music faded away down the street. Sterling patted his face, but Buddy's eyes stayed rolled upward, like he was looking inside his own head.

"Hey, Buddy. Remember me? Sterling! I got yo' horn right here, and someone comin' to he'p ya'. Don't ya worry, now."

It might have been an hour or only a few minutes later—Sterling could not guess, because it seemed time had slowed down, like a clock that needed winding. Dismay sat like a rock in the pit of his stomach as he stayed close to Buddy, talking to him. "Someone comin', don't fret. Someone comin' to help." He touched Buddy's hand, cold, while sweat stood out on the man's face. He brushed it away, feeling the heat rising from the clammy skin.

"He a gonner, kid. Let 'im be,' called a man nearby.

There came a commotion behind him, and the crowd gave way.

"Let me see 'im. Out o' my way!" A woman pushed through the crowd, her head high, carrying beauty and grace in her face and carriage. Two men hurried along behind her.

"Get out o' the way, kid," someone called.

The two lifted Bolden with ease to carry him between them as, silent and proud, the woman led the way back along the boardwalk. Sterling followed. Buddy's chest heaved as he panted for breath, but his mouth remained closed as froth pushed out between clenched teeth, till Sterling could no longer stand to see it, and ran past the bearers to reach the woman up ahead.

He held out the cornet. "This belong to Buddy."

She glanced briefly his way, her fine eyes taking in the instrument, shook her head no, and her step quickened till the crowd swallowed her, and Bolden, too.

TWENTY-FOUR

Sterling trod home with heavy steps, worried about Buddy. As he opened the front gate, the sound of piano music tinkled lightly through the open window. He paused a moment to listen. *His* notes—"Colonel Rag," played by an accomplished hand. He took the steps two at a time and barged into the front parlor. His teacher sat at a piano beside the window.

Sterling stood listening, holding the King's horn. It felt good to stand back and hear his music in someone else's hands. But Mr. Trask played the piece too slow. "Colonel Rag" was meant to show a lively beat, just the way the Colonel himself moved when he carried the Captain on his back. The music stopped as his teacher noticed Sterling. He pushed back on the bench and greeted him.

"These are fine compositions, Sterling. You show promise." He rose to fill his pipe, tamping down the tobacco. "You have been well taught, it seems."

"You playin' that too slow," said Sterling, in his eagerness forgetting he was talking to his teacher. "Here, I'm gonna show how it s'pose a-sound."

Sterling put down the cornet and sat at the piano. As his fingers played the first line of music, he remembered that night with Bernier. "Step up, my beauty," Bernier had called, and the Colonel had begun prancing along the fence line, proud to be of service. Sterling's fingers played the piece lightly, the notes as high-stepping as the Colonel's gait. Freedom had come so close during that moment, when all his dreams seemed possible and nothing could shatter them. He finished the piece and sat still, his hands resting on the keys, then swung into "Sundown Blues." Into his mind rushed pictures of evenings after a hard day's work, happy for some rest, but always tinged with thoughts of more hard work the next day and the next. He sounded the final mellow notes. *Rest, boys, rest.*

"Very fine tunes, Sterling. Very fine." Mr. Trask gave Sterling's mother a meaningful look, then gestured to a chair in the parlor. "It's time for us to sit down and have a talk." His mother turned to go back into the kitchen. "Maria, please stay. This concerns us all. Sit down, Sterling."

Here it come, thought Sterling. What they gonna do with me? I ain't goin' back to school no more!

"Sterling. Your mother and I want you to come back to school to catch up on your learning, then go on to a junior college when I think you're ready."

Sterling did not answer.

"Speak up, Sterling," urged his mother. "We wanna do the best for you."

"I need a-learn 'bout music," said Sterling. "Schoolin' ain't gonna help me, less'n it be music schoolin'."

"I can find you more lessons in music theory. But in the meantime, you will attend school and catch up on all the missed learning."

It was not a question, but Sterling shook his head. "They done teach me real good, Cap'n Jones and Miss Vine. You see if they ain't. I ain't gonna need no more learnin' less'n it be music learnin'."

"This is not negotiable. You're turning twelve next month. Some twelve-year-old children are not as lucky as you—working in cotton mills and coal mines. I'll see you have your music training, and until that is arranged, you will come back to my school, so I can test your skills in reading and writing and arithmetic."

"But I ain't need no ..."

"Sterling ..." His mother's mouth set in a firm line. She shook her head in warning.

"Okay, I guess."

"Okay, *thank you,*" said his mother.

"Thank you," he muttered. Seemed like his teacher was tricking him, offering the music help in one hand, but with a hard condition in the other. He didn't need to go back to his classroom. Barrel had quit. Didn't seem fair.

"Clancy still in school?" he asked, hope in his voice.

Mr. Trask shook his head. "That boy was never meant for higher learning."

"Sydney? His foot good, now?"

"Sydney lost his foot, amputated at the knee."

Sterling gasped. Poor Sydney. He hoped he still had his trumpet to play and ease all his cares.

"I seen him workin' with his dad," said his mother. "He seem okay, Sterl, but he sho' be glad a-see you again."

"He still play horn?" Sterling asked his mother.

"He's driving a coal wagon with his father," said Mr. Trask. "He has a hard path in life without your advantages."

"I got me a job," said Sterling. They might as well know straightaway. "I'm gonna visit Armand Piron and c'llaborate, him and me and Clarence. An' I got a job playin' piano for folk right after church."

"Sterling, you got a job? How'd you get a job so quick?"

"I done met Clarence Williams in town. He want me to come work with 'im, Sunday, playin' tunes an' all."

"You'll have to put those plans on hold," said Mr. Trask. "No more running about the streets. No one should be working on our day of rest. You had strict orders from the judge to settle down. We don't want a repeat of the trouble you had that put you in prison. Expect some hard work from now on."

"But I done promise Clarence a-give 'im back this music." Sterling picked up the sheet music Clarence had given him. "Sunday tomorrow. Please, Ma, can I go tomorrow? They gonna be waitin' on me. Won't take but a few minutes. I'm gonna be back in time for church."

"Best not break a promise," said his mother. "But go first thing tomorrow an' hurry on back."

That day, Sterling tried to get used to living with his teacher, and though the man treated him with kindness, he did not feel easy in his presence. His formal manner, as stiff as his starched shirts, was hard to get used to. He was demanding but fair, and Sterling supposed he should feel lucky his mother had chosen someone dependable. Someone who loved music. He owned a good piano and piles of sheet music that Sterling had yet to explore.

Sunday arrived to the bellow of a freighter's horn. Sterling awoke and listened to the hum of New Orleans outside his window. His skin prickled with excitement at the thought of visiting Armand and Clarence this morning.

"Put on your good church pants today, son. I've pressed your white shirt," said his mother as he sat down for breakfast. She searched his face, as if looking for that stubbornness he had worn ever since his homecoming. "Clarence and Armand, they good boys?"

Sterling shoveled down grits and ham. "Stop worryin', Ma. They both real good fellas. I'm gonna run there real quick. Make sure Clarence get his sheet music back."

"Be sure you come back in time for church, Sterling." Mr. Trask walked into the kitchen, tightening his tie. He wore a good suit, and his starched collar rose around his skinny neck. He took out his pocket watch, checked the hour, and snapped shut the case. "You have just one hour to travel there and back."

Sterling moved to wipe his mouth on his sleeve, but his mother told him to go wash his face and hands at the sink. He dipped his hands into the tub of washing-up water, and hurried to his room to put on the pressed white shirt and long pants she had laid out for him.

Armand lived about a twenty-minute walk away, but Sterling decided to take the streetcar to save time. His teacher stood at the front door, gazing out at the morning and sniffing the air as if it were a fine cigar. A brief rain in the night had left the day smelling fresh, and dew sparkled on the lawn.

Yesterday, he had given Sterling a list of chores— trim the hedge, polish the brass, and wash the windows. For that, Sterling had earned ten cents pocket money to save or spend as he liked.

Not wanting to spend it today, he turned back to ask his mother for streetcar fare. His teacher reached into his pocket and gave him a coin. "Don't be too long, Sterling."

"Yessir, Mr. Trask." Sterling pocketed the coin, grabbed his music, and dodged around him to leap down the steps.

"And ... Sterling. You may call me Robert when we are at home together. But at school, it remains Mr. Trask. Does that suit you?"

Sterling nodded. "Okay, Mr. Tr ... Robert," he amended. He felt relieved that the man did not expect to be called "Uncle."

Released at last, Sterling ran toward the streetcar stop at the corner, where a large crowd of Sunday picnickers waited to get an early start on the day. There, he paced and hopped about with impatience, gazing down the street and listening for the musical clang of the car.

As it drew up, he slipped unnoticed in front of a woman, carrying a wide wicker basket of food, and pushed his way up the narrow aisle. At the back, it was standing room only, and passengers clung to the leather straps dangling from the ceiling. Through the open windows, he glimpsed the shops all shut tight, but white men spilled out of sporting houses to join the throng of church-goers. Beignet sellers and newspaper boys sang out their wares, and carts full of fresh produce, recently unloaded from the freight boats, rumbled along the avenues.

At last, Sterling stepped down and hurried along the road and up to Armand's front door. The sound of piano music drifted through the open window. Sterling hoped that Rose was home, and his heart beat faster. He was all grown now, and Syl was gone. Maybe he had a chance.

"Come in," Armand called in answer to his knock.

Sterling walked into the parlor. The same stuffed bird of prey with cruel talons guarded its place on the mantel. Two violins lay on a side table. Armand's carved walking stick leaned against his desk. The musician sat at his piano, formally dressed in a black suit and tie. He turned to greet him with a gentle smile.

"Mornin', Sterling. It's been a long time. You are looking mighty prosperous. Family well?"

Encouraged, Sterling stepped into the room. "Mighty good seein' you again, Armand." He looked around. "Rose at home? You still writin' music? Bet you got some real good tunes."

"I hear from Clarence you have some fine compositions." He nodded at the bound music Sterling held. "You had some good teaching at the Waifs Home? Rose is married now and lives along the street. You might see her later today."

"I done wrote lotsa tunes since you gave me lessons," said Sterling, trying to hide his disappointment at

Armand's news. Rose *married?* Seemed like years ago he had hoped she might wait for him. Just stupid kid dreams. He hoped she had married someone kind, someone she deserved to have.

He thrust the penciled sheets at Armand, feeling a swell of pride. "Got a good one here that I'm maybe gonna ask Buddy Bolden a-help me finish."

Too late, he remembered Armand's bad opinion of Bolden, but Armand took the music without comment. He stood up and reached for his cane, leaning on it as he limped over to his desk.

"Looks very professional," he said, studying the top page. "You've come a long way with your notation. Now, let's hear how it sounds."

"Yessir, I can play some for ya."

Sterling sat down on the bench and wiped his palms on his pants. "This the 'Plaquemine Blues.' You remembers the story?"

Armand nodded. "I remember it."

Sterling found he played better when he allowed the images in his head to tumble through his fingers and out onto the keys—that time on the railroad track when Syl left him behind. The horn lying bent in the bushes, its flashing arc as he tossed it away in anger and pain.

He relaxed his shoulders and sat up straight, the way Miss Vine had taught him. He closed his eyes for a moment to block out everything but his memories of that distant morning, when he had set out with Syl. He started into "Plaquemine Blues," nervous that Armand sat listening and judging. He played up to the middle part with its bluesy prisoners' lament, then stopped when the music ran out. He looked up from the keys at Armand and saw that the young man's eyes were closed. Did he like it?

"I'm still workin' on the next part," he explained. "I been workin' on it a whole year. Still can't find how to end it."

"Well, Sterling ..." Armand began, his face lit with a curious expression, as though something unexpected had leaped out at him.

The parlor door swung wide and banged against the frame, startling them both. Clarence swept in. His red bow tie and purple silk vest drove a dazzling punch of color into Armand's calm, orderly space, and his large presence seemed to shrink the room. His wide grin and high spirits were contagious. Armand's eyes lit with pleasure, and Sterling felt his worry evaporate. The young man tossed his hat onto the desk and beamed down at them.

"You lookin' might' fine, Armand. You rest well this mornin'? An' how's our boy doin'? Didn't expect you till after church, Sterling. I was just listenin' outside the window. That one of your new tunes?"

"I stay workin' on it a long time," said Sterling. "You like it?"

"Well, it is sure good!" said Clarence. "What do you think, A.J.? But I gotta say ..." He frowned, hesitating. "Even so, I gotta tell ya, Sterl, an' don't take it personal, but folks are not gonna be interested in that way of playing. You got any ragtime? A nice four-four beat works wonders!"

"I gotta few," said Sterling. "'The Colonel Rag' an' all." He turned to Armand, worried. "So, you ain't like my 'Plaquemine Blues,' neither?"

"Clarence is right about that. Not something folk care to listen to for Sunday entertainment ..."

Armand might as well have aimed a boot into Sterling's gut—that's how much his words hurt. He felt his hopes crushed like a roach. Seemed nothing was quite good enough for Armand.

"... Nor should it be," he hastily added, seeing Sterling's disappointment. "Not something folk care to listen to, Sterling, because it does not have a dull, predictable ragtime beat."

"Say," Clarence broke in. "Nothin' wrong with a little ragtime."

"Ragtime is fine for the after-church crowd," said Armand. "But this piece is wasted on them. You have blended different influences into a musical collage. Delicate and tuneful. I hear a story in your composition, something of Bolden—bluesy, but not in his usual loud, grating way."

"So, you like it?"

"I would say the piece shows great promise. With hard work it could even be orchestrated, but for that, you need a good grounding in classical music theory, something you don't yet possess."

Not that *dicty* music again!

"How old are you, Sterling?" Armand studied him, sizing him up.

"Twelve."

"Only twelve. One of my criteria for judging music is, do I feel what you intended? Here, my answer is yes—I hear the strong emotions you felt when you wrote it—proof, indeed, that it's good. You show promise."

Sterling felt a rush of heat to his face as his heart thumped with excitement. Praise from Armand, at last!

But the musician frowned. "I cannot discourage you from a music career, but I warn you, Sterling, if you pursue this career, then get used to a daily diet of disappointments, discomforts, sacrifices ... a composer's life is not an easy one. It is a damn hard one ..."

Clarence had been pacing the room as Armand spoke. He gave an impatient snort. "Armand, you scarin' the boy! Go easy on 'im."

"I ain't a-scared o' hard work!" Sterling squared his shoulders. Hard work! He knew all about hard work! That didn't matter. Deep down, he knew that music was going to be his life, no matter the hardships.

"We livin' with a schoolteacher, now. Mr. Trask. You know 'im, Clarence? He got some money an' he aimin' a-help me."

"If you like, I can speak to him about you," said Armand. "Explain that ..."

"Money ain't gonna be no problem," interrupted Clarence. "You tell Sterl the good news?"

"I was saving that for you."

In answer, Clarence pulled open a drawer in the sideboard and took out a small metal change box. He rattled the coins inside.

"Hear that, Sterl? That's the sound of money earned. And you earned it while you was away, diggin' potatoes or whatever they make you do in them places. Ha ha! They tryin' to keep you down, and all the time you was makin' money and didn't even know it!" Clarence tipped the box and a cascade of silver coins bounced and rolled in all directions over Armand's desk.

"Watch my papers," protested Armand. He slid the coins together and began to stack them into neat piles.

Clarence gestured at the piles. "Take 'em, Sterling. All yours."

Sterling felt a fluttering in his stomach like a flock of butterflies had taken up space there. "How come? Why y'all givin' me this? Must be all o' twenty dollar here!" Sterling looked from one face to the other, trying to glean some understanding about this windfall.

"You remember your tune, 'Bouncy Feet'?" said Clarence. "What a grand tune that turned out to be. Everywhere I play it, folk want to buy it. All them people sittin' home after Sunday dinner, just lookin' to be entertained, waitin' for a simple, easy tune to come along they all love to play. Me and Armand printed it out and sold it, and that pile is your commission, Sterl."

"Can't be true?" Sterling looked from Clarence to Armand to the pile of money.

"Sterling, my man," crowed Clarence. "You got a future in music!"

"Le' me see it," said Sterling. "I wanna see my name on it!"

"We got any left?" Clarence asked.

Armand shook his head. "Sold them all. We need to print more."

"Next week, I'll give you a copy," said Clarence. "We are goin' around to show you off this afternoon. You practice that other sheet music I gave you?"

"I know all of it," Sterling confirmed with a nod.

"Today we introduce Kid Sterling to New Orleans. Good thing you wearin' your churchy clothes. They are gonna love you!"

Sterling remembered his promise to his teacher.

"I can't today. I come here to tell ya. Mr. Trask say I gotta go to church. I only got one hour gettin' here and back. But I'm gonna leave my music for y'all to take a look, an' I'm gonna come back Sunday next. An' I done learn all the tunes you gave me, Clarence. I brung 'em back. I'm sorry I can't come along an' play 'em." He gestured to the sheet music he had placed on the piano.

"You made a promise, you gotta keep it," said Clarence. "But work on some rags if you got the time."

"Yessir, I got the 'River Rag' you ain't seen. I ain't wrote it down yet. I gotta get back, now. Mr. Trask waitin' on me."

"See you here next week, for sure. Don't forget to take the money with you. Your ma and new pa goin' to be real impressed!"

Sterling hesitated. "Maybe better I leave it here. He kinda stric' that way. Specially it bein' Sunday an' all. An' he ain't my father. An' I gotta call him Robert at home, and Mr. Trask if'n I go back to school."

"We'll keep it for you," said Armand. "Get on home, Sterling. Don't be late back."

Sterling said goodbye and left their good company with reluctance. Before he had gone out the door, the two men sat down at the desk and bent over Armand's paperwork, to begin a serious discussion. He wondered what it was about and paused at the door, trying to catch a few words, but they were speaking in French. He heard the word, "Chicago," then Armand looked up. "Hurry home, Sterling."

A streetcar was just pulling away, and he managed to catch it because his feet moved extra fast. They seemed to dance with the thrill of knowing at last he could call himself a real musicianer. People were paying money to play his music! The days of shining shoes were gone! From now on, it was Kid Sterling! With his head in the clouds, Sterling found the journey took no time at all. He got off to run the final distance home, pausing at the curb while a lumbering wagon passed.

Someone bumped up against him and knocked him off balance.

It happened fast. One minute, Sterling was upright, the next, the world tipped sideways. Hands gripped his arms and hauled him back.

"Say! Le' go! Le' go o' me!" Sterling struggled, feeling outrage and terror mixed. His feet dragged along the ground, and he dug in his heels, leaving two lines in the dirt as he was propelled backward. A hand clamped down over his mouth, pushing his head till he was staring at the sky, unable to see his attackers, for there were two of them, one on each side. He struggled, but their hold on his arms felt like iron manacles. He bit down on the hand covering his mouth, and received an oath and a punch to the side of the head that made his ears ring.

He glimpsed a face with eyes hard as pellets of black coal, olive complexion, thick black brows. Hands lifted him with ease, dumped him into a cart, and rolled him over and over, as rough sacking was wrapped around his face and body, till he was trussed like a squealing pig ready for roasting.

"Le' me up! Le' me go!" Sterling wriggled and fought, but it was no use. A hand shoved the sacking hard into his face till he could taste it, closing his nostrils till his breath stopped.

"Shut your mouth if you wanna live," said a gruff voice.

Sterling went limp, an animal playing dead. The hand lifted. He gulped air. The wagon made a sharp turn and his head bounced against the side. The familiar streetcar sounds meant they were traveling along Canal Street. After some right and left turns, the steady clip-clop of the horses' hooves echoed, as if the sound bounced against buildings in a narrow alley. The wagon slowed to a halt and Sterling braced himself. Hands seized him, dragged him over the side, and dropped him. Sterling's feet hit the ground. He stumbled and fell. Someone yanked the sacking away and he sat, blinking, in the alley behind Paulo's shop. There stood the wide delivery doors and, just inside, Paulo himself, nodding in satisfaction.

"Inside," he said, with a jerk of his thumb.

Sterling rubbed his head and stood there. One of his captors looked at him through one good eye that showed no emotion, the other closed tight and crossed by a red scar. The second man tied up the horse, then slouched against the wall, watching.

Sterling remembered them both—they used to sit around the table in the back room, deep in discussions amid a haze of tobacco smoke.

One-Eye shoved Sterling into the storeroom.

"Look-a here," said Paulo, as if continuing a conversation already begun, "your brother no pay, you gonna pay. Two hundred he owe me. Two hundred dollar." He gestured to One-Eye. "Guido, get the book."

"I ain't got no brother. Why you brung me here?"

Sterling played for time, his eyes darting this way and that, looking for an exit. Behind him, two burly men. In front of him, Paulo. No way out.

"Sterling Crawford, thata you name!" Paulo reached behind him for a wooden box on the counter. The old shoeshine box. "You teenk I stupido?" He jabbed his finger at its underside, where Sterling had scratched his full name. "Syl Crawford you brother. You no lie no more."

"Syl done gone."

Paulo pointed a stubby finger at him. "He gone—*you* worka for me now."

Guido moved to a shelf, took down a thick accountant's book, and slammed it onto the wooden counter. Paulo opened it and thumbed through the pages, each one scrawled with spidery writing. "Come. Look." He gestured.

Sterling moved closer and Paulo shoved his head forward to bend over the pages, to give Sterling a real good close-up view. A tobacco-stained finger pointed at a few lines of writing.

"Job no finito." The finger jabbed a line, then another. "Job no finito. Job no finito. He take money and no pay back. You, you gonna pay back."

Syl loved to gamble. Seemed he had used Paulo's money for it. Sterling remembered his brother's late-night disappearances—was this to be his own life from now on? Would he end up crawling home at dawn? And his music—when would he ever have time for it if he worked for Paulo?

In a rush of courage, Sterling stood tall and looked him in the eye. "I ain't doin' it."

Paulo's eyes glistened. "Nobody gonna cheat me. Syl, you brother. Ned, you uncle. You no pay, uncle gonna pay."

Sterling knew about the *pizzos* Paulo's men extorted from grocery store owners. He knew about the beatings, too. His uncle was already sick. Things were looking worse and worse.

"But I got school," protested Sterling.

Paulo nodded. "School okay. School good. Night, you come here, worka for me."

"How long I gotta work for you?"

"Lotta special job ..." Paulo gave a shrug.

"What kinda job?"

"Luigi?" He jerked his head at One-Eye's partner.

Luigi moved toward Sterling, giving off a whiff of body odor masked by expensive cologne. Sterling stepped back in fear, but the man handed Sterling a package wrapped in cloth and tied with string.

"You gonna find the *Pardo*, cargo ship. Got that? P-a-r-d-o. Midnight. Give the Captain this. He gonna give you a envelope. Bring it here. Watch, so no one see nuttin'. Police see you? Question you?—you know nuttin'. You say nuttin'. You talk, Guido gonna cut your tongue out. You got that?"

"That's all I gotta do? Don' hafta work but this one job?"

Paulo laughed without humor. "You crazy? You brother owe me ten job." He held up ten fat fingers. "You work ten job, then finito.

"Now, go. Out. Get out."

TWENTY-FIVE

Monday night. Sterling waited in his room in the dark. He heard Robert tapping his pipe against a saucer. It must be close on midnight.

Yesterday afternoon, when Paulo had let him go, Sterling had thought hard and fast about a story he could make up for Robert and his mother. He'd slipped through the back door and into his room, slid the package under the bed, and walked into the kitchen. His mother had lit up with relief to see him. She still wore her good church clothes. The table held the remains of their dinner.

Robert looked coldly at him. "What's your excuse, boy? It better be a good one."

"Where was you, Sterling?" asked his mother. "Why you run off? And lookit your clothes!"

Sterling turned toward the river and picked up speed, hugging the shadows alongside trees and fences, building to a sprint. Two men lay on the boardwalk in a drunken stupor and muttered obscenities as he tripped over them. He picked himself up and ran on before they could open their bleary eyes.

The sight of two policemen walking toward him stopped him in his tracks. They carried night sticks. Guido's warning resounded in his ears. *"Gonna cut out your tongue ..."*

He ducked for cover behind a pile of crates, clutching his package and scarcely breathing. They walked on by, moving toward the louts lying in a heap further along. They kicked the men awake and, in the ensuing yells and curses, Sterling ran unnoticed down the street toward the river.

At the waterfront, lanterns bobbed like oversized fireflies. The docks were alive with the creak of ropes and the shouts and grunts of men working through the night.

Sterling picked his way among the barrels that lay along the levee. As he approached, dark shapes appearing as high as mountains became piled bundles of sacks, filled with raw cotton. He yelped as he trod on

Sterling figured half-truths were better than lies.

"Some men done grab me an' tie me up. They come tellin' me some story that I owe 'em money. When they see I ain't the right boy, they le' me go."

His mother came close and prodded a sore spot on Sterling's face. He winced.

"Who done this? Who these men you say take you off o' the street? They hit you?"

"No. They done toss me in a wagon an' I hit my head. I never seen 'em afore. They run some opium dive other side o' town. I got out o' there real fast and come right back home.

"They white men?"

Sterling nodded.

"They mess with you?"

"No, they jus' talkin'; they ain't done nothin' a' me."

"You never met these men before?" Mr. Trask's mouth set in a grim line, his expression hard and distrustful. "This something to do with your brother?"

"You ain't runnin' with them bad men like your brother done?" asked his mother.

"Maybe Syl knowed 'em," said Sterling, relieved to have another line of inquiry for Robert. "Syl always git in with some bad people, gamblin' an' all. He most always at the Twenty-Five, playin' Kotch an' all. Maybe they all them gangster fellas. They sure done look that way."

"These folk is white," said his mother. "An' Sterling already known to the police. Ain't nothin' we can do."

She stared into Sterling's face, likely guessing he was not being truthful. He saw the struggle in her face, but she sighed and turned away, wanting to keep the peace at all cost and take comfort in practical things.

"Sterling, your clothes all ruin. Go put 'em in the basket, I'ma wash 'em today. Lord know if'n that dirt gonna come out."

"Tomorrow, you start school," snapped Robert. "Work hard and stay off the streets from now on."

Sterling did as Robert asked. The next day, he sat in a class of boys who whispered and muttered about him. They knew he lived with their teacher and were watchful for any sign of favoritism. But they soon understood that Robert treated Sterling like all the rest, and even more strictly, since there were arithmetic problems that he could not solve. Numbers had never been his strong point, and the Colored Waifs Home did not have a program, except for learning how to weigh potatoes and

measure out ingredients for kitchen chores. He worr about the night ahead and could not concentrate. H could he learn his times tables now, when he had bigg problems to work on after dark?

"Pay attention," Robert snapped as Sterling's min wandered, and the other boys snickered and whispere "Dunce!"

The long day ended at last. That night, Sterling wen to bed in his street clothes. He lay awake, eyes wide open, trying to keep sleep at bay. Around midnight, the faint blast of a freight ship from the harbor called Sterling from his half-slumber. There came the sound of the bolt sliding across the front door as Robert locked up. A door closed. All quiet.

He pushed back the covers, picked up his shoes, felt for the package under his bed, and crept to the window. He slid it wide open, swung over the sill, and dropped to the ground. He opened the front gate slowly to stifle the squeal of its hinges, and stepped onto the street, looking right and left for any human traffic. All that stirred was a skinny stray cat that leaped for cover through the garden fence, eyes flashing. The houses along the street sat in darkness, lamps dimmed for sleep.

something soft and alive. The prone form of a worker, who was snatching some rest among the piles, grumbled curses at being so rudely wakened.

The night breeze brought sharp pricks of rain against his cheeks. He moved from one loading dock to the next, searching for the right freighter. At the end of the line, a hulking shape proved to be the ship he was after. In the dim light, he could read the letters on her bow.

USS Pardo.

On board, hurrying figures lifted crates and sacks of produce. As Sterling moved closer, a man shouted commands to men plodding up and down the loading dock. Each carried a sack on his back or a crate on his shoulder. Men on board unpacked the next crate or sack of vegetables, and swung them from hand to hand along the deck in a rhythmic manner. A stout man stood beside the gangway, holding a lantern close to his face as he looked down at a list. The lamplight revealed short-clipped graying hair and a handlebar mustache. His thick brows furrowed into a frown.

"Cap'n?"

The captain looked up from his list, impatience written on his face.

"Paulo di Christiano done send me. I gotta give ya this." Sterling thrust the package at him as the captain turned the lantern to illuminate Sterling's face. He softly cursed.

"You kinda young for this work, ain't ya? He takin' bag boys from the cradle now? Cheap bastard."

He set down the lantern and took the package. From its weight and size, Sterling had already guessed what was inside—cocaine. It was just like the package he had found in Syl's drawer under his clothes, that day a year ago when Sterling had searched everywhere for his missing eight dollars. The captain took out a piece of paper. He licked the end of a pencil, scribbled some words, retrieved an envelope from his back pocket, and stuffed the paper inside.

"Here's your receipt and payment. Give it to your boss and get on home where you belong, boy."

Behind them, a few voices began a bluesy chant in time with the rhythm and beat of the lifting and hauling. Others joined in. Sterling paused to listen as the captain turned back to the men. They would work and sing through the night. Music was their solace, but cocaine was the fuel that made it all bearable. Syl once told him that dock workers who snorted the white powder could work for three days and nights without any sleep, enough time to get the ship unloaded and back upriver. Syl had tried it once and said it felt like he was flying like a bird. Something about it had frightened him, because it left him feeling empty and craving more. He told Sterling how he had seen friends on cocaine, wasting away into skeletons. He had let it alone and advised Sterling to do the same.

Sterling ran on into the night toward Paolo's shop, the envelope tucked into his pocket, fighting the tiredness that descended like a weight upon his back, longing for his bed, hoping Mr. Trask had not discovered him gone. He tried to remember the dock workers' song. A good tune in his head would help his feet move faster. But no matter how hard he tried, the tune would not come. His mind seemed to have emptied itself of music and become filled to the brim with fear.

TWENTY-SIX

Sterling's daylight hours were full of safe routines—meals, school, chores. He wished he might stay protected inside the sunny world of days. But cloaked and menacing nights always waited. The world of night was full of hidden byways where vermin scuttled. He learned to navigate the maze—vital to keep away from lighted streets and the policemen who patroled, swinging their nightsticks. He soon became known to the denizens of this world. A word to bouncers gave him entry into rooms crowded with gamblers, bent over gaming tables. Unnoticed, he scurried past them and on into backrooms, where accountants handed him the night's take.

A shadow with a suitcase, he scampered out the back doors into the alleyways, like the rats of the city as they gnawed on piles of garbage. He might as well be one of them, moving as he did from one rubbish-heap joint to another. His bones and muscles begged for rest. If only he were free from worries, free from the secret midnight journeys, free from Paulo di Christiano. But each morning, Sterling crawled from his bed and sat at the table, a rag doll with head heavy from missed sleep.

"Sterling. Ain't you sleep good, again?" His mother's voice broke into his thoughts.

"Dunno ... not so good," Sterling said, then improvised to gain sympathy. "Keep dreamin' 'bout them gangster grab me off o' the street."

"Robert, maybe the boy might stay home today. Jus' rest."

"What's troubling you, boy? You need a doctor?" Robert studied him from across the table.

His mother felt Sterling's forehead.

"Feel like he got a little fever."

"Stay home today," said Robert. "If you're no better tomorrow, we'll send you to Doc Hébert. Maria, maybe give him one of your tonics?"

Sterling grimaced. His mother's tonics tasted foul, but at least it would give him a day to sleep. Tonight, he had another job to do for Paulo. He swallowed the homemade medicine his mother brought from the pantry. She tucked him back into bed, the way she used to when he was a little boy. He slumbered, dreamless, till the afternoon, when she woke him and coaxed him out to the kitchen to eat his dinner.

"You feelin' okay now?" she asked, touching his forehead again. "You ain't hot no more. No fever, thank the Lord. Robert come home but you sleepin'."

She laid a plate of rice and red beans in front of him and sat at the table, leaning forward to look him in the eye. "You gonna tell me what really happen that day last week you was late? I know you lyin'. You always was a bad ole liar."

Sterling felt his stomach clench. Caught between telling lies or the truth, he kept silent. Best say nothing, finish the jobs till it was all over.

"Sterling, my boy, somethin' wrong, you best tell me. A boy owe his mother the truth."

As always with her, he could not stop the story from tumbling out. Syl's gambling. Paulo's account book. The job down at the levee when the *Pardo* came into port. He told it all as best he could, keeping to half-truths. He did not tell her about the cocaine, or the threat to his uncle, or about climbing out of the window at night.

"I done the one job for him after school las' week down at the levee. He happy with that. Say I ain't gotta do no more."

"So, it all finish?" His mother looked at him steadily. "You don't gotta work for that man no more?"

He shook his head. "No."

"You promise?"

His fingers crossed underneath the table. "Promise. You ain't gonna tell Robert, is you?"

She shook her head. "Best I say nothin'." She took away his empty plate. "You go on back and rest some more. Tomorrow you be ready for school, an' we all gonna get pas' this."

Sterling did as she asked. In his room, he noticed a piece of newsprint had slipped from his desk to the floor—*The Chicago Defender*. A breeze had sent the stray page of newspaper along the street toward him on his first day back, that morning Paolo had threatened him with a clenched fist. Sterling had turned and fled. How foolish of him to believe that just by running, he could escape Paolo. He reached for the page and studied it. A headline caught his eye.

Black Pugilist Defeats Jim Crow Laws

Sterling read on about a famous black boxer who had broken the law and ridden on a Pullman train carriage meant for whites only. The conductor explained to the police that the boxer had bought tickets for the whole car so that he could sleep in a berth, undisturbed. The law could do nothing about it.

Can't be true! One of us, buyin' up a whole carload of white man seats?

Images of the train to Plaquemine flashed in his head—the baggage car, its smoke and cinders, a prisoner in chains, a glimpse through the connecting door into the Pullman car for whites only, its comfortable seats that turned into sleeping berths. And here was a fellow had the brass to buy up all those seats and sleep in comfort! And the advertisements on the page offered all kinds of promises—jobs, college education—there seemed nothing his folk could not do or become in Chicago. At the bottom, he read a line that froze his blood.

Louisiana 1907, number of lynchings 9.

He shoved the newsprint in his drawer and slammed it shut, wishing he could just as easily put away his sudden terror.

His mother sent him to bed early that evening.

Sterling figured half-truths were better than lies.

"Some men done grab me an' tie me up. They come tellin' me some story that I owe 'em money. When they see I ain't the right boy, they le' me go."

His mother came close and prodded a sore spot on Sterling's face. He winced.

"Who done this? Who these men you say take you off o' the street? They hit you?"

"No. They done toss me in a wagon an' I hit my head. I never seen 'em afore. They run some opium dive other side o' town. I got out o' there real fast and come right back home.

"They white men?"

Sterling nodded.

"They mess with you?"

"No, they jus' talkin'; they ain't done nothin' a' me."

"You never met these men before?" Mr. Trask's mouth set in a grim line, his expression hard and distrustful. "This something to do with your brother?"

"You ain't runnin' with them bad men like your brother done?" asked his mother.

"Maybe Syl knowed 'em," said Sterling, relieved to have another line of inquiry for Robert. "Syl always git in

with some bad people, gamblin' an' all. He most always
at the Twenty-Five, playin' Kotch an' all. Maybe they all
them gangster fellas. They sure done look that way."

"These folk is white," said his mother. "An' Sterling
already known to the police. Ain't nothin' we can do."

She stared into Sterling's face, likely guessing he was
not being truthful. He saw the struggle in her face, but
she sighed and turned away, wanting to keep the peace
at all cost and take comfort in practical things.

"Sterling, your clothes all ruin. Go put 'em in the
basket, I'ma wash 'em today. Lord know if'n that dirt
gonna come out."

"Tomorrow, you start school," snapped Robert.
"Work hard and stay off the streets from now on."

Sterling did as Robert asked. The next day, he sat in
a class of boys who whispered and muttered about him.
They knew he lived with their teacher and were watchful
for any sign of favoritism. But they soon understood that
Robert treated Sterling like all the rest, and even more
strictly, since there were arithmetic problems that he
could not solve. Numbers had never been his strong
point, and the Colored Waifs Home did not have a
program, except for learning how to weigh potatoes and

measure out ingredients for kitchen chores. He worried about the night ahead and could not concentrate. How could he learn his times tables now, when he had bigger problems to work on after dark?

"Pay attention," Robert snapped as Sterling's mind wandered, and the other boys snickered and whispered, "Dunce!"

The long day ended at last. That night, Sterling went to bed in his street clothes. He lay awake, eyes wide open, trying to keep sleep at bay. Around midnight, the faint blast of a freight ship from the harbor called Sterling from his half-slumber. There came the sound of the bolt sliding across the front door as Robert locked up. A door closed. All quiet.

He pushed back the covers, picked up his shoes, felt for the package under his bed, and crept to the window. He slid it wide open, swung over the sill, and dropped to the ground. He opened the front gate slowly to stifle the squeal of its hinges, and stepped onto the street, looking right and left for any human traffic. All that stirred was a skinny stray cat that leaped for cover through the garden fence, eyes flashing. The houses along the street sat in darkness, lamps dimmed for sleep.

Sterling turned toward the river and picked up speed, hugging the shadows alongside trees and fences, building to a sprint. Two men lay on the boardwalk in a drunken stupor and muttered obscenities as he tripped over them. He picked himself up and ran on before they could open their bleary eyes.

The sight of two policemen walking toward him stopped him in his tracks. They carried night sticks. Guido's warning resounded in his ears. *"Gonna cut out your tongue ..."*

He ducked for cover behind a pile of crates, clutching his package and scarcely breathing. They walked on by, moving toward the louts lying in a heap further along. They kicked the men awake and, in the ensuing yells and curses, Sterling ran unnoticed down the street toward the river.

At the waterfront, lanterns bobbed like oversized fireflies. The docks were alive with the creak of ropes and the shouts and grunts of men working through the night.

Sterling picked his way among the barrels that lay along the levee. As he approached, dark shapes appearing as high as mountains became piled bundles of sacks, filled with raw cotton. He yelped as he trod on something soft and alive. The prone form of a worker, who was snatching some rest among the piles, grumbled curses at being so rudely wakened.

The night breeze brought sharp pricks of rain against his cheeks. He moved from one loading dock to the next, searching for the right freighter. At the end of the line, a hulking shape proved to be the ship he was after. In the dim light, he could read the letters on her bow.

USS Pardo.

On board, hurrying figures lifted crates and sacks of produce. As Sterling moved closer, a man shouted commands to men plodding up and down the loading dock. Each carried a sack on his back or a crate on his shoulder. Men on board unpacked the next crate or sack of vegetables, and swung them from hand to hand along the deck in a rhythmic manner. A stout man stood beside the gangway, holding a lantern close to his face as he looked down at a list. The lamplight revealed short-clipped graying hair and a handlebar mustache. His thick brows furrowed into a frown.

"Cap'n?"

The captain looked up from his list, impatience written on his face.

"Paulo di Christiano done send me. I gotta give ya this."
Sterling thrust the package at him as the captain turned
the lantern to illuminate Sterling's face. He softly cursed.

"You kinda young for this work, ain't ya? He takin'
bag boys from the cradle now? Cheap bastard."

He set down the lantern and took the package. From
its weight and size, Sterling had already guessed what
was inside—cocaine. It was just like the package he
had found in Syl's drawer under his clothes, that day
a year ago when Sterling had searched everywhere for
his missing eight dollars. The captain took out a piece
of paper. He licked the end of a pencil, scribbled some
words, retrieved an envelope from his back pocket, and
stuffed the paper inside.

"Here's your receipt and payment. Give it to your
boss and get on home where you belong, boy."

Behind them, a few voices began a bluesy chant in
time with the rhythm and beat of the lifting and hauling.
Others joined in. Sterling paused to listen as the captain
turned back to the men. They would work and sing
through the night. Music was their solace, but cocaine
was the fuel that made it all bearable. Syl once told him
that dock workers who snorted the white powder could

work for three days and nights without any sleep, enough time to get the ship unloaded and back upriver. Syl had tried it once and said it felt like he was flying like a bird. Something about it had frightened him, because it left him feeling empty and craving more. He told Sterling how he had seen friends on cocaine, wasting away into skeletons. He had let it alone and advised Sterling to do the same.

Sterling ran on into the night toward Paolo's shop, the envelope tucked into his pocket, fighting the tiredness that descended like a weight upon his back, longing for his bed, hoping Mr. Trask had not discovered him gone. He tried to remember the dock workers' song. A good tune in his head would help his feet move faster. But no matter how hard he tried, the tune would not come. His mind seemed to have emptied itself of music and become filled to the brim with fear.

TWENTY-SIX

Sterling's daylight hours were full of safe routines—meals, school, chores. He wished he might stay protected inside the sunny world of days. But cloaked and menacing nights always waited. The world of night was full of hidden byways where vermin scuttled. He learned to navigate the maze—vital to keep away from lighted streets and the policemen who patroled, swinging their nightsticks. He soon became known to the denizens of this world. A word to bouncers gave him entry into rooms crowded with gamblers, bent over gaming tables. Unnoticed, he scurried past them and on into backrooms, where accountants handed him the night's take.

A shadow with a suitcase, he scampered out the back doors into the alleyways, like the rats of the city as they gnawed on piles of garbage. He might as well be one of them, moving as he did from one rubbish-heap joint to another. His bones and muscles begged for rest. If only he were free from worries, free from the secret midnight journeys, free from Paulo di Christiano. But each morning, Sterling crawled from his bed and sat at the table, a rag doll with head heavy from missed sleep.

"Sterling. Ain't you sleep good, again?" His mother's voice broke into his thoughts.

"Dunno ... not so good," Sterling said, then improvised to gain sympathy. "Keep dreamin' 'bout them gangster grab me off o' the street."

"Robert, maybe the boy might stay home today. Jus' rest."

"What's troubling you, boy? You need a doctor?" Robert studied him from across the table.

His mother felt Sterling's forehead.

"Feel like he got a little fever."

"Stay home today," said Robert. "If you're no better tomorrow, we'll send you to Doc Hébert. Maria, maybe give him one of your tonics?"

Sterling grimaced. His mother's tonics tasted foul, but at least it would give him a day to sleep. Tonight, he had another job to do for Paulo. He swallowed the homemade medicine his mother brought from the pantry. She tucked him back into bed, the way she used to when he was a little boy. He slumbered, dreamless, till the afternoon, when she woke him and coaxed him out to the kitchen to eat his dinner.

"You feelin' okay now?" she asked, touching his forehead again. "You ain't hot no more. No fever, thank the Lord. Robert come home but you sleepin'."

She laid a plate of rice and red beans in front of him and sat at the table, leaning forward to look him in the eye. "You gonna tell me what really happen that day last week you was late? I know you lyin'. You always was a bad ole liar."

Sterling felt his stomach clench. Caught between telling lies or the truth, he kept silent. Best say nothing, finish the jobs till it was all over.

"Sterling, my boy, somethin' wrong, you best tell me. A boy owe his mother the truth."

As always with her, he could not stop the story from tumbling out. Syl's gambling. Paulo's account book. The job down at the levee when the *Pardo* came into port. He told it all as best he could, keeping to half-truths. He did not tell her about the cocaine, or the threat to his uncle, or about climbing out of the window at night.

"I done the one job for him after school las' week down at the levee. He happy with that. Say I ain't gotta do no more."

"So, it all finish?" His mother looked at him steadily. "You don't gotta work for that man no more?"

He shook his head. "No."

"You promise?"

His fingers crossed underneath the table. "Promise. You ain't gonna tell Robert, is you?"

She shook her head. "Best I say nothin'." She took away his empty plate. "You go on back and rest some more. Tomorrow you be ready for school, an' we all gonna get pas' this."

Sterling did as she asked. In his room, he noticed a piece of newsprint had slipped from his desk to the floor—*The Chicago Defender*. A breeze had sent the stray page of newspaper along the street toward him on his first day back, that morning Paolo had threatened him with a clenched fist. Sterling had turned and fled. How foolish of him to believe that just by running, he could escape Paolo. He reached for the page and studied it. A headline caught his eye.

Black Pugilist Defeats Jim Crow Laws

Sterling read on about a famous black boxer who had broken the law and ridden on a Pullman train carriage meant for whites only. The conductor explained to the police that the boxer had bought tickets for the whole car so that he could sleep in a berth, undisturbed. The law could do nothing about it.

Can't be true! One of us, buyin' up a whole carload of white man seats?

Images of the train to Plaquemine flashed in his head—the baggage car, its smoke and cinders, a prisoner in chains, a glimpse through the connecting door into the Pullman car for whites only, its comfortable seats that turned into sleeping berths. And here was a fellow had the brass to buy up all those seats and sleep in comfort! And the advertisements on the page offered all kinds of promises—jobs, college education—there seemed nothing his folk could not do or become in Chicago. At the bottom, he read a line that froze his blood.

Louisiana 1907, number of lynchings 9.

He shoved the newsprint in his drawer and slammed it shut, wishing he could just as easily put away his sudden terror.

His mother sent him to bed early that evening.

"School tomorrow," said Robert. "No excuses."

Sterling muttered his good nights and sat for a while at the desk in his bedroom, pencil in hand, to notate a fragment of music he had heard the other day on the street. A fruitseller's call had caught his interest, set in motion a melody in his head. He tried to remember it, pencil at the ready. Nothing came. Vanished. Ever since working for Paulo, the tunes in his head had faded almost to silence. He knew they were there, somewhere. He just couldn't find them. He lay down and fell into a half-sleep. Hours passed. He sprang awake to familiar sounds from the parlor—the pipe tap-tapping, as Robert emptied its spent tobacco into a saucer, the front door bolt rasping shut. The crack of light beneath his bedroom door faded to darkness. All was quiet. He threw back the covers and put on his shoes, crept to the window, slid it gently open, and climbed out. Tonight, he was to pick up a package from Paulo's for delivery. That's all he knew about it.

He headed for the lane behind his street, knowing every twist and turn in his inner map of the city at night. He kept to the shadows, his feet gliding along the rutted path. When his route crossed roadways, he stopped to watch and listen for any threat—policemen on night duty, roaming gangs of kids looking for trouble.

All clear.

He ran with his head down, as if curling into himself rendered him invisible, till he was safely in the dark byways once again. He entered the lit streets of the District. The city sang out in all its voices, pulsing with music and laughter that flooded through the open doorways of clubs and dance halls. Another hundred steps and he reached the dark lane that led northward to Paulo's shop, and there he approached its back door, locked. Someone swung it open to his signal, three taps ... pause ... three taps. He entered.

Inside, two tall white boys stared down at him. A shiver of alarm swept up and down Sterling's spine. He looked down at his feet. Safest not to look them in the eye.

"I'm lookin' for Paulo," he said, swallowing back the tremor in his voice. He kept his eyes lowered. "He aroun' somewhere?"

The first one stepped up, his lip curled. "You the best they got? Paulo says you gotta do a job with us. Our lookout boy. Stick with us. Do what I say. Keep your mouth shut. Or else ..."

A flash of silver appeared in his hand, a switchblade. Sterling snatched a glance at the boys before staring back down at his feet. They were both large and muscular. The leader had a thatch of yellow hair that fell forward, and a mean pinched mouth that barely moved, as it spat out his words in a monotone. The other boy, his muscled body in a posture of challenge, stood back a little behind the first, watchful.

"What I gotta do?" Sterling kept his head bowed. Ice-cold terror crept through his veins. Paulo had made him believe he was picking up a package for delivery. He had lied.

"What I gotta do?" mimicked the boy.

The other one snickered. "Just keep it shut and do what I say. Got it?"

Sterling nodded.

"Let's go."

The leader went first. The second pulled up the rear. Misery and fear clouded Sterling's thoughts. He must be alert if he was to get free. He knew the city's back lanes, maybe even better than they did. If he could escape, he could easily disappear into the maze of hidden byways. As if guessing his thoughts, the leader muttered, "No funny stuff."

Into the streets they walked, the leader softly whistling a cheerful cakewalk. At the sound of voices up ahead, he shot out his arm and pushed Sterling back against a wall till it was quiet again. They crossed Rampart and entered the Vieux Carré, passing terraced homes that lined narrow roads. A power outage had plunged the streets into shadow. But they were not entirely under cover of darkness. Gas lamps flickered from their brackets along the streets. The boy led them down a grassy laneway between two buildings. At the end, a brick wall blocked their entry. Set in the wall stood an oak gate, decorated finely with iron fretwork.

The leader pushed Sterling into a crouch, stepped onto his back, and heaved himself up and over the wall. After a moment, the inside bolt slid back. The gate swung open. The second boy shoved him through the entrance. Inside lay a darkened courtyard, filled with palm trees and flowering bushes. The scent of mimosa drifted in air moist from trickling fountains.

Wordless with horror, Sterling gazed around him. "You ain't gonna rob this place, is ya? Please, le' me go. I don't wanna do it!" He felt his knees go weak, almost buckling to the ground in terror.

"You do what I say, or I'm gonna crack open your head, right here." With a rough shove, the first boy encouraged Sterling to move along. The building they passed seemed divided into separate apartments. He stared into lighted windows as the boys crept on through the shrubbery. Here, an elderly woman sat alone at a table, bent over her cards. On the floor above, a man and woman danced slowly to phonograph music. The boys found easy concealment among the moving shadows of the palm fronds that wafted gently in the breeze. It seemed to Sterling that he himself had become just a shadow, a thing of no substance or will of its own.

On they went through flowering shrubs, to a wall at the opposite side of the garden. Sterling was made to crouch again. Hope stirred. If the two ended up on one side and he on the other, what was to stop him from running? But his plan was foiled. One boy stepped on Sterling's back, heaved himself up, and remained straddled on the wall. The second gave Sterling a boost upward as hands reached down from the top and yanked him up. Sterling swung his legs over, his chest against the edge, his feet scrabbling for a foothold. Blackness beneath. He hesitated.

"Git over."

One shove and he plunged downward. His feet hit uneven ground and he fell backwards, knees and hands scraped bloody from the quick descent. He found himself in another courtyard. The leader jumped down beside him. From his vantage point, the second boy scanned the grounds before dropping down to their side. The windows overlooking them were in darkness, except for two on the top floor. There, a group of revelers sat outside on the verandah, unaware of the three who stole through the shadows below.

"Cin Cin! Alla tua salute!" Glasses clinked.

The boys kept to the back of the garden and climbed over into a third courtyard, where a building loomed three stories high. All its windows were dark, its wooden shutters closed. Unlike the other buildings with their air of neglect, this one looked well kept. On each floor, a verandah with polished decorative railings swept its length. A fine gas lamp flickered over the arched service entrance, illuminating a narrow window to one side.

"See that window?" muttered the leader. "You small enough to fit. Ya gonna climb inside and open the back door. Ain't no one home."

"How I gonna get in? It all lock up."

But the leader had already taken surgical tape out of his pocket. He ripped off pieces and taped the window end to end, then took off his shirt. He picked up one of the smooth rounded stones that bordered a raised flower bed and wrapped his shirt around it. With gentle taps, he made several cracks in the glass, applying more and more pressure, till it fell inward with a muffled sound. He pushed out the remaining shards from the frame.

"Get in and open the back door. No funny business."

He flicked the knife open and Sterling felt it prick his neck. He stood caught between two terrors, a knife blade and an open window. Both held unimaginable danger. Sterling moved to the window, lifted one leg over the sill, perched there, and ducked his head, his back just scraping beneath the upper frame. He began to swing his other leg over when he felt a sharp pain in his shoulder from a stray shard of glass stuck to the frame. As he recoiled, his foot hit something on the verandah. There came a loud grating noise—a wrought iron chair. Sterling froze in motion.

The leader cursed under his breath. "Get in. Open the door," and he shoved Sterling through to land on broken glass.

Pricks of pain to his chest and shoulder. He stood waiting a second, to allow his eyes to adjust to the darkness. Glass crunched underfoot. Beside him, the service door with a set of two sliding bolts. In front of him, an open door leading to a hallway. His only chance! He would not let them inside. If people were sleeping somewhere in the house, he would wake them and warn them.

"Open the door or you're dead!" raged the leader, leaning in through the window to reach for him.

But Sterling stepped away and took the door to the hallway. He sprinted along it, his footsteps muffled by soft carpeting, past a ticking clock that might be measuring off the remaining seconds of his life. He reached the front door. It had even more bolts than the back.

"Qui va là?!"

Steps moved across the floor above, toward the rear. The sound of a window sliding up, a shutter banging open. Sterling imagined the man was on the upper verandah, leaning over it to search the gloom below.

The first bolt on the front door proved to be stiff. Sterling struggled to slide it open.

Another shout.

"Parle! J'ai une arme!"

A roar of gunfire shattered the quiet. Footsteps. The man was descending from the upper floor.

Hide! Hide! But where? Sterling slipped into a dark room off the hall. Drapes covered the windows. Frantic, he flung one panel aside and stepped behind it.

"Parle, ou je tire!" The voice again, closer now. The man was on the main floor, heading toward the rear. Sterling waited, ready to run. A thin beam of lamplight shone through a crack in the curtain. A moment passed. Quickening footsteps back along the hallway. The muffled sound of the front door bolts sliding open. A voice shouting.

"Au secours! Au secours! Vôlé!"

People and things dear to him flashed through Sterling's head—his mother, his music, Cap'n Jones, King Bolden. He had come so far. Was he about to lose everything? He had only one chance.

Run!

He stumbled out from his hiding place. Through the front door, wide open. The man stood in the street, shouting his alarm. Sterling's first glimpse of him revealed a frail and bent old man, but the pistol made him lethal. He fired at the sky, his gun erupting in a flash of light and blue smoke. As Sterling leaped down the front steps, windows and doors along the street opened and residents looked out.

"There he goes. Thief!" called a voice from an upper storey.

"*Fermati, ladro!* Stop heem!" shouted another.

The man swung toward him, gun pointing his way. Sterling was away and running. A third gunshot ripped the air. Sterling flinched, feeling the bullet entering his flesh and tearing into his pounding heart before it had even happened. But it hadn't. Still unscathed. Either the man was half-blind, or luck was with him. Feet scarcely touching the ground, he reached the corner. The sound of a chase behind him, shouts, running footsteps. A police whistle shrilled. He knew this neighborhood and all its streets. No back lanes here. He crossed into an empty lot. The dim outline of a pile of crates nestled in a corner. No time to think. More shouts. Closer. He dived behind the crates and waited.

The shouts grew fainter, but a low humming broke the stillness. Electric bulbs strung alongside the buildings flickered and flashed.

"No! No!" whispered Sterling.

More flickers. Brighter. The electricity was coming back on. A full blaze of light illuminated every crate and pile of rubbish in this corner lot, seeking him out and showing him no mercy. He recognized his location— only two streets down from a gaming club on Royal Street, where he had once done a suitcase pick-up for Paulo. To reach it, he would need to walk down a fully lighted street. If his luck held, maybe the name "Paulo" would gain him entry to the club. He hoped the same bouncer still guarded the entrance. His back and arm throbbed. He could see a dark bloodstain on his sleeve.

He walked the lit street, taut with fear, and hurried past each accusing electric light strung above him. Not many folk were out at this hour, but he felt the stares of those who walked by. First would come a brief casual glance, next, a double take at the blood on his shirt. Finally, a recognition that here was a young boy who was up to no good. By the time these details had registered with passersby, Sterling was already away down the street, feeling their eyes on his back, terrified that he would hear a shout, running feet. At last, he reached the gaming house. A doorman stood out front, a club in his hands.

"Move along, boy. Get off this property."

There was something about the voice and the tall bulk of the man. Black Benny! Sterling ran up the steps, risking a club to the head.

"Benny! It me. Sterling. I'm in trouble. Le' me in, Benny?"

A clatter of wheels made him turn. A police wagon at the top of the street moved slowly down toward them. The policeman perched up behind the horse looked from right to left, intently searching. For him.

"That you, Sterl?" said Benny, lowering his club. "You look a sight. Get in here."

He pulled Sterling inside. Just in time. The wagon came closer and drew up. Sterling pressed himself into the corner behind the doorway. He listened to the conversation.

"You seen a colored kid passin' this way?"

"Ain't seen nothin' nor nobody, Suh."

"That you, Benny? When they let you out? Thought you was in five years this time."

"No, Suh. I'm workin' now. Got a good job. Straight and narrow, Suh."

"Maybe I gonna take you in, anyhow. We got too

many empty cells right now. Got a comfy one'll fit you just right."

"I'm jus' fine, Suh. No need to trouble you."

The sound of the wagon moving on.

"Stick here a while," said Benny. "Stay out o' sight if'n anyone come through. Police lookin' for you? What you done?"

"Some white folk done made me help 'em rob a house. I ain't no thief. Say they gonna cut my throat if'n I don' help 'em. You see inside that wagon? White boy in there?"

"Seen one inside there. He already in trouble. No worry," said Benny.

"He have yella hair?"

"Might be. I'm tellin' ya, don' worry. He goin' a-jail."

But Sterling doubted even Benny was any match for Paulo's thugs. Benny allowed him to rest there in the shadows. His eyes heavy with the need for sleep, Sterling sank into a stupor, oblivious to customers who pushed in and out through the inner door. A hand on his shoulder startled him to wakefulness.

"You safe to go," said Benny. "Ain't no sign of the police this past hour, an' ain't nobody come lookin' for ya.

"C'mon this way." Benny skirted the gaming room and led him along a passageway to unbolt a side exit door. "Git over to Rampart an' git on home. Don' wanna see you in trouble no more."

"Thanks, Benny. You ain't gonna see me, for sure."

"Ain't seen that brother o' your'n. Where he at?"

"Chicago."

"Chicago a good place. Git along now."

Sterling no longer cared to hide and blend into shadows. He cast aside reason and common sense, and ran like a wild thing down the middle of the street, desperate to leave the Vieux Carré behind. In his exhaustion, he saw the stars above him, spinning in the black sky. One last burst of energy and speed would loosen him from this net that entangled him. If anyone dared stop him, he would scratch and claw and fight them to the death to get free. Joy and relief flooded him as he crossed Rampart Street and took a snaking path toward home.

But the night was not over. Lights blazed in the front parlor. He looked in the window. There sat his mother, head bent over her sewing. He stopped still. *They know!* He wanted to run. But where? He slipped through the gate, ran along the side of the house and up to his window. Closed. He tried to force it upward. Locked. A lamp came on in his bedroom. Robert looked out at him. He slid the window open.

"Good morning, Sterling."

Part 5

SHAKING
THE BLUES
AWAY

TWENTY-SEVEN

"I have some money. I can pay off Syl's debt, Maria."

Sterling's news had hit hard. He had to tell them the whole truth. All of it. The lines in Robert's face dug deeper, mouth pulled downward, eyes shot with worry.

"I should a' stop Syl. Somehow," said his mother, her eyes red from weeping. "I knowed he up to no good, and now Sterling made to pay. Wish I done somethin' back then."

She finished bathing Sterling's cuts and scrapes. She picked out some grit from his knees and applied a soothing ointment.

"What's done is done," said Robert. "Those boys are off the streets. They hardly know if Sterling's alive or dead. First, we wait. Sterling, you must just lie low."

"But they gonna rat on 'im, Robert," wailed his mother. "I'm scared the police gon' come knockin' on that door, today, an' take 'im back to prison like some kind o' criminal.

"They know your name, Sterling?"

Sterling shrugged. "I dunno. They never call me nothin', don' guess they know it." He slumped in his chair, dizzy with exhaustion.

"Mighty sorry you said nothin' to me or your mother," Robert said. "For now, stay off the streets. School's the only place for you. Let's hope Paulo leaves us alone."

Sterling sank into bed, his thoughts in a whirl. He was home but felt no safety here. The police might come for him and take him away to jail, the proper jail this time. The Waifs Home would look like heaven from a cell inside the parish prison. His head had scarcely touched the pillow when it seemed a hand was shaking him awake again. A whisper of pain in his shoulder brought back a sharp memory of the night before.

"Breakfast, Sterling," said Robert.

"Aaah ... I need sleep." He shielded his eyes from the bright sunlight streaming in the window.

"Up you get. School day. We must treat this like any other day. Get washed. Get dressed."

And so the routine began. Breakfast. School. Dinner. School. Chores. Supper. Bed.

And no word from Paulo. Every morning, Robert scanned the street before he and Sterling set out for school, and muttered a warning to Maria to bolt the front door behind them. The sound of that bolt sliding closed brought on a dark mood inside their house—like the expectant hush before storm clouds burst and every creature runs for cover. Ever watchful, Sterling stayed close to Robert on his way to and from school, thinking this might be the last time he'd see home again. Were Paulo's thugs waiting out there to snatch him? Would the police wagon be waiting at the curb?

One day passed. Two. Three. Four days went by and no police at the door. No word from Paulo. Could they stop worrying and breathe easy? But they each carried a dread deep inside them. As sure as the breath in their bodies, they knew this wasn't over. On the fifth day, Mr. Trask sent Sterling home from school alone. "Won't be long. Got some inquiries to make. You get home, tell Maria I'll be along in awhile for supper."

"Where ya goin'?"

"Never mind. You get home quick. Straight home, now."

But supper time came and went, and no Robert.

"What he say agin?" asked his mother for the third

time. "You see where he went? He so late for supper."

"He ain't tell me nothin'." Sterling picked at his food, not hungry.

His mother moved to the window again and again, peering out to look for some sign of him. "Where can he be?" she muttered. "I pray he safe."

She hummed her bluesy tunes as she paced to and fro. Steps came up the front path. A sharp knock.

"Maria. Let me in." called Robert.

Sterling rushed to slide back the bolt.

"Where was you?" Maria hurried to him. "I bin worryin' somethin' happen!"

Robert took off his jacket, humming softly to himself, and pulled out his pipe from the inside pocket.

"Robert! Ain't you gonna tell us?"

He grinned from ear to ear. "Give me a moment, Maria. And where's my supper?"

"Why, you sit right down. I'm too scared to eat, but I got supper waitin' in the pot." She scurried into the kitchen but turned back, hands on her hips. "I ain't givin' you nuthin' till first you tell me where *was* you!?"

For answer, Robert tossed a rolled-up *Picayune* newspaper onto the table.

"Page three," he said. "Take a look, Sterling. Read it aloud."

Sterling picked up the newspaper and opened it to the right page. Robert pointed at a headline midway down.

Mafia Boss Shot Dead

Sterling began to read aloud.

"At about 10:30 PM on Thursday, April 25, three men entered the grocery owned by Italian Gangster and Crime Boss Paulo di Christiano, and upon going to the rear of the grocery, they opened fire upon di Christiano, who at the time of the shooting was just coming from a toilet at the rear. The crime boss received gunshot wounds to the body and was removed to New Orleans Hospital, later dying at said Hospital from his bullet wounds. The following are notes taken by a member of the New Orleans Police Force, at di Christiano's bedside. 'I gonna get the dirty rat who done this.' His three attackers are still unknown. Witnesses are encouraged to come forward with any pertinent information."

Before he reached the end, Maria let out a shriek and clapped her hands for joy. She hugged first Sterling, then Robert, then tried to hug Sterling again, but could not catch him as he jumped up and down and danced around the room.

"I'm safe!" he yelled. "That rat can't get me no more! An' I ain't gotta be a rat like him no more, neither!!"

Robert caught his hand and shook it. "You never said a truer word, Sterling. You ain't gotta be a rat like him no more!"

In the midst of their joy, there came a knocking on the front door and the three froze in place, Sterling midway through the kitchen to the parlor, Maria with the dinner pot in her hands, Robert ready to fill his pipe with tobacco.

"Did you bolt it?" whispered Robert.

Sterling shook his head. No.

"Stay quiet."

Another knock. Louder. "Anybody home?" called a voice.

"Why, it Clarence Williams!" Sterling hurried to open the door to his old friend. "I bet he gonna ask me why I never come on Sunday like I promise."

Clarence barreled in, good humor shining on his face, eyes beaming through his round spectacles. "Well, well, mighty good to see you all, Sterling! Mr. Trask. Maria. Looks like I caught you at supper, but I got some good news can't wait."

"Clarence, sit down, have supper with us," said Maria.

"No, thank you. I just gotta share somethin' that you gon' be might' proud to hear 'bout our boy, here."

He beamed at Sterling. "I always knew he was special. Took the liberty of sendin' away a composition of his. Me and A.J., that is. Tell the truth, I never knew it was that good. But Armand, he knew it. 'Plaquemine Blues,' he calls it."

"But that ain't even finish," said Sterling.

"And some other things he wrote—'Bouncy Feet,' for one. We call it 'Bouncin' Around.' 'Sundown Blues.' 'Colonel Rag.' We sent the application to Chicago Musical College. They lookin' for colored talent. Just cost us a dime. An' guess we was real proud when they send back a letter sayin' they want to audition the boy. Here it is. Got it right here in my pocket."

Clarence unfolded the letter written in fine handwriting. "If the audition is good, they are puttin' him in line for a bursary. Room and board. Lessons. He is gonna be a music scholar! He'll have piano lessons. Composition. Theory. Harmony. History, even. An' one day, he'll be our own Kid Sterling, great composer. Armand an' me are proud to help. All you gotta do is sign, Mr. Trask."

Robert read the letter. "They know how old he is?"

"The boy maybe too young?" said Maria, worried.

"They say he is exactly the right age. They want 'em young, untrained—empty sponge, just mop up all that learnin'. What do you say, Mr. Trask? Maria?"

Robert turned to Maria. "This may be just the answer. Get Sterling out of this city, away from the police, to a good school."

Sterling looked from one face to the next. *Why they ain't askin' me what I want?*

"They want the answer soon as can be. Term startin' next week and they got one space. I'm headin' to Chicago myself next week—recording deal to make. I can take him up. If they want him, I can help him get settled."

"How about askin' me? Ain't no one sayin', 'Sterling, what you want?'" Sterling burst out. "You talkin' like I ain't even in the room!"

"Sterling, what you want?" asked his mother. "I guess we know already."

"What I want? This the best damn thing ever happen a-me! I want a-go to Chicago an' learn an' learn, an' Clarence gonna go along with me, so it all good! An' that's what I want!"

TWENTY-EIGHT

There it sat. Buddy Bolden's cornet. Tarnished now. No loving hands had cradled or polished it since that day Sterling saved it from the gutter. So much going on that Sterling had not given it much thought. Until today, his last in New Orleans. Tomorrow morning, he would be on the train to Chicago.

Robert had signed the music school papers. A confirmation arrived by return mail. Sterling had already said goodbye to his aunt and uncle, and to his cousin Barrel. They had come for supper to wish him well. Told him not to get too uppity when he became a famous musicianer.

Sterling folded some clean clothes for his trip and wondered about Buddy. Was he still sick? He glanced at the horn now and again. He had always meant for the musicianer to play a solo part in "Plaquemine Blues." It still was not finished.

The King might be feeling better, might even help him find the ending, show him some licks. His only chance was right now, right this minute. Robert was teaching. His mother was busy in the kitchen. He picked up the horn, walked by the kitchen door, and called out, "Just goin' out awhile. Wanna take this horn back to Bolden."

"Sterling! That ain't wise. We tole you, stay off the street ..."

"Back soon," he called, and was out the door in a flash. He boarded a streetcar that took him close to Buddy's neighborhood and ran the last few blocks to his cottage on First Street. The musician's front door stood half-open. He knocked and it swung wider. "Buddy?"

A shuffling sound.

"Hey, King Bolden? It me. Sterling Crawford. I come a-visit."

"C'm on in," Buddy's voice called in a sing-song way.

Sterling stepped inside. Buddy stood with hunched shoulders, his back toward Sterling as he looked at a wall calendar. The sharp odor of sweat and dirt and beer stung the air, and something more. If sadness was a smell, then Buddy had a whiff of that on him, too.

"I'm jus' visitin'. Got yo' horn, right here."

As Buddy turned, a beam of sunlight fell across the glass of amber liquid in his hand and lit his gaunt face. *Look like he done been starvin' hisself,* thought Sterling.

His skin had lost its luster. The rips in his shirt, the grubby pants, and bare feet suggested a tramp just crawled out of a rubbish heap. There was no hint of the Bolden that Sterling used to know—someone strong and fit, sparkling clean and handsome, someone who wore the best clothes to show off his good looks, right down to the shine on his shoes. Sterling felt sick to see Buddy in this shape.

"... come a-visit?" Buddy muttered.

"I'm Sterling! Remember? I been shine your shoes up at the station. But I ain't shine 'em goin' on a year now."

Recognition flashed. Buddy shuffled closer. Smiling, he lifted a trembling hand to shake Sterling's. "I remember you."

He stood taller for a moment, and Sterling saw a hint of the man he used to be. "Come on in. Don't be a-scared. I ain't crazy, though they say I am."

Sterling offered the cornet. "I brung your horn. You

left it side o' the road when you sick. You feelin' better?"

Buddy flinched. "Keep it. I don' want it." He looked Sterling up and down. "You grown some, ain't ya? You the one always sayin', 'Buddy, teach me some licks! Teach me some licks!'" His expression softened. "I'm sorry I never had time. Just too damn busy. Ain't so busy no more. Can't even play no more."

"Here, you can play. I got your horn right here, Buddy. I even got a tune for ya."

Sterling gestured at a piano in a corner of the room. "I got this music I done wrote, 'Plaquemine Blues.' You wan' a-hear it?"

Buddy glanced at the horn but made no move toward it. "You better git goin'. Take the horn. I'm done with it. If my sister see that thing, no tellin' what she liable a-do."

"I can't believe you ain't playin' horn no more. Why ain'tcha?"

Buddy turned away to stare at a poster tacked to the kitchen wall. Sterling stepped closer to take a look. The artist had captured Buddy the way he used to be, a man bursting with strength and fire, the horn raised to his mouth. The poster was dated a year ago. *King Buddy Bolden,* read the text. *Oddfellows Hall. Two nights.*

"'Play it, Buddy!', you all shoutin'. 'Play it, King Bolden!'" Buddy muttered. "But you all copyin' my licks. Mighty flatterin', fellows. Mighty nice. But hey, now you stealin' 'em. Buildin' on 'em. Can't keep up. Can't do it no more."

He gulped some beer, glancing at Sterling. "You better git. My sister find you here ... she gonna throw yo' ass out." He gestured to the cornet. "And take that along."

"But my music got a solo part jus' for you." If Buddy would only listen, maybe he might pick up that horn once more. "Here, I'ma play it."

Sterling placed the horn on the sideboard and sat down at the piano. With his fingers poised over the keys, he looked up at Buddy. "See, it start out like this, when me and my brother on that train to Plaquemine. It have the sound of a train on the track. Whyn't ya pick up the horn and get ready."

Sterling began his piece, his breath ragged, hoping against hope that Buddy would play. He had always dreamed that he might take Bolden's place on the stage. Now he knew better. Just to sit down with the King and play *together*—*that* would make him happy for the rest of his life!

He gulped air and began the clickety-clack rhythm

with his left hand, adding the bluesy notes with his right. His fingers shook. The keys felt slippery with his sweat. He hit a few wrong notes, but he stopped for nothing. As he reached the part that called for Buddy's horn, he paused and looked over at the musician.

"This the horn part, where a train whistle come in," Sterling urged. "Remember that note you can hit that ain't even on this keyboard? The train whistle got some sad in it, 'cause it guess some bad news gonna be comin'. But my tune got some happy part, too."

Buddy looked at him, eyes blank. Sterling repeated the notes. "This your part, right here. The train whistle, that's where you come in."

Sterling willed Buddy to pick up the horn and play just like he had that time inside the Globe Ballroom, when his golden note made everyone stop and listen. Buddy shook his head and turned away. He reached for the jug and poured another drink.

Through the stillness came the laughter of children playing on the street outside, the rattle of a wagon, a clinking sound as Buddy's glass tapped the pitcher. Sterling bowed his head, stung.

Was no one true anymore?

His brother had let him take the punishment, and left Sterling wide open for all kinds of trouble. Bernier had run away with his train ticket, and Sterling had paid the price for that, too. The one person he had always believed in, Buddy Bolden—was he just a drunk, with nothing left in him? Angry words boiled up in a red heat, words that Sterling couldn't swallow. His fingers crashed on the keys in one ugly chord. The piano bench screeched as he shoved it back and stood up.

"Well, I guess you *is* finish! Guess you jus' a good-for-nothin' now, like they all say."

He stomped toward the door as tears spilled down his cheeks. "I'm mighty sad for you, Buddy Bolden. Seein' you this way. I guess you ain't good for nothin' else!"

Buddy looked up from his drink, puzzled. "Hey, you got no cause to get mad. I ain't worth it. Why you so angry?"

Sterling paused at the door, his voice loud and tearful. "I done wrote this tune, see? An' it need your horn. I always countin' on you a-help me. You ain't never help me. You ain't never got time a-teach me some licks. So, jus' this one time. I done been writin' this tune one whole year, just so some day ... some day, I can hear you play it. I always thinkin'—the King, why, he ain't no ornery musicianer. He the best! But I guess jus' maybe you ain't the best no more."

A flicker in Bolden's eyes. Maybe give it one last try? Sterling took a step back into the room.

"This tune about me and my brother. See, we all fixin' a-go to Plaquemine, an' we got into some bad luck there, all 'cuz o' one white man try an' hurt us. See, we ain't never know that my brother never gonna come back home. His whole life done change an' he run for it, an' they took me away to prison. But I done learn a-write my own music. I done wrote this tune, 'Plaquemine Blues.' But it ain't finish. It need your help. Look, I'ma play it one more time, so you listen good an' help me. An' I askin' you again. Please, King Bolden, teach me some licks!"

Sterling sat down at the piano, wiped his hands on his pants, and rested them on the keyboard. He began to play. His fingers felt clumsy but that did not matter. Fingers were just tools to express the memories that flooded his mind—that time he and his brother had set out on their journey, looking for adventure. A glint of sunlight on the winding river, its silvery gold sparkle, the excitement he had felt to explore the world outside New Orleans—his tune captured it all.

In his mind, the train whistle let out its mournful note to tell him that the world outside was not like home. Out there, danger lurked. He imagined he could hear the sound of Buddy's horn.

But it was not just his imagination! He could hear it! Buddy had raised the horn to sing out that train's piercing wail. At first, his notes stammered, called from a dreary place, but soon they came loud and true. They echoed Sterling's melody, built on it, and soared. Lively cadences streamed free, wove around and over Sterling's melody, like pebbles skipping across a river. Sterling felt joyful as the two instruments danced and blended their sounds as one.

Sterling's notes sang out the middle part of his story—the bluesy sadness from inside the dank prison cell, the prisoners' longing to return from the shadows into the safe and familiar. Buddy's horn invented new patterns. Horn and piano helped each other find the way and Sterling felt he was bursting free, through a door that swung wide to let him out. All the weight and burden floated up and away from him. This way and that, Buddy's horn weaved in and out, following Sterling's melody, sometimes pushing out in front while

Sterling chased behind. Buddy owned the melody for a moment, and Sterling followed to see where it went.

They reached the "stuck place" that Sterling could never get past. Sterling's notes faltered and faded but Buddy played on, slowed it to search out an ending, and Sterling's notes charged ahead of Buddy's with a new idea. As Buddy played some last dissonant notes, Sterling took them and built a phrase full of lingering questions that hung in the air.

Where do I belong? Where is home? Sad, so sad. All gone, forever, sang the piano. Childhood. Home. Friends.

Buddy answered his sadness with a melancholy that only a horn could voice. Horn and piano slid into one chord that sang out a hard truth—Sterling could never go back. The childhood he had known was over. All Sterling had of the past was this moment full of memories, fragile as a cobweb.

Even so, the last dying note sounded a spark of promise. He would see Syl again. Work things out. Clarence and Armand believed in him. His mother always loved him just the same. Maybe something good waited for him around the next corner. Who knew what Chicago had in store!

Before the vibration of horn and piano had melted away, Buddy added a light cascade of notes like a dazzling sunbeam inside a dark corner.

"Plaquemine Blues" was complete.

Buddy lowered the horn and gazed at it, turning it this way and that. "Ain't that somethin'! This horn still got it."

"You play so fine!" said Sterling, bounding up from his bench. "I knowed you still the King! I tole ya! You the best musicianer in New Orleans. Ain't nothin' change."

"I like your music," Buddy said softly. "The bluesy parts is real good."

Sterling could hear Buddy's notes still shimmering, floating in the air like gold dust. "You sure done help me finish my tune!"

He looked around him for pencil and paper. "I gotta write it all down 'fore I forget it." He spied a pencil stub hanging by a string from the wall calendar. He grabbed the pencil, string and all.

The pages of the calendar showed only blank days. Buddy had not been working for some time. Sterling tore a page out and hurried back to the piano, sat down, and quickly drew the notation lines to mark Buddy's melody. He filled in some of the notes as best he could from memory, playing them on the keyboard before scribbling them down. They would serve to remind him, later. He worked in silence and Buddy gazed over his shoulder at the notations on the page.

"You got talent, boy. I never did learn to read an' write music."

"That why you play so free," answered Sterling. "Don't need no notation tyin' ya music down."

"You sure learned somehow. Willie teach ya?"

"Nah, I done been gone away, but someone teached me. It ain't hard." He finished and stood up from the piano. "I know you still got it! I ain't never give up on you. You still the King!"

Buddy shook his head and placed the cornet on the table. His body drooped as though the music had drained right out of him.

"All the times you ask, 'Teach me some licks.' Well, there it is. I done show you some licks." He gestured to the horn. "Ain't playin' no more. Take the horn for yoursel'. You better git home now."

Sterling shook his head. "I'ma leave it right here. You gonna change your mind. Start playin' again. You gotta!"

Buddy moved toward a cabinet against the wall and

opened it with trembling fingers. "Maybe one day, you gonna understand better." He reached inside and took out a wax cylinder.

"Here. Take it. We done record this a while ago. Willie on it, Bunk, and the rest of the fellas. Tha's before they threw me out. 'Teach me some licks,' you always sayin'? Well, this tune got some licks. You got a gramophone at home? Just listen to this an' remember how it all use a-be." He handed Sterling the cylinder in its paper sleeve. "Keep it safe, now. No one gonna ever hear me again, 'cept you. There. Now, git."

"But ..."

"Just git. Don't come back."

He turned away, eyes blank.

There was a motion at the front door and a young woman hurried in. "Buddy! I'ma take you to the doctor." Her eyes flicked a glance at Sterling as she passed him.

"Gonna find you a fresh shirt. An' your shoes. Where you leave 'em?"

Sterling remembered the woman from that day when Buddy had collapsed into the gutter—the sister who had fetched the men to carry him away.

An older woman bustled in behind her and stopped

when she saw Sterling. "Who are you, boy? You better get on home. You live aroun' here?"

"No, ma'am. I jus' visitin' Buddy."

"Well, get on, now. My son ain't takin' no visitors. Off you go, chile."

Sterling gripped his calendar page and the cylinder, and she eyed both. Before she could ask what he was holding, he hurried outside.

At the curb, a police wagon waited. A policeman stood smoking and talking idly to the wagon driver, who held the reins of two black horses. Sterling shrank back against the wall. The police officer noticed him but, to Sterling's relief, did not seem interested.

"Get along, kid, or I'll put the cuffs on ya an' take you to the madhouse, along with Bolden."

He shook the handcuffs dangling from his belt and took a step toward Sterling.

Sterling dodged away in terror and ran down the street. He looked back. The policeman stood slapping his thigh as he guffawed with the driver.

Buddy going to the madhouse? His own mother! How could she send her son away? As he reached the corner he turned again to wait and watch.

Buddy shuffled out of the house. He wore polished shoes and a clean white shirt that hung loosely on his thin frame. His sister led him to the wagon, talking into Buddy's ear as they walked. Buddy's head was down, but when he looked up and saw the police wagon, he jerked back and turned away. His sister urged him forward. Buddy's mother watched from the doorway and wiped her eyes with her fists. The policeman cuffed Buddy's wrists, shoved him up into the wagon, climbed in after him, and slammed the door shut. The horse set off at a trot, and Sterling gazed after it, till the wagon turned the corner and was gone.

Was this the last time he would ever see King Bolden? With care, Sterling placed the cylinder in his pants pocket. It might be all that was left to remember him by.

Tomorrow, he and Clarence would be on that train to Chicago. He made a silent promise that when he got there, he would tell anyone who would listen about King Buddy Bolden—the way he could send his special sound clear across Lake Pontchartrain, how he made that horn moan till the girls went weak for love of him, and how his sweet low-down music could gather in all the people, understand their hurts, and make their spirits rise.

"Buddy Bolden! I'm gonna see they remember you," he said out loud. "I swear, I'ma use my music, an' my words, an' I ain't never gonna let 'em forget you! Never!"

CODA

The track unfurled like a spool of ribbon. Its gleaming silver rails lengthened as the train gathered speed. The figures of his mother and Robert receded with every passing second. Sterling leaned out the window as far as he could and waved, his body swaying with the train's motion, till the two figures, the station, the skyline of New Orleans, all faded away into the haze of heat. Sterling felt as though he were caught in a dream, struggling to stay inside it, yet feeling its tug on him loosen.

Clarence gave a whoop.

"Well, that's goodbye to Nawlins. Chicago, here we come! Sit down, Kid Sterling. Your mother says I gotta tie you to me. Don't want you fallin' off no train before we hardly left the station."

"Jus' wait a second," said Sterling, his eyes fixed on

the view as the train left the winding Mississippi River behind, and he turned his gaze away from New Orleans. On each side of him, the green fields passed in a blur, but up ahead, as the train rounded a bend, he had a clear view. There lay his future!

He wanted to spread his arms wide to embrace the rush of landscape toward him, all its greenery ladled with the broth of sunlight. He wanted to grab armloads of it, to breathe it in with deep, heaping gulps. If his life were like a music book of stories, Sterling felt as strong as the spine that bound and divided it down its center. One part was finished, its pages full. The rest contained empty notation lines, waiting to be filled.

What musical notes would those pages soon hold?

The train whistle blew loud and long, heralding his journey onward.

"Here I come!" it called.

And, for a moment, he could have sworn he heard another sound cloaked within its blast—the crystal voice of King Bolden's horn, that wondrous, golden note bursting loose from its captivity, tugged upward with the breeze, soaring free.

ACKNOWLEDGEMENTS

I acknowledge the assistance of Canada Council for the Arts.

I'm very grateful to Peter Carver for his faith in this story, and thanks to Richard Dionne for his support.

Thank you also to those archivists, educators, historians, linguists, poets, and writers who guided and assisted me: Lynn Abbot, Associate Curator, Recorded Sound, Hogan Jazz Archives; Suzanne Blaum, Director of Education & Outreach, Preservation Resource Center of New Orleans; Alaina W. Hébert, MLIS Associate Curator, Graphics, Hogan Jazz Archives; Leon Miller, Archivist, Head of Louisiana Research Collection, Tulane University; Dr. John B. Raeburn, Assistant Dean of Libraries, Special Collections, Tulane University.

For help with dialect, I'm grateful to Dr. Lisa Green,

Department of Linguistics, University of Massachusetts at Amherst and Dr. Andrea Kortenhoven, Department of Linguistics, University of Michigan. Also, Chris Benjamin, Managing Editor, *Atlantic Books Today*; George Elliott Clarke OC, ONS, Professor of English, University of Toronto; Ajay Heble, Professor of English, School of English and Theatre Studies, University of Guelph; and John McCusker, *Times Picayune*, who guided me through Buddy Bolden's neighborhood and my character's special haunts; Thomas Henderson, African Canadian Services Division, Nova Scotia Department of Education, for his valued advice; Robert Appel, Sheila and Garry Cook, Eleanor Gasparik, Gab Halasz, Glenna Jenkins, Mark Miller, Tela Purcell, Caroline Pignat, Brenda and Kenneth Privat, and to Gill Osmond, whose writers prompt about an open door enabled me to conjure my protagonist, Sterling.

GLOSSARY

Battle royal—A free-for-all boxing match with few rules, this form of fighting began during the 1700s in the United Kingdom, and eventually spread to the colonies in America. The battle became racially motivated from 1890 to 1910, when white promoters used the contest as a crowd pleaser for white audiences before a boxing event.

Bayou—These beautiful marshlands and sluggish streams, bordered by moss-covered trees, cross Louisiana's lowlands. Bayous are full of wildlife, including alligators. Sterling and Syl crossed a bridge over a bayou when they were running away from Danny.

Beignet—A deep-fried sweet pastry. Clancy brought this treat for Sydney after his accident.

Chicago Defender—A newspaper written by and for African Americans that still exists today. It fought against racial injustice. Railway Pullman porters and traveling entertainers, on the trains from Chicago to the Deep South, would smuggle copies into the southern states. There, the papers were passed hand to hand among the black population. Each edition listed the monthly number of lynchings that had taken place in the southern states. It printed train schedules to Chicago as well as job listings. The paper encouraged African Americans to come north and enjoy a society that was freer from the rampant racism of the Deep South. Sterling found a page of this newspaper just before he met Paulo near the station.

Creole—The term Creole does not refer to race. Louisiana was once a colony of France and then of Spain. The word means "native-born"—born in Europe (either France or Spain). It later came to include the people of European, or African, or Native American descent, or of any mixture therein, who were born in Louisiana. The Creoles lived in "downtown" New Orleans, and felt a pride in their heritage, going back generations. They were wealthier and better educated, so felt superior to the black newcomers who lived uptown. Armand's reaction to Buddy Bolden's music illustrates this feeling of superiority. A legal amendment in 1894 defined Creoles legally as blacks, and this event increased the tension for many years.

Curfew (See Jim Crow)—A law imposed upon blacks in the Deep South to stay off the streets after 10:00 PM. Sterling worried about being out after ten o'clock because police patroled the streets at night.

Dicty—A term meaning snobbish, haughty. Sterling thought Mozart was "dicty" because his music was sophisticated, and images of the composer revealed to Sterling that he wore very fancy clothes.

Fever—Yellow Fever is a virus caused by mosquitoes. An outbreak in 1905 in New Orleans killed 452 people, especially young children. It was discovered that open cisterns were responsible for breeding mosquitoes, and orders were issued to screen all cisterns.

Jim Crow car—Closest to the engine, this car was reserved for baggage, smoking, and for segregating black passengers. Whites also used it as a smoking car, as happened on Sterling's train ride to Plaquemine. Smoking was not allowed in the passenger cars.

Kid—A term used to describe young musicians who were being noticed because they showed talent.

Klan—The Ku Klux Klan is a white supremacist hate group that targeted African Americans in Sterling's time, and still exists. Today, it also targets immigrants, Jews, and Catholics.

Levee—A flood barrier either naturally formed or built to prevent a river from overflowing. In my story, Sterling loved to sit on the levee looking over the Mississippi River, to watch the river life—the barges and oyster luggers, and to create tunes from the calls of the stevedores who worked along the shore.

Lynching—A total of 3,446 African Americans in southern states died at the hands of angry white lynch mobs during the period 1881 to 1968 (data collected by Tuskegee Institute Archives). The term refers to mob killings without legal permission, usually by torture and hanging, for an alleged crime. Lynching was a form of racial control to terrorize African Americans into an inferior social and racial position.

Kotch—A card game, one of many that were usually played by "card sharks"—people who played professional card games for profit. Sterling's brother Syl has an addiction to all kinds of gambling, including Kotch.

Nickelodeon—A "nickel theater" that presented short movies from five minutes to one hour long. Children like Sterling likely watched a few short films in New Orleans as a treat now and again. Admission was five cents.

The pizzo—"Protection" money paid to the Mafia by forcible means. The term is derived from the Sicilian *pizzu* ("beak"). To let someone "wet their beak" is to pay protection money to Mafia criminals. Syl sometimes collected *pizzos* from shop owners for his boss, Paulo.

Ragtime—the precursor to Jazz, ragtime features a ragged or syncopated beat. Composer Scott Joplin, named King of Ragtime, wrote many such pieces. Sterling and the band at the Colored Waifs Home practiced the "Maple Leaf Rag," one of Joplin's popular compositions.

Rougarou—Derived from the French "loup-garou," the rougarou is a creature similar to the werewolf, and a common legend in southern Louisiana. Danny scared Sterling when he spoke of the rougarou during that dark night on the track.

Second liners—It is a tradition for New Orleans brass bands to march along the streets of the city. "Second liners" are those who walk or dance along behind the band to enjoy the music close up.

Sharecropper—After slavery was abolished, poor tenant farmers, both black and white, worked a small piece of land rented from a landowner. In return, they were allowed to keep a share of the crops they produced, but often went into debt for money owed. Freed slaves, like Sterling's great-grandfather Ned, were compelled to seek a living by sharecropping for survival.

Spasm band—First formed on the streets of New Orleans, bands made up of children played homemade instruments such as a chair leg for a drumstick, or a comb and paper for a horn. Young musicians often started their music careers with a spasm band of their own.

Tonk—The shortened form of Honky Tonk, the term refers to cheap bars and clubs where ragtime music was played on upright pianos. Gamblers and working-class drinkers patronized these tonks, that were usually located on the lower floor of a venue, while the upper floor was often a place of business for prostitutes. Sterling likes to listen outside tonks and clubs to hear Bolden's music.

Wax cylinder—A cylindrical device made of soft wax that had an audio recording on its outside surface. They would wear out after a few dozen playings, and were played on a phonograph, a machine for reproducing the sound. In real life, Willie Cornish attested to the existence of a recording made of Bolden's band. This wax cylinder has become something of a legend. Was there ever such a cylinder containing the sound of Bolden's music? If so, does it still exist? What do you think?

WHAT HAPPENED TO ...?

Armand Piron and Clarence Williams eventually started a business in New Orleans known as Armand and Williams Publishing Company. Armand's biggest hit song was "I Wish I Could Shimmy Like My Sister Kate." In 1917, he started an orchestra and took it to New York City. After a successful career, he died in 1943.

Billy Kersands, born in 1842, was a well-known comedian during Sterling's time. A dancer, singer, and acrobat, he played blackface roles in minstrel shows. He was over six feet tall, weighed two hundred pounds, and was famous for placing a variety of objects in his mouth during his performances. "If God had made my mouth any bigger, he would have had to move my ears," Billy would say. He performed for kings and queens, and died in 1915.

Black Benny Williams, a handsome, charming musician, bouncer, boxer, and expert drummer, often spent time in jail. One police record shows him booked for driving into a streetcar, assault and battery on the scene, using obscene language, and disturbing the peace. When he was 34, he was stabbed in the heart by a jealous woman and taken to hospital. A blood transfusion revived him, but he died the next day of pneumonia.

Bob Bartley was a hot air balloonist who entertained the crowds at parks in New Orleans during Sterling's time. Part of his act was to have a marksman pretend to shoot a hole in Bob's balloon and bring it down.

Booker T. Washington. Born into slavery in 1856, Booker T. became a strong orator, educator, writer, and eventually, an advisor to President Theodore Roosevelt. He was the first African American to be invited to the White House. He believed education was the pathway to social, racial, and political equality for African Americans, and he became the leading voice for former slaves and their descendents.

Charles Joseph "Buddy" Bolden, said to be the inventor of jazz, could not read or write music. He was an "ear" musican and improvised with music he heard, creating loose versions of the blues, hymns, and ragtime. He began to complain of severe headaches in 1906—when this story begins—and gradually lost his ability to play. Alcoholism played a part in his decline as a musician. By April 1907, he was committed to a psychiatric hospital for treatment of schizophrenia, a mental disorder. There, with no memory of his previous success, he died in November 1934.

Clarence Williams enjoyed a successful career as a pianist, composer, singer, publicist, theatrical producer, and publisher. He lived a rich, full life and died in 1965, at the age of 67, in New York City. His grandson, Clarence Williams III, is an American film actor, currently living in New York City.

Joe Never Smile, who owned a stable of horses in New Orleans, is often mentioned by musicians of that period. He played a large part in helping to arrange funerals, and used onions to make his horses cry. He was known for his unsmiling face. Nothing more is known about him.

Joseph "Captain" Jones was 27 when he founded the Colored Waifs Home with his wife, Manuela, in New Orleans in 1906. He was enabled to do so with the help of a court judge. Before this Home was established, young boys were forced to mix with hardened criminals at the parish prison. A commissioned officer in the Spanish American War, Jones used military techniques to organize the boys, offering rescue and safety from the streets of New Orleans. One of his students was Louis Armstrong. Not much is known about Jones today. He died and was buried in a common grave in New Orleans some time in the 1940s.

Willie Cornish, a member of Bolden's band, led bands of his own and taught music for decades. When he suffered a stroke in 1931 that paralyzed his left side, he fashioned a strap to hold his trombone so that he could continue to play. He died in 1942.

INTERVIEW WITH CHRISTINE WELLDON

What made you want to tell Kid Sterling's story in the first place?

I disliked history as a kid in school. I found it dry and dull, but I loved reading first-hand accounts, stories told by people who lived through difficult times— their voices resonated. Much better than reading a dry presentation of dates and facts and events. Most of the books I've written contain the voices of people who lived through interesting times in Canada's history.

I had been asked by my publisher to write a children's book about jazz history in Canada, but it wasn't going well. I found myself writing in the same way as those dull old textbooks. How to convey the richness of jazz by means of a rather dry format—words on paper? I found it very difficult. Before I gave up, I spent a year researching jazz history, trying to find a way in. And that's when I discovered Buddy Bolden, whose genius in creating a new musical expression spread outward from the cradle of New Orleans to influence musicians all around the U.S. and beyond.

Again, I turned to voices. There must be some voices from that time, buried in old recordings, transcripts, out of print autobiographies. So I went to New Orleans and found them, all there to be discovered—what a find! The voices of Clarence and Armand, Willie Cornish, Bunk Johnson, and through the recollections of his friends, Buddy Bolden himself. And, somehow, I conjured up Kid Sterling's voice to help tell their story at the same time as I was telling his.

How did you come to learn about life in New Orleans at the time the story is set?

Two years of research in all, and very layered research. If Sterling picked up a pencil, did they have pencils in 1906? If he ran along the street, what would he see? What was the ground like underfoot? Paved? Dirt? What recording devices had been invented? Was there electricity? Could one smell the salt marshes? What does a paddlewheeler horn sound like? I was compelled to explore all these elements to be able to set myself in that time and place.

Of course, the actual time I spent in the city was a vital part of my research. It's not the same city today as it was then, but if you look closely, you can find the old New Orleans as it was, in its architecture, cuisine, languages. And in subtle ways, the spirit of the city finds its way into your awareness, through its heightened colors, flavors, voices, and, most importantly, its music.

What is it like to tell a story set in a time and a place— and a culture—which is outside your own experience?

I was a little frightened to venture into this territory, writing as I was from outside my experience and race and culture. I naively thought I was setting out to write about the birth of jazz, but discovered that the story would not be authentic if I didn't bring in the rampant racism that prevailed in the Deep South and elsewhere. And as a storyteller, I'm unable to limit my imagination to only my own race, culture, and creed.

As in jazz composition, writing can only be performed best if the imagination is free to roam. My obligation is to tell a story well, with authenticity and truth. The Jim Crow era was horrific. I didn't experience it, but I set out to try and convey my empathy and respect for these characters without becoming clichéd in my descriptions of their lives. I was intent on providing an authentic portrait of life in those times as seen from an African American child's point of view.

Literature is where we go to explore beyond our own small world, and gain empathy for other cultures and peoples. My story needed to be authentic and honest and as true as I could make it. That's my duty as a storyteller.

One obvious aspect of the story is the way in which characters speak—in other words, their dialect. Why was it important to you to capture that part of the New Orleans African American culture? Why do some

English speakers speak differently than others and why was it important for you to capture this dialect in this story?

The African American dialect conveys much about the speakers' cultural history. Its roots are found in both the English spoken by slavers, and the native languages of West Africa, spoken by those brutally captured from their homes and enslaved in the Americas.

With this in mind, the characters in my story deserve the respect of having their speech portrayed accurately. So, with the help of two African American linguists, I delightedly discovered that the dialect is rich and complex with clear rules of grammar. For example, there are five present tenses in African American English compared to the four in formal English. I did my best to learn the rules before I wrote the dialogue, or "speaking" parts.

There are a total of 160 dialects in the English language, and even more accents that convey each one! The African American dialect, among others, helps us understand the traditions, history, and culture of the community in which it's spoken. It is worthy of respect and admiration—English would be so much less rich and vibrant without it!

Why is this period in New Orleans such an important one in history?

It was a turbulent time in the history of African Americans. Jim Crow laws in the Deep South enforced racial segregation in every area of society. Facilities for African Americans were inferior and underfunded or non-existent. Racial hatred was rampant.

But within this dark period sprang the native art form of jazz. African Americans, and Buddy Bolden in particular, invented a music that offered an escape, a momentary release from their struggles, the creative freedom to make a wild and joyful music that combined blues, folk, European, spirituals, marching band, Latin, and African influences. Today it is played all over the world. And it all sprang from the cradle of jazz— New Orleans.

In this story, Kid Sterling has a hero in whom he invests great faith. Do you think it's wise for young people to have heroes in their lives to whom they look for inspiration, as Sterling does with Buddy Bolden?

Heroes often tend to have feet of clay, as Sterling discovered about Syl and Bolden. But Sterling demonstrated a forgiving nature. He found the positive traits in them just as he eventually recognized their shortcomings and failures. Ultimately, this was a necessary lesson toward his emotional growth. Young people today might seek out people who inspire them, but they must recognize that no one is without faults of one kind or another.

Not only have you written about the music that came to life in New Orleans, but you have also given us a powerful adventure story. What can you tell us about how you came up with Sterling's story?
Hard to explain. I guess I first saw the story as a jazz piece, the Mississippi river providing the main melody, long and unwavering, winding its way through the city, absorbing the improvisations, embellishments, the cross melodies and rhythms provided by an assortment of characters. The characters improvising to protect their own survival or happiness or success—all playing with different tempos, and beats, and moods, the dissonance and harmonies, but, in the end, managing to create a meaningful composition.

I wrote about King Bolden and about New Orleans' rich gumbo of cultures, languages, musical influences, and races, from a child's point of view, and the child had to be someone who is sensitive to the colors and flavors, sights and sounds, and, most importantly, the music of that time. To children of Sterling's age, it seems everything is possible, no dream is too daring. Sterling's role in the story is meant to be one of exploring both the musical elements and the tough gritty elements of life in the Jim Crow era as he pursues his dream. I envisaged the story beginning with Sterling being invited to walk through an open door. I knew the ending before I began. I didn't know what would happen in the middle bit—it seemed to just go where Sterling wanted to take it, a true jazz artist!

The relationship Sterling has with his brother is a complicated one. Why was this part of his story of particular interest to you?

Syl is a complex young man, anger always seething beneath the surface, seeking instant gratification, but tender, too. Sterling admires and looks up to him, and hates and resents him by turns. Syl changes Sterling's life for the worse, and puts him smack into some brutal situations. But throughout all that, they're bonded: "... our music, it gonna always fit together like one tune ..." says

Sterling, as he comes to recognize this life lesson—love is unconditional, no matter the grief that comes with it.

What has been the place of jazz in your life?
I was schooled in classical piano. When I was around nine or ten, I used to sit at the piano and write little compositions of my own on notation paper, simple little tunes in three-quarter time, complete with clefs and bars. Very controlled and following the rules. I enjoyed the creative buzz, but didn't feel I was creating anything special. I was always scribbling down stories, too, and found it was much more satisfying creatively to go where my imagination pleased.

It was much later, when I began to appreciate jazz and be touched by it, that I set out to learn the jazz scale. I can't play in that style, but I have my favorite musicians, especially John Coltrane, who wrote transformative music, and tapped into a transcendent creativity. I find the music of jazz serves to cross all cultural and racial boundaries; it speaks a language anyone can understand. It's freeing. It puts you into the present moment. It's a mystical thing to me. Spiritual. It has the strength and power to connect us all.

Sterling is ten years old when the story begins, eleven when he heads off for Chicago. This seems very young when we think of young people that age today. Is it true that children had to grow up much faster in 1906 in New Orleans?

This is true of that era, in general. Children did not have much of a childhood. Child labor laws were not in effect until the thirties, and even then, not many industries complied. So they were seen as a resource to be exploited. Those under fifteen were put to work toiling in mines, selling newspapers, shining shoes, picking cotton. By 1904, 50,000 children under the age of twelve were employed in the cotton mills of the Deep South. There were few if any safety regulations, so accidents were inevitable. Children might easily be caught or trapped in machinery. Sadly, there were some deaths.

In the end, Sterling is given the chance to go to the Chicago Musical College. In reality, were there black "musicianers" who were able to attend the college in the early 1900s?

In 1900, Rudolph Ganz joined the piano department of the Chicago Musical College. Called "one of the most successful musicians with children," he eventually conducted and recorded young people's concerts. It is known that, noticing children on the streets of Chicago, selling newspapers and shining shoes near the college, he offered them opportunities to learn music and play in bands. I took artistic license with having Sterling trying for a place at the college, but it is highly possible that Ganz offered these opportunities. Many African American students from that era attended the school and distinguished themselves in later life: Florence Cole Talbert-McCleave, named "The First Lady of Grand Opera," by the National Negro Opera Guild; Johnny Hartman, jazz singer who eventually performed with John Coltrane; Walter Henri Dyatt, violinist and musical educator; Eddy Otha South, jazz violinist, among many others.

Thank you, Christine, for the powerful insights you have given us.